BLOOD LOVE

GOD WARS SERIES, BOOK FOUR

CONNIE SUTTLE

Print Second Edition (2018)
Print ISBN: 1-63478-049-3
Print ISBN-13: 978-1-63478-049-0
eBook ISBN: 1-93975-924-2
eBook ISBN-13: 978-1-93975-924-5

Published by:
SubtleDemon Publishing, LLC
PO Box 95696
Oklahoma City, OK 73143

Cover art by Renée Barratt @ The Cover Counts

To Walter, Joe, Larry, Lee, Dianne, Sarah and Mark.
Thank you.

And for Grant, who seriously beat cancer up and left it in the dust.

ACKNOWLEDGMENTS

As always, this book is the result of collaboration. If it weren't for the support of my editor, my cover artist and my beta readers, it would be less than it is. All mistakes, as usual, are mine and no other's.

About the Author:
Connie Suttle lives in Oklahoma with her husband and a conglomerate of cats. They have finally banded together to make their demands, which has proven disconcerting to all humans involved.

You may find Connie in the following ways:
Facebook: Connie Suttle Author
Twitter: @subtledemon
Website and Blog: subtledemon.com

ALSO BY CONNIE SUTTLE

~

R-D Series:

Cloud Dust

Cloud Invasion

Cloud Rebel

~

Latter Day Demons Series:

Hot Demon in the City

A Demon's Work is Never Done

A Demon's Due

~

Seattle Elementals Series:

Your Money's Worth

Worth Your While*

~

BlackWing Pirates Series

MindSighted

MindMage

MindRogue

MindMaster*

~

Black Rose Sorceress Series

The Rose Mark

Rose and Thorn

Black Rose Queen

Queen of Thorns and Roses

~

Future Wars Series

Buffer Zone

Black Zone*

~

Other Titles from SubtleDemon Publishing:

Malefactor

Transgressor

Underhanded*

by Joe Scholes

*Forthcoming

CHAPTER 1

issa's Journal
There comes a time when the tears will not fall. A time when you're just too numb to cry. That's how I felt.

Breanne had wasted her life, defending two who didn't deserve her sacrifice. Yes, I recognized Ashe easily enough, but the Mighty Mind was unfamiliar to me. He, Ashe and the dark-haired god knelt beside Breanne's body, likely discussing her death in mindspeech.

I blinked in confusion when the Five Larentii Wise Ones and their Protectors appeared. I was afraid to hope. My confusion only increased when another Larentii appeared. Taller than the others, he was like no Larentii I'd ever seen. Dressed in a leather jacket, dark denim pants and boots, he had deep, red hair worn long and loose about his shoulders.

If he'd been human, I'd have expected a Harley to be parked nearby. Ashe, the dark-haired god and the Mighty Mind stepped back to allow the Wise Ones to approach Breanne's body. The Wise Ones weren't the ones to act first, however.

The red-haired Larentii stepped forward and formed light about him. The others followed his example and began trilling. They were quickly joined by their Protectors.

Suddenly, the massive building was filled with Larentii. So many of them I knew—Pheligar. Renegar. Lenigar. Nefrigar. My Reemagar and Connegar had come. All joined their voices to that of the five Wise Ones and the red-haired Larentii. The air became thick with their song and their brightness, blinding me.

Throwing an arm over my eyes to block the light, I dropped to the floor and sleep descended.

~

Avendor—present

"Boss, do you think she'll make it?"

Trajan wanted to hold Breanne's body. His wolf wanted to howl to the moon outside, pleading for the safety of his mate.

"I don't know." Ashe shook his head. "They managed to heal the breaks and torn blood vessels. Most of the bruises are gone, too, but we don't know what kind of emotional damage happened or whether her mind might recover from that."

"My memory was modified in the past," he growled. "I don't remember that Lissa is alive or that I saw her then."

"Traje, that's for the best, don't you think?"

"I don't know what to think, except to be mad that somebody fucked with my memories."

"I understand," Ashe raked fingers through his hair. "Who's with Breanne now?"

"Lissa and Karzac," Trajan muttered. "It's been four days. Karzac stuck that stupid feeding tube in yesterday. I don't like that one bit."

"It's necessary to preserve her body," Ashe sighed.

"Bill just sits out on the deck—when he isn't with Bree or doesn't have to feed Kay," Trajan pointed out. "He's kinda pissed that his memory was tampered with, too, and he's really upset that Bree is like she is."

"You think we're not all worried?" Ashe blinked at Trajan. "If she doesn't come back from this," he shook his head in frustration. "Traje, I'm still trying to work out who the Mighty Mind is," Ashe flopped onto a padded chair in his den and blew out a breath. "Once the Larentii managed to bring the body back to life, Wisdom took off like a shot."

"You think maybe Breanne is somewhere else, now, deciding whether it's worth it to come back?"

"It's possible," Ashe said, rubbing his forehead. He hadn't had a headache this bad in almost a decade. He'd had this one for four days.

"She may not want to stay here if she wakes up," Trajan sounded troubled.

"I know. Sometimes I want to kick my own ass over that."

"I'll do it for you."

"Look, you're still the better fighter, so no, thanks," Ashe held up a hand.

Earth—past

"Charles, this saddens me." Wlodek shook his head as Charles and Gavin finished their reports to the Head of the Council.

"And we are no closer to solving this mystery," Gavin muttered. "The church was destroyed not long after Breanne died, but I cannot say how that was accomplished."

"I want you to investigate this—I hear from Bill Jennings that vampire rogues were involved in many deaths in the destroyed churches. This is unacceptable, and places all of us in danger. Find the ones responsible and ensure they are dispatched."

"With pleasure, Honored One," Gavin inclined his head to Wlodek. "Charles and I discussed this with Director Jennings before our return," Gavin added. "He feels the same, and requests that either I or another be sent back to help him and his agents track these rogues."

"Honored One, please allow me to accompany Gavin," Charles pleaded.

"Are you sure, Charles? Will has been effective as a temporary assistant, but this could place your life in danger."

"I want to do this, Honored One. I cared for Breanne."

"Then I will allow this," Wlodek agreed. "Tell Will everything he needs to know. I expect you to begin this assignment as quickly as possible."

~

Campiaa—present
Tybus' Journal

"Reah, how nice to see you," I greeted her as she stepped timidly inside my study. Yes, it was my study, now, and that hadn't fully settled in. Reah was accompanied by Aurelius and Edward, who walked in behind her.

"How is the baby?" I asked. She had no idea how much I adored children. The fact that I'd only had one child in my previous life always troubled me, although she was eventually made Queen of Le-Ath Veronis.

"Lexsi is doing fine," Reah nodded to me and accepted the chair I indicated with a sigh. Aurelius and Edward took the other seats available and once they'd settled, I returned to the chair behind the desk, waiting for them to ask their questions.

"I think we should allow things to remain as they are between us—between Teeg and me," Reah began. I watched as her fingers twisted together in her lap. I wanted to reach out and tell her that her fears were unfounded—that I would never harm her. She seemed overly troubled to me, and there was no need for that.

"If that is your wish," I inclined my head to her. She was a Queen, after all, in addition to being High Demon enough to turn Thifilatha. That wasn't all she was, and I wondered—yet again—how anyone might fail to see the faint glow of power about her.

"How old are—were you?"

"I was thirty-seven thousand years a vampire when I fell in the destruction of Le-Ath Veronis," I replied. I had no reason to hide anything from these present. "I was near death after an accident when I was comesula, at barely sixty-three years of age. I only had one child at that time, and she was ten when I was turned. My vampire sire allowed me to continue with her rearing and education. He also helped with that, and she grew in wisdom quickly."

"Amazing," Aurelius shook his head slightly. Like any good vampire, his emotions were tightly controlled. This one, though, allowed them through if he were with those he trusted. I was not trusted. I would have to earn that.

I seemed to have all of Gavril's talents, and if my suspicions were correct, Breanne may have left me with a few extra. She realized I might need them, I suspect, to maintain my masquerade. Without any trouble, I could tell by scent that Aurelius was Gavin's sire. I already knew that through Gavril's memories, but without them, I'd still have known.

Edward glowed with a power similar to Reah's, so I knew they were the same. Aurelius' power was lesser and different, but he had it, nonetheless.

"I will be available for any events, should you require it," Reah said.

"My dear," I said gently, "I will only require it if you stop trembling in my presence." Reah jerked her head up in surprise.

~

Avendor—present

Lissa's Journal

"Karzac, what will we do if she doesn't wake?" I'd been at SouthStar for four days and the only signs that life might still be present were Breanne's chest rising and falling and the heartbeat, faint as it was, in her chest.

Even the Larentii couldn't detect brain activity, and that terrified me. Were we keeping her body alive just to leave our hopes intact?

"Lissa," Karzac scolded gently, "We do not know what may happen. Please do not upset yourself. There is more than enough distress as it is."

"I need to get back to Le-Ath Veronis, but I don't want to leave her here like this," I was close to tears and struggled to hold them back. I'd sent mindspeech to Griffin, but he wasn't answering. That was no surprise. I held back from attempting to locate Wylend—if anybody might know where Griffin was, it would be him.

"My love, she is safer here than anywhere else while this condition persists," Karzac soothed. "And you need a break. Tell me this is not so."

"Yeah. I need to go home and get work done," I muttered, hugging myself. "At least we know who the dark-haired god is," I added. Ashe had informed me that it was Li'Neruh Rath, Kifirin's overseer. Karzac and I discussed that briefly over dinner the night before. Kifirin likely had his work cut out for him with a Ko'Ahmari for a supervisor.

"Ashe will alert you if anything changes," Karzac said, glancing at Breanne's body. "Kevis is coming, too. He is taking time away from Sea Winds, and plans to devote his full attention to Kay—and to Breanne's care."

"Then ask Kevis to send mindspeech if there is any change at all," I said. "We'll have to get Ashe or Trajan to take us out of here," I added.

"I know. I just sent mindspeech. Trajan is on the way," Karzac said.

~

Le-Ath Veronis—present

Lissa's Journal

"How is she?" Gavin rose from a chair inside my study the moment I landed there.

"No change." I hunched my shoulders.

"Cara, it has been such a short time. Even a vampire might not recover for many days from something such as this."

"I know. Karzac inserted a feeding tube. He's worried; he just won't say so."

"We are all worried," Gavin shook his head. "Breanne is the only child I have left, and she may leave me, too."

"Gavin?" I stared at him in shock. This was such a turnabout from his original feelings, mind cloud or not.

"Lissa, I cannot begin to describe how things are for me, now. As if the blindfold has been removed and I see clearly for the first time."

6

Gavin turned away—something troubled him greatly and he found it difficult to put in words.

"Things changed when she sent *Love* to you, didn't they?" I blinked at him. His dark eyes fastened on my face and he breathed a sigh.

"Yes. Gavril's death—I doubted I would survive it. Yet here I am. I realize all the mistakes I have made, and hope that I may not repeat them in the future."

"I hear Tybus has not only survived his ordeal, but is thriving and handling his duties easily. Tell me that would be if Breanne hadn't done something for him."

"I believe the old Gavin would not have reacted well to someone else in my son's place. Now, I am merely grateful that Tybus was able to assume that role as easily as he has."

"Yeah. And he seems to be a decent person, on top of that."

"I might have persecuted him—as I did in the past with Breanne, had things not changed for me."

"Gavin, it's the same soul. Conner says so, and she'd know. We didn't give birth to him, but the important part is the same. We need to support him in any way we can."

"And I will, cara. I promise. Just as I will support Breanne in any way I can, should she survive."

"Gavin, I'm so worried." I went to him. He pulled me into his embrace and kissed the top of my head. "What would hold the universes together, if Love didn't exist?" I said.

Gavin pulled away and stared at me. "Lissa, that is the most frightening thing I've heard in a very long time," he whispered.

"Yeah," I agreed.

Earth—past

"Mr. President, we lost that round," Bill sighed. "I don't know where all the rats went after the church went down, but I'm certain they're out there somewhere, waiting to spread their plague again."

"This doesn't sound good at all," the President shook his head at

Bill. "I realize you don't have a better chance at nailing those responsible than the ones I have in other agencies, but I have to tell you, you're the only one who managed to get any information on what we're facing. You say the woman's dead?"

"Yes." Bill lowered his gaze to the floor.

"I realize she was important to you and I'm sorry for your loss. Keep me posted, Director Jennings, and if you need help from anyone else—anyone—let me know. I'll make sure they're available to you."

"Thank you, Mr. President." Bill nodded respectfully and turned to leave the Oval Office.

"We need to track Vernon Clark," Bill said the moment he arrived at his office. He'd asked Opal, Hank and Jayson (whom everyone else called Matt) to wait there for him after the meeting with the President.

"The conspiracy nutcase?" Jayson asked.

"Yeah. I think he's up to his hairline in this," Bill replied before taking a seat behind his desk. "And since he's human—or was the last I heard, he may be easier to track. Maybe we can get information from him on some of the others. We don't need more death and destruction, and I'm grasping at flimsy straws as it is. Vernon Clark may be the first step in a long battle."

"We may not get anything useful out of him, if he's carrying an obsession," Hank pointed out.

"That's all right—I wouldn't mind watching him die like the Sirenali you killed in San Francisco. The fact that he targeted Breanne and Jayson with that idiotic website he runs is enough for me to want him questioned and dead. If he's obsessed, then dead only will do."

"I think I can handle that," Hank agreed, his eyes turning dark and feral.

"You haven't heard anything—have you?" Bill watched Hank carefully. He knew Breanne's body had been moved and was no longer on Earth. He had no idea if she'd been taken for burial or some other purpose. Regardless of the reason, he grieved for her.

"No, Director. There is no news." Hank's eyes regained their normal appearance as he shook his head.

"This sucks," Jayson muttered.

"I agree completely," Bill said. "But we have a job to do, now, and we have to get on it. The last reliable sighting of Vernon was in New Mexico. Are you packed and ready to go? If not, get that way. Hank, can you transport?"

"I can."

"Good."

~

Kifirin—present

"This is Lexsi?" Jayd watched as the baby's hand curled around his finger. "She's so precious," he smiled at the tiny girl in Tory's arms. Reah, Edward and Zendeval stood nearby, trying not to appear impatient as Jayd and Glinda played with the baby.

"This one you will not command," a newcomer appeared, with Kifirin beside him.

Jayd blinked at the new arrivals. Yes, he'd seen Li'Neruh Rath once before and the meeting had been particularly one-sided. Li'Neruh pointed out Jayd's shortcomings, and Jayd had bowed to Kifirin's superior. One of the things Li'Neruh had changed for the High Demon race—dramatically—was the tradition of placing claiming marks.

No longer would the female become ill. The bulk of the responsibility fell on the male, who was now required to care for his mate by rendering her unconscious with their first kiss, then healing the bite marks afterward, so she wouldn't suffer.

Jayd didn't know what to think of the changes. Yes, it would be much better for the female, but he felt it reduced the male's show of strength and virility. It didn't matter; Li'Neruh had decreed the change, therefore it was law.

"Dark Lords," Jayd bowed to the new arrivals.

"You would be wise to conceal your contempt," Li'Neruh snapped at Jayd. "Only Kifirin promised not to interfere. I have not made that promise, and I will not. The Dark Realm required a steady hand upon it, by its very nature. That hand will fall heavy in the future, should it be required." Li'Neruh's eyes were completely black and stars fell and burst in their depths. Jayd was learning that it meant Li'Neruh was angry.

"My apologies, Dark Lord," Jayd lowered his eyes.

"Do not anger me again over such inconsequential nonsense," Li'Neruh breathed smoke with his displeasure. "Strength and virility? There are other, more effective ways to display those. There is no need to harm an already frightened female." Li'Neruh crossed well-muscled arms over his chest.

"You call it harm?" Jayd asked.

"Yes. It is harm. As you have never been ill, you have no idea how your mate suffered when you claimed her. I can rectify that, if you'd like." Li'Neruh uncrossed his arms and lifted a hand.

"No—no, there is no need," Jayd backed away. "I was merely reflecting on tradition."

"At times, traditions are not only harmful; they are ill-conceived from the beginning." More smoke escaped Li'Neruh's nostrils.

Jayd's eyes turned to Kifirin, who glowered. He resented his overlord—a great deal indeed.

~

Earth—past

"It was a mistake, building only one to start," Acrimus observed. "Don't these humans have a saying—about not putting all your eggs in one basket?"

"I agree," Calhoun nodded. "Actually, why build at all, when there are so many throughout this planet? We can target those most amenable to our agenda, and take over from within."

"That may be the best idea I've heard from you," Acrimus' grimace barely resembled the smile intended. "Why stop with only this planet? Are there not religious establishments throughout the worlds?"

"There are," Calhoun's nod became more animated.

"Excellent. Bring a list of targets, and we will devise our plans."

~

"Here's your first target," Vernon Clark pointed to the website he'd pulled up on his laptop.

"I see," Calhoun nodded. "I had them on my list as well. There's no need to instill hate when it's there already."

"One less task for ours to accomplish," Vernon agreed. "These already picket funerals for the dead and hospitals for the wounded, claiming they're all going to hell."

"Hell. Such a delicious concept," Calhoun chuckled. "How easy it is to dupe or mislead these; they so readily believe anything fed to them. Such apt pupils they are."

"You don't believe in hell?" Vernon turned muddy green eyes on Calhoun.

"Oh, my dear, dear, misguided human," Calhoun patted Vernon's shoulder affectionately.

~

Avendor—present

"Hey, Frank." Bill sighed as Franklin chose a lounge chair next to his. Bill had taken to sitting on the wide, back deck outside his bedroom. He'd almost stopped cooking altogether, allowing Sharon O'Neill, Adele Evans and Lavonna Anderson to cook. They usually prepared meals in their homes for *the big house*, as they called it, and Trace or Trajan picked up the food and brought it in.

The only thing Bill did was take Kay's meals to her, and Franklin currently alternated days tending Kay so Bill could have time alone or with Breanne.

"I looked in on Breanne," Franklin said, making himself more comfortable on the deck chair.

"Yeah." Bill's shoulders drooped.

"Hey, none of us have treated one of her kind before—except Karzac, that is, and he only healed superficial stuff. None of us know what any of this means." Franklin stared across miles of gishi fruit trees below the house. He knew the trees would soon flower and grow tiny knobs of green fruit, heralding another harvesting season on Avendor.

"It doesn't matter whether I'm in there or not. Whether I'm talking to her or not. She's not there," Bill whispered.

"Bill, I'm asking you not to give up hope," Frank leaned over and rubbed Bill's back.

"Nine days, Frank. It's been nine days, and no sign. Nothing. Yeah, she's breathing on her own, and her heart is still beating, but —that's it."

"If she weren't breathing on her own, I'd be more worried than I am," Frank said, giving Bill's back a final pat before pulling away. "For me, that spells hope. If she needed help to breathe, then I'd worry. Her vitals are strong for someone in her condition."

"I thought the Larentii had a hand in that," Bill said.

"Up to a point," Franklin agreed. "But you see they're not here sustaining that, don't you?"

"This is so confusing," Bill covered his face with both hands.

"And wearying, I know," Franklin sympathized. "If that were one of my mates in there, I'd be freaked out, too. Bill, she'll get the best of care, and if there's any way," Franklin left the sentence hanging.

"Yeah. I know that. Ashe says that he won't attempt to call her back, because of their history. He's worried that he'll just drive her farther away, and that will make it worse."

"Not good," Franklin sighed. "Look, Kay ate her lunch, and I'll be back to take dinner to her. She still has that permanent blank look on her face, but that's nothing new."

"Yeah." Bill dropped his hands and blinked to adjust to the light again. "Both of them—wandering who knows where, and we can't get to either one."

∼

Kevis changed the bag of liquid sustenance attached to Breanne's feeding tube. His father inserted the tube five days earlier, so Breanne's body might be kept healthy. Kevis knew, just as his father did, that there was no brain activity. That might mean something to most people. He knew his father was waiting to make a judgment on one of the Mighty, however.

"You'd make a lot of people feel better if you'd just wake," Kevis hung the new bag on the pole beside Breanne's bed. "You're safe where you are, I promise. I talked with Graegar—he came to see me. He says that he loves you. Barrigar does, too. You've never really talked with Barrigar. He's one of the best Larentii I know. Doesn't say much, but he sees everything around him." Kevis took a chair beside the bed with a sigh.

"I think Barry's talent for noticing everything around him makes him a really good Protector. I know Conner loves him a lot—just like she loves Graegar. Connegar is Barrigar's son, you know. Barrigar is a wonderful parent. Connegar was Conner's first Larentii child, so he was named after her. Garegar is Graegar's child with Conner, and since he was second-born, he took a variation of his father's name for himself. Are you cold?" Kevis leaned forward and pulled the blanket up a little, covering Breanne's body up to her chin.

"Now," he said, "Pheligar is Renegar's father. Kiarra is Renegar's mother. Renegar is Graegar's father; Grace is Graegar's mother. Graegar is Garegar's father, Conner is Garegar's mother."

"If you don't shut up with Larentii lineage, I may punch you," Breanne's cobalt-blue eyes opened and she blinked in the light filtering through a nearby window. Even Bill heard Kevis' whoop of joy and popped out of his deck chair at a run.

CHAPTER 2

reanne's Journal

The light hurt my eyes as I squinted at Kevis Halivar. I'd never seen a psychiatrist do a victory dance, but he was doing a good job at it. Bill bolted through a nearby door and stopped abruptly, staring at me for a moment before falling to his knees beside the bed and pulling me into his arms.

Trajan wasn't far behind, and if Kevis hadn't started doing weird things with his arms and legs, I'd have wept instead of bursting into laughter. "Wooh-wooh," Kevis chortled while waving his arms. I laughed so hard I cried.

"Here, now, don't pull on the tube," Karzac arrived to dampen the festivities.

"Huh?" Bill let me go and stood aside so Karzac could make his way to my bed. Did I know how long I'd been out? No. I couldn't even say I'd known I was alive. I lowered my shield and read Karzac.

Nine days. Nine days had come and gone since I'd—well, it was better not to think about that. It was too terrifying. Too depressing, too, to realize I'd had absolutely no effect against what I'd faced. Acrimus I might have dealt with. The General? He was too frightening to contemplate.

"Where am I?" My skin quivered as Karzac's fingers explored the area surrounding the feeding tube.

"Hush; I think I can remove this, now. You'll feel a tugging," Karzac announced as Kevis *Pulled* gauze and a small bottle of antiseptic to him.

"Wait," I gasped as stitches were removed with a thought and the tube pulled from my body. Karzac ignored me completely and left me breathing in shock and a small amount of pain.

"It's better if it's done quickly," Karzac soothed, brushing hair back from my face while Kevis dressed the small wound left behind.

"Up to now," my voice shook, "I said you were my favorite Refizani."

"Is that no longer true?" Karzac's green-gold eyes gazed into mine while a smile tugged at a corner of his mouth.

"Jury's still out," I wheezed as Kevis covered the wound with treated gauze and set about healing it with power.

"No harm was intended," Karzac's fingers brushed my forehead again. "I suggest clear broths and simple soups at first. We will check on you regularly, but report any illness or discomfort to Kevis, or directly to me if you wish. If I am not here, send mindspeech."

"Kevis is staying?" I squeaked. I wasn't sure how I felt about that. He'd never mistreated me—not really—but he'd not done anything when Teeg, well, Teeg was gone. Dead. I wondered if Lissa and Gavin were still in mourning.

"Is Lissa still," I began before rethinking my words. *Is she still in mourning for Gavril?* I finished my question in mindspeech.

Yes, but she says you made it easier for her. I have not spoken to Tybus after he was transported to Campiaa, but I hear he is doing well.

"Lissa is still on Le-Ath Veronis, but we can bring her if you'd like," Karzac grinned. He'd covered for me, and I was grateful.

You're still my favorite Refizani, I sent.

Good. I will attempt to keep that honor. Karzac rose from his spot on my bed. "Kevis will care for you, but you may speak with me whenever you like."

"I'll think about it," I nodded.

"I've already alerted Lissa, so she may be here very soon," Karzac turned to go. "I will do my best to return soon as well." Karzac nodded to Trace, who'd stepped inside the bedroom. He and Karzac disappeared.

"Dad says to tell you that you have to take it easy for four to six weeks," Kevis grinned at being left in charge of me.

"Honey, I don't know that I could fight a fly right now," I said. I felt weak, and that worried me. There were things to do; I had no idea where to start and all those things required me to be at full strength. Even that might not be enough if I faced the General alone again. I shivered at the thought.

"Are you cold, sweetheart?" Bill's fingers were tugging at my blanket, working to pull it over my body.

"A little," I nodded. Even nodding tired me.

"Baby, I'll work with you. Get you back in shape," Trajan promised.

"I'll work with you, too. You've been in that bed nine days and all we've done is move you around to prevent bedsores," Bill sighed.

"It may feel like we're pushing too hard, but it's to get you back like you were," Trajan added. Well, he ought to know. He was the one who trained Winkler's werewolves.

"When?" I asked.

"Tomorrow," Kevis said in a commanding tone. The doctor on duty had spoken. "For half an hour, at the most. You can increase it gradually each day, until she's at full strength. Lots of rest in between, too."

"You like that, don't you? Laying down the law?" My eyes felt heavy. "Don't let me sleep too long," I grasped Bill's fingers weakly.

"I won't. I'll wake you for dinner, if you're not awake already."

"Good." I let my eyes close and heard nothing more for several hours.

~

Lissa's Journal

She's sleeping, so you may consider coming for dinner, Kevis sent mindspeech.

Again? Yes, I knew she had to be weak, but she'd only been awake and alert for less than half an hour.

She's been down for nine days. That will debilitate anyone, and we still don't know the extent of the emotional damage.

Yeah, I understand. I just wanted to see her. Talk to her, I amended.

Come for dinner, Kevis repeated. *Trajan will come for you.*

All right, I agreed with a mental sigh.

"What did he say?" Winkler asked.

"To come for dinner. She ought to be awake again around that time."

"Who's going with you?"

"I guess anybody who wants. Why?"

"Because I want to go."

Earth—past

"I hear Obediah headed south," Winkler informed Weldon Harper. "Not much chance to keep an eye on him if he's not in the country. If he's in Mexico, there's no way we can track him there."

"Agreed. Just ask to be informed if he shows up in New Mexico again," Weldon said. "I heard from Wlodek last night, too. He says he's sending Gavin and Charles back to investigate those rogue vamps. Do you have anybody available to put with them?"

"Trajan can go. Trace, Ace and Grady can keep up with things here."

"You think that's enough?"

"For now. I have a feeling Director Bill and those two new agents of his are gonna get involved with this, too, so there's more than enough."

"I'll have some of mine watching for any signs of the enemy," Weldon said. "I expect you to do the same."

"Already on it, Grand Master," Winkler said. "Already on it."

17

~

"These are the ones we're searching for," Bill handed photographs to Dan Kelsey.

"I recognize Vernon Clark—he's been on our radar for a while. Nasty piece of work," Dan acknowledged.

"I have intel that says he was responsible for those border guard murders a couple of years back," Bill said. "He's likely involved in this mess, too."

"I love his minions, who always spout the bullshit that Vernon's working for the people by working against the government," Dan huffed. "He's got his hand in a lot of murders, if my suspicions are correct. It doesn't surprise me at all that he'd be involved with this."

"This one, too," Bill handed a photograph of Janine Webster to Dan. "She's likely connected to that last bombing in San Francisco."

"That's where one of your agents killed that—thing?" Dan had seen the scaled body of an amphibian that bore a rough resemblance to humans.

"Yes. That's a Sirenali, remember? It was fortunate that we managed to kill it before it placed an obsession."

"You say there are four more out there?"

"That's what my source said, and there's no reason not to believe it."

"What kind of attack do you think they'll plan next?" Dan asked. "I'm almost afraid to hear an answer," he held up a hand.

"We don't know. We have feelers out for any new churches being built, but so far, there's nothing that's on the scale of the one in Dallas. Before the building ended up in a pile of rubble, we found a basement filled with equipment, all of it designed to torture people. We found a huge altar, too, and it was covered in human blood."

"I saw those photographs," Dan said. "Forensics is working on identifying the bodies we found. Any new ideas on how the building was destroyed?"

"Nothing concrete, although I have a few suspicions," Bill replied. "At least the building didn't go down until after we gathered evidence.

As for the bodies we cleared out of there, I wasn't expecting to find those. We thought they were feeding all those people to some of their creatures, but that didn't turn out to be the case. Some, it looks as if they just wanted to hear them scream before they died."

"This is fucked up," Dan shook his head. "Mighty fucked up."

Le-Ath Veronis—present
  Lissa's Journal
"Ready?" I studied the ones who'd asked to go with me to Avendor. Drake, Drew, Winkler, Gavin, Rigo and Merrill were lined up and waiting. Those were just my mates who'd expressed a desire to accompany me. Also prepared to go were Graegar, Barrigar, Kiarra, Adam, Pheligar, Chazi, Perzi and Bekzi.

The two extra Larentii, Kiarra, Adam and Pheligar I could understand. The reptanoids? I had no idea. They'd been ferried to Le-Ath Veronis by Edward, who smiled at me, told me they wanted to see Breanne and left before I could ask questions.

"Ready," Winkler grinned.

"Everybody here?" Trajan appeared in my library, prepared to ferry us to SouthStar. He whistled at the crowd. "Ashe told the cooks to prepare for a bunch. Now I know why," Trajan said before folding us to Avendor.

Breanne's Journal
"Sweetheart, are you hungry?" Bill's kiss on my forehead woke me.

"Bill, I need a bath," I moaned before opening my eyes. I wanted one, whether I needed it or not.

"I think we might arrange that, if you'll let me help." Bill's brown eyes smiled at me as I blinked at him.

"But," I said.

"No arguments. I'll carry you in and run water in the tub. Time may be different for you, but I haven't touched you in a long, long time."

"Bill, I don't know," I frowned at him.

"Kevis may kill both of us if I get frisky," Bill grinned. "Come on, pretty girl. Let's get you cleaned up. We'll get frisky when Kevis and Karzac say we can."

I chewed my lip and thought of Hank. There's no way the term frisky would pass his lips—he'd just say fuck. No embarrassment—that was Henry Hank Bell's M.O.

"What are you thinking?" Bill asked as he lifted me from the bed.

"About Hank, and the fact that he'd never say frisky. Not in a million years," I said.

"You're right," Bill agreed, carrying me through a door and into a beautiful bathroom. "He'd just say fuck—about a dozen times, at least."

"I was just thinking about the terminology, not making a comparison," I lifted a hand and brushed hair away from Bill's forehead.

"I hope not," Bill leaned in and kissed me carefully. "There, I kissed you first. Ha!"

"I love you so much," I tucked my head beneath Bill's chin.

"Bree, do you know what that does to me?" Bill whispered.

"What?" I sighed.

"It makes me feel like the luckiest man ever. Plus giving me a rock-hard, well, you know."

"That thing we can't do anything with, right now?"

"Yeah. That thing."

"What thing?" Trajan walked in. "Are we giving our girl a bath?"

"I believe we are," Bill said. "Want to hang onto her while I run the water?"

"It would be my pleasure," Trajan's Texas accent became evident.

I was passed from Bill's arms to Trajan's, who wasted no time in getting his kiss. "I missed you," Trajan whispered before kissing me again.

"Yeah," I huddled into Trajan's warmth.

"Bill, do we have fuzzy pajamas for our girl? I think she's cold," Trajan said.

"I'm not wearing fuzzy pajamas to dinner," I mumbled against Trajan's chest. As a werewolf, he heard me easily and chuckled.

"There's a bunch of folks waiting for you in the kitchen," Trajan said softly against my hair. "I won't let any of 'em get too close unless you want it."

"What about Ashe?" His presence troubled me. I knew I was at SouthStar—how could I not know?

"He says he's real sorry, baby. You're here so he can protect you."

"I'm here because he wants something."

"Sweetheart, Kay needs something. Wait until you meet her to pass judgment," Bill said. "Water's ready, Traje."

"Don't take your anger with Ashe out on Kay," Trajan mumbled as he lowered me to the tile floor and lifted my pajama top over my head.

"I can't do anything for anybody until I feel better," I wheezed. Just wiggling out of pajamas with help from Trajan wore me out.

"You think we don't know that?" Bill swirled a hand in the bathwater, then stepped back so Trajan could place me in the tub. "Kevis and Karzac would punch all of us if we tried to push you too hard. Hell, I'd kick my own ass if I did something that stupid."

"I'll push you some, but I'll take care of you, too," Trajan grinned and *Pulled* a mesh sponge and a bottle of liquid soap into his hands.

"Somebody's way more talented now than he was the last time I saw him," I pointed out.

"Yeah. Ashe happened," Trajan nodded. "We're gonna get you clean, so just relax and enjoy," he said.

After my bath and a considered decision on how to dress me (I ended up in fleece pants, a T and a matching fleece jacket), I was folded into the massive dining room at SouthStar. Bill and Trajan had that talent, now, but Trajan did the honors. Both settled me on a chair between them, while people, already seated, watched. Was I embarrassed? *Yes.*

"I suppose you're all wondering why I called this meeting," my voice wobbled on the much-used joke. Drake and Drew snickered. Well, at least I didn't feel horribly uncomfortable around them.

"How are Travis and Trent?" I asked Lissa's Falchani mates.

"Getting in trouble on Falchan," Drake grinned.

"You talked about our kids?" Lissa blinked at Drake.

"She knew, just from looking at us," Drew nodded in my direction. "So we talked about them for a little bit when we moved her out of that closet office she had and into yours, after they made her look like you."

"That's when I didn't know how to shield, so I was forced to read everybody," I said, staring at my plate.

"How did you learn how to shield?" Ashe asked. He accepted a plate of food from a servant and nodded his thanks.

"From Kalenegar," I said. "Do you know who he is? I still want to kick his ass. He thought the best way to correct my behavior and inability to learn was to give me severe headaches."

"Larentii have not used that method of training in a very long while," Graegar said softly. "And he regrets those things, now." Several Larentii sat at the table—all of them together, and they'd altered their bodies so they'd fit with the rest of us on the chairs provided.

"He can't say that to me himself?" A bowl of soup was set in front of me, while everyone else was served a regular meal.

"He worries that you may be unwilling to listen."

"He may have to wait awhile, until I feel more charitable toward him. And a little stronger," I added.

"I have a question," Winkler said.

"I hope I can answer," I replied.

"What happened to Erithia Cordan's casino?"

"Ah. Well. That." My shoulders drooped. "I blew it up." Drake and Drew chuckled at my admission.

"Why?" Lissa asked, holding back a smile.

"Because Erithia Cordan wasn't dead," I said. "She was Sirenali, and she's the one who placed the obsession on Cheedas to kill you. She also had a lot of other people obsessed to kill, too. Ildevar was a target. Teeg was a target. She had her scaly claws in lots of people. Most of them were in her casino when I chased everybody else out and blew it up."

"She wasn't dead? Rathik didn't kill her?" Gavin stared at me in surprise.

"No. She set somebody else up to be killed in her place. Somebody surgically enhanced to look like her. Rathik was her lapdog. He'd never lay a hand on her unless she told him to."

"You were doing this investigation while you lived at the palace?" Rigo asked.

"Yeah. I sent a message to Kooper, telling him that Erithia was still alive. I don't know whether he ignored it, didn't get it or had already forgotten about me by that time. Either way, there was no response, Erithia was still plotting murder and nobody was willing to listen to me. What else was I supposed to do?"

Gavin cursed softly in Italian at my explanation. Lissa frowned at him. I could tell she was having a mental conversation with my sire, but I didn't want to guess what it might be.

"Was this the only Sirenali you destroyed?" Pheligar asked.

"No. I killed another one on Bexari," I said. "He was Erithia's brother. Hank killed one in San Francisco, but there were four others working with that one," I said. "I really need to go hunt them down."

"Breanne, you're not going anywhere until you recover," Kevis pointed out.

"Kevis, I can't walk from here to the door without feeling faint. What makes you think I could go anywhere right now?"

"Are we sparring?" Kevis grinned mischievously.

"If that's what you want to call it," I shrugged uncomfortably. Everybody was watching me again, and I felt as if I were the only fish in a fishbowl, surrounded by children who were all tapping on the glass.

"Dearest, Kevis only means to keep you from harming yourself," Graegar pointed out.

"I know."

"Eat, now. Your food is getting cold. We will speak of other things later."

I was tired when I dipped into my soup, although the soup was good. Someone knew how to make miso soup with seaweed and small chunks of tofu, so I almost emptied the small bowl placed in front of me.

Lissa's Journal

Breanne almost passed out after eating, so Trajan put her back in bed. Graegar and Barrigar went with him. Surprisingly, all three reptanoids followed.

"Ashe," I said, while setting my fork down with a sigh.

"Lissa?" The Mighty Hand gazed at me from across the table.

"Can you remove compulsion?"

"Ye-es," he said cautiously.

"Good. Will you come with me after dinner? There are three instances of compulsion that need to be removed, with no trace left behind."

"That may be a little harder, but I think I can do that," Ashe nodded.

"Great. Thank you. I'll explain on the way."

"I'd appreciate that." Ashe went back to his chateaubriand with a nod.

"Kooper, this is Ashe." Ashe and I walked into the office Kooper kept inside my palace.

Kooper looked up from the comp-vid in his hand, a puzzled expression on his face. "Lissa? I thought you were off-planet for the evening."

"We made an unplanned trip back. I found out how Erithia

Cordan's casino was destroyed," I began. Ashe moved carefully behind me, and I knew he was gathering energy to do what needed to be done.

"How?" Kooper's interest was immediate. "Trevor and I have been trying to solve that conundrum for a while."

"The compulsion is removed," Ashe stepped forward, his eyes darkened and filled with stars. "You will not recall it or who placed it," he added compulsion of his own.

Kooper blinked for a moment, before his eyes focused on me again. "How?" he repeated his question.

"Breanne destroyed it," I explained, almost holding my breath. Would he remember her now?

"Bree?" Kooper stood almost faster than I could follow the movement. "Where is she? Is she all right? I want to talk to her. Now."

"Kooper, we need to talk," I said, gesturing for him to sit down again. "But there are two more we need to talk with at the same time. Ashe, will you get Trevor and Stellan for me?" I turned to Ashe, who nodded silently and disappeared.

"Is Breanne all right?" Kooper repeated. He was worried. Terrified, actually. He loved her, there was no doubt, and I silently wept for him, Trevor, Stellan and my son.

"She was wounded?" Stellan looked as if he wanted to rip something or someone apart.

I didn't tell him she'd died. Somehow, the Larentii had managed to heal her body and hold it in stasis while waiting for her to return to it. Ashe had gone home, leaving explanations to me.

"She was wounded. Severely," I acknowledged.

"Lissa, what is her condition?" Trevor had remained silent for the most part, but I could tell he was seething; he just wasn't exhibiting outward signs.

"She is very weak. The Larentii helped heal her body, but the damage took a toll. She was only awake for around two hours today. We're hoping she's better tomorrow."

"I never received a message from her," Kooper had gone through his comp-vid twice, searching. There'd been nothing. I knew Gavin had deleted it, but all three who sat in front of me in my study were upset that they'd gotten nothing from Breanne for months. I'd explained that she'd attempted a message to Kooper.

"Gavin, as you know, prevented contact," I began. "But that has since been rescinded."

"I hope Gavin has been reprimanded," Stellan hissed.

"Gavin is sorry for his behavior," I explained. "He was affected—as were others—by something beyond his control. He admits he mistreated Breanne, and hopes for a better relationship now."

"Has someone else taken over her education? What about Casimir? I heard she was engaged to him—without her consent." Trevor wasn't just seething—he was about to reveal claws and fangs. That wasn't a good thing.

"Trevor, that engagement was a sham and I recognized it as such. That has also been rescinded. Breanne is free to choose her own mates. As for her education, let's say that it has been completed. If Breanne needs further instruction, Adam Chessman or I will supply it."

"I'm satisfied with Chessman," Trevor leaned back in his chair. He knew, just as I did, that my education had never been completed, either. In his vampire opinion, anyway.

"Look, I may be able to get you to SouthStar tomorrow to see her," I said.

"I don't want to see her. I want to stay with her. Protect her while she's down," Kooper said. "I have plenty of time, and frankly, Norian owes me—and Breanne."

"I have time as well," Trevor said.

"I'm taking off, whether Teeg says it's all right or not," Stellan added.

"He'll agree," I nodded at Stellan.

"Yeah. He's been a lot better lately. More approachable. No idea what changed, but I don't think it'll be a problem."

"He and Breanne are friends now, I think," I said. "He won't mistreat her, I know that much. He owes her too much."

"Definitely," Stellan agreed. "Where should we meet tomorrow? I'll have my bags packed and ready to go."

"Meet me here; I'll have to tell the people at SouthStar you're coming."

"There's enough room," Ashe raked fingers through his hair when I broke the news to him. "And I probably owe her that. I just don't want to scare Kay, if she happens to see them in the house."

"Why don't you go ahead and ask Breanne to read her, so you'll know what you're dealing with?" I suggested.

"Yeah. I guess we could do that, and maybe it'll help Kevis. It might be better if Bill or Trajan asks her," Ashe sighed.

"True. She cares for both of them," I agreed. "If she needs anything, let me know. Gavin has placed money in an account for her."

"Lissa, I can handle anything Breanne might need, as can Trajan and Bill," Ashe replied with a smile. "Tell Gavin to invest for Breanne, so she'll be taken care of in the future."

"I'll see to it," I said. "Will Trajan come to Le-Ath Veronis tomorrow?"

"He'll be there," Ashe nodded.

Breanne's Journal

Something tickled my chin, waking me to sunlight shining through a bedroom window. The suite I'd been given at SouthStar was quite large, as it turned out, with a separate sitting area, a vidscreen, the huge bath I'd seen the day before and an enormous closet space with an island in the center, which held drawers and storage spaces all around.

Someone had also provided clothing, and I had no idea who that was. My chin was tickled again as I stared at the sunlight filtering through wide, pale wood blinds, made from a tree that only grew on a few worlds.

Lifting a hand to my chin, I immediately understood the source of the tickling. "How did you get here?" A friendly lion snake blinked at me as I touched the top of his head. Two more snakes popped up around me, bringing the total count to three lion snakes. They all blinked hopefully at me, as if they expected something.

"Hey," I stroked the head of the first one gently. No, these weren't as long or as broad as the friendly snake on Le-Ath Veronis, but I had the idea he was an anomaly and they weren't normally that big.

Eventually, all three snakes curled about me while I petted them with both hands. They seemed to enjoy that immensely, and blinked pitifully if I pulled my hands away for any reason.

All three lifted their heads when Bill walked in. They didn't hiss at him, which meant they recognized and liked Bill.

"Time for breakfast," Bill announced. "Want to help get her dressed?" he spoke directly to the snakes.

"We help." I gasped when the first one changed to humanoid. These were lion snake shapeshifters—I just hadn't thought to read any of them. The other two changed, then, and my bed was suddenly crowded.

All three were around five-six, had dark hair, handsome features and lovely smiles as they slid off my bed, completely naked. Well, most shapeshifters didn't have a modest bone in their bodies—Opal didn't. I didn't even want to start with the werewolves. Yeah, I'd seen Trajan, Winkler and the Grand Master naked. It didn't bother them a bit.

"Where clothes?" one of them asked Bill. They intended to dress me first, looked like.

"Chazi, why don't you and your brothers dress while I pick something out, and then you can help her," Bill suggested. I watched him—he had a grin on his face, the schmuck.

"Sound good," another said. "We dress. You find something for Love."

Lowering my shields, I read them. I wanted to smile. They had a peculiar shortcut through Alliance common, plus another language they only spoke with each other.

There were eight reptanoids—all brothers, but these three felt I was theirs. I read in them why they thought that, and added another task to a growing list I kept in my head. It didn't matter—they were loyal to a fault and would defend my life with theirs. I'd seldom seen that kind of devotion in anybody.

Bill picked out fleece trousers, socks, a soft T-shirt and comfortable underwear. I ended up in the bathroom while Chazi, Perzi and Bekzi dressed me. That was certainly a different experience for me, and I struggled to hide any embarrassment as one lifted me while another slipped my feet into panties and pulled them up.

They gabbled amongst themselves while they dressed me, discussed how things fastened and warned one another not to pinch me anywhere. I felt I had to tell them that I understood what they were saying. "Honey," I tapped Chazi's chin as he smiled at me, "I understand all languages, including the one you use with your brothers. I hope that doesn't upset you."

"You understand?" Chazi's eyes lit up.

"Yes," I nodded.

"We glad." He pulled me against him and tucked my head against his shoulder. "Nobody else understand," he breathed. "This good. Very good."

"We have guests at breakfast," Bill said when three reptanoids herded me out of the bathroom after slipping socks on my feet. "Want to walk or fold?" Bill was almost bursting with something—his eyes twinkled mischievously. I forced myself not to read him.

"Fold; I don't want to faint before I get there," I said.

"Good enough." Bill folded me and my three lion snake shapeshifters to the kitchen.

∾

The cook's back was turned to us when we arrived, and Bill and Chazi fussed about getting me settled on a barstool at the massive island. I blinked in shock when the cook turned our way—he was grinning hugely at me. Fes. Fes Desh had come. Who had known to bring him?

"Fes," I wanted to weep at seeing him, but I settled for holding my arms out instead. He came immediately and wrapped me in a tight hug.

"Reah told Ashe to come for me," Fes admitted when he pulled away. "I guess she got tired of hearing me ask about you. Nobody ever had any answers," he admitted.

"It's a long story," I said. "Ask Bill."

"He'd rather hear it from you, sweetheart," Bill said. "Kevis says you can have eggs and toast this morning, and some vegetarian yogurt, if you're still hungry."

"Eggs and toast," I nodded. "Please." I was ready for solid food, and my stomach rumbled at the thought.

"I'll make anything you want as soon as you can eat it," Fes declared and went to the stove.

Trajan wandered in and dropped a kiss on top of my head before settling on a chair beside Bekzi.

"Look at this." Gentle hands cupped my face from behind. I went completely still. I knew that voice. That scent. *Kooper.* I sobbed; I couldn't help myself.

"It's all right, go ahead and cry," Bill soothed after Kooper lifted me off my seat and held me. I gripped the jacket he wore so tightly I ripped it in my fingers, attempting (uselessly) to hold back tears.

"Bree, anybody you can't read won't be hurt by your tears; Graegar said that last night," Bill soothed. Other hands and scents came. Trevor. Stellan. Trevor lifted me away from Kooper and kissed my tears. That had never happened. Ever.

"Teeg sends this and his best wishes," Stellan held out a silk handkerchief.

"Stellan, I missed you so much," I blubbered.

"I know, baby. But that's in the past, now," he crooned before leaning in and kissing me.

CHAPTER 3

*B*reanne's Journal

Five-pound weights did me in. Trajan probably should have laughed his head off. He didn't. I was grateful. "Your body has to come back to normal. Gradually increasing your exercise will help a lot," he said. "I'm gonna make you sweat," he added. "But somebody will help you wash it off."

"Sure," I sighed. I lay flat on my back in Trajan's dojo, staring at his face, which hovered far above mine. I'd done three push-ups after lifting five-pound weights for ten minutes. *Three* push-ups. I was a vampire, for Pete's sake. Weak as I was, I should have done better than that.

"The body goes downhill fast if it does nothing but lie in bed," Kevis' face appeared beside Trajan's. "Muscles don't respond well to that."

"Thanks for the medical opinion," I rasped.

"Anytime," Kevis grinned.

"Are you breathing normally, sweetheart?" Bill's head appeared in my line of vision.

"Yeah. Absolutely. Any day, now," I said.

"We can work with you again later," Kooper, Stellan and Trevor appeared on my other side. "In the pool," Stellan added.

"The pool is warm," Bill said. "It would be ideal."

"We get in pool," Chazi, Perzi and Bekzi appeared at my feet.

"Come on," Bill knelt beside me and helped me sit up. "I'll take you to the hot tub. Then you can nap before lunch."

"Okay, who's making these plans?" I asked while Trajan and Bill lifted me off the mat.

"We are," Bill said. "Can you walk, or do you want to be carried?"

"I can walk," I muttered, wanting more than anything to walk away and leave them behind. I needed a hand to steady me, however. I got two. Stellan and Kooper stepped in, with Trevor right behind. At that moment, I wanted to growl at all of them. I was tired, out of sorts and practically helpless. I didn't like that at all.

"Breanne, that reaction is understandable," Kevis said behind me. "Don't let it harm you or those around you. They only want to help."

"She's not used to that—people wanting to help," Bill muttered. "She's used to people using her. She's not used to being loved, either, so we have to do something about that."

"I'm right here," I pointed out.

"We know that," Trajan snickered. "We just want you to argue with us," he added.

"What Trajan is saying is that he—and the others—want your attention. If it takes an argument to get it, that's what they'll do," Kevis informed me.

"Is that what you're doing?" I stopped for a breather and to turn and look at Trajan.

"Baby doll, you're the most important thing here to us, so yeah, we want some attention."

"This one needs attention, too." I whirled to see Merrill and Kiarra's son, Franklin, standing before us, his hands gripping the shoulders of the most beautiful woman I'd ever seen.

Piercing blue eyes gazed blankly at me, while a river of black hair fell about her shoulders and almost to her waist. We were nearly the same height; I saw that immediately. I lowered my shields to read her. This was Kay—the one Bill and the others were so worried about.

The information hit me like blows. So much. So much had happened to this one, and little of it had been kind or with her well-being in mind. I wanted to scream. I couldn't. The best I could do was moan as the images proved to be too much and darkness took me.

~

"Dearest, what did you see?" Graegar had arrived, with Barrigar right behind him. Somehow, I'd ended up back in my bed while two Larentii bent over me and the others stood around the bed, looking halfway guilty. I couldn't read most of them, but it didn't take a genius to figure out why they felt guilty.

"Graegar, I saw awful things." I covered my eyes with a shaking hand, as if that would block the visions now buried in my brain.

"Kevis needs to know those things, in order to help Kay," Bill said softly.

"Kay needs *my* help, Bill Jennings." My retort was harsher than I meant it to be. "Kevis can work with her all he wants after I get done, but without my help, she'll never be close to normal."

"Bree, I didn't mean," Bill began.

"Honey, I know that. I'm sorry. Where's Kevis? I'll tell him what I know, but until I get some strength back, I can't do much for her."

"I'm here," Kevis stepped through a crowd to get to my bedside.

"You can stay. Graegar and Barrigar can stay. Everybody else needs to go," I sighed.

There was grumbling, but I didn't want all of Kay's secrets poured out to everybody. At the last moment, someone else popped in. I should have expected it. *Ashe.*

At least Ashe didn't speak, or demand that I spill everything immediately. This would take time, and frankly, I wanted to throw up. Was reading Kay a trigger? Oh, yes. It made me wonder if I'd ever get past my early life and be anything close to normal.

"Kay is two people," I began.

33

"Huh?" I'd taken Kevis off guard.

"This is difficult for you, isn't it?" Barrigar said.

"Yeah."

"Then let me help." Graegar moved aside so Barrigar could sit on the side of my bed. Lifting me into muscular blue arms, he smiled gently at me before tucking my head beneath his chin.

"Now," his chest rumbled with the word, "tell us."

Barrigar and Graegar were sending me energy and emotional strength, and I had no idea how they were accomplishing that feat. It didn't matter—I felt so much better because of it, and might be able to get through what I had to say.

"Kay has two souls inside her body," I said. "One is named Kalia, and she is horribly damaged. The other is named Kay—really—and she's somewhat damaged, too. Kay is more coherent, but Kalia's fears override everything. Right now, that's what is going on inside her body—Kay's consciousness is being squashed by Kalia's terror."

"A walk-in soul? Are you sure?" Kevis breathed. "I mean, I've heard of it, but I've never seen it. Always thought it might be a myth."

"It's true in Kay's case," I said. Barrigar's fingers stroked my face gently, while Graegar reached for one of my hands and kissed the palm. Both Larentii were as warm as a summer day, which was more than welcome—I felt chilled.

"Are they fighting? The souls? Is that why she acts as though she's not really there?" Ashe broke his silence, then. He was terrified for Kay—I could tell from his voice.

"Yes and no," I said. "Kalia is so afraid that she takes over everything with her fear. Kay can't withstand that."

"What makes Kalia afraid, dearest?" Graegar asked softly. He was asking the big question, when he knew how awful the answers might be—for me to tell and for the others to hear.

"Kalia was a sex slave," I said. "She was trained as such from the age of six, and sold to a pedophile criminal when she was nine. She's terrified of women, because women trained her—hurt her—when she was little. She's afraid that any man will ask her to perform, well, you know," I sighed. "There has never been real love in Kalia's life. Obsession and torture, yes. Love—no."

"How did Kay's soul get there?" Ashe asked.

"Kay is from Earth," I said. "She was disfigured from injuries received in a fire that burned her house and killed her parents when she was tiny. She wasn't accepted because of the way she looked." Yeah, I knew exactly how that felt.

"But that doesn't explain," Ashe began.

"I'm not done, yet," I said. "Kay was shot in a bank during a botched robbery attempt. Somehow, her soul was transferred to Kalia's body, just as Kalia was being tortured by Iversti Foculis. Kay has a peculiar talent that Kalia doesn't," I said. What I was about to say made me tremble, and that caused Barrigar to hold me tighter against him.

"What is that?" Ashe's voice was softer. Gentler. As if he'd been told that this upset me a great deal. It did. I had images burned in my brain of the criminal sadist, Iversti Foculis, cutting designs into Kalia's stomach and grinning while she screamed.

"Show us," Graegar suggested. "Just let the images play while you connect with us," he said.

"All right." I huddled against Barrigar and sent the images.

Ashe's Journal

I saw it. It was horrible. Kalia was chained to a wall, her mouth open in a terrifying scream as Iversti Foculis cut into her belly with a knife. He'd already drawn smaller sun wheels into her flesh. This one was larger.

He laughed while she screamed. Then I saw the sudden difference in her. Kalia's eyes changed and the scream cut off. Iversti jerked his head up—he imagined she'd fainted. That wasn't the case. Kay looked out of Kalia's eyes, and I knew in that moment that her soul had been transferred into Kalia's body.

"You die," Kay hissed, and Iversti dropped to the floor, quite dead.

"How?" I spoke aloud. Yes, Breanne suffered to give these images to me. How could she not? I knew that her past was just as horrible as Kalia's, and at that moment, her terror washed through the images, making my heart speed up and filling me with fear.

That was what she faced daily. The potential triggering of memories so terrible they could be debilitating. Kalia was much the same, although most of her abuse was sexual and not just physical.

"Kay can see most people's aura lines," Breanne sighed while Barrigar began to trill softly.

Breanne's Journal

"Not just auras?" Kevis asked. He sounded confused.

"There are lines of basic colors that form secondary aura colors," I explained. Barrigar had begun trilling softly, and frankly, it helped me push the awful memories aside so I could explain Kay's talent. "Kay can see the lines," I said. "Not only can she do that, she can change them, too. She can make someone who's sick well. If you were vampire and wanted to be able to eat normally, she could do that. If you were human and wanted to be werewolf, she could do that. Obviously, she hasn't done any of those things. So far, Kay has only used her talent twice, and both times it was to do the same thing."

"What was that?" Ashe asked. He suspected, now, but he wanted to hear it anyway.

"If she turns the aura lines all black, that person dies. She's killed twice. First, it was the gunman in the bank robbery, after he shot her. Second was Iversti Foculis, for torturing Kalia."

"She can do this to anyone?" Kevis breathed, sounding shocked.

"If she can read your lines. Anybody with power she generally can't read. That means Larentii. Gods. Saa Thalarr. Some wizards and warlocks. A few others, maybe."

"The Elemaiya have a term for this," Ashe rose and raked fingers through his hair. "It's a myth to them," he added. "They call the one who holds this power Ri'Kita—the Changer."

"Kalia is a pureblood Elemaiya," I said. "Kay was a quarter." Ashe's head jerked around and he stared at me. "Kalia's parents sold her when she was tiny to those fucking women who train girls for pedophiles," I gritted. "As soon as I'm able, I'm hunting those women down and making them dead."

I didn't add that Hordace Cayetes, the criminal who'd purchased Kalia, was also on my radar, as were several others—Rezil Foculis and Q'And and Q'Ind Ribalo, to name three.

"Dearest, there are others who need dispatching first," Graegar reminded me.

"Yeah." My anger deflated, leaving me beyond weary.

"How soon, Breanne? How soon can you help Kay?" Ashe had turned back to me again. Barrigar increased the volume of his trilling, making my eyes droop.

"Don't know," I whispered before falling asleep.

"Traje, the next time I start to yell at anybody, punch me in the mouth," Ashe mumbled as he took a chair next to his Second.

"Be happy to," Trajan nodded.

"Try this," Fes set a slice of cake in front of Trajan, before cutting a second piece and offering it to Ashe.

"This smells like heaven," Trajan grinned and cut into the cake with a fork.

"It's really good—one of Reah's recipes," Fes grinned.

"Oh, yeah, this is amazing," Trajan spoke around a second mouthful.

"There's food?" Stellan walked in, followed by Trevor, Kooper and the reptanoids. Chazi, Bekzi and Perzi recognized Kooper as a lion snake shapeshifter from the beginning, and admired him greatly after he'd shifted for them earlier. All of them felt better, too, when Graegar came and explained that Breanne was sleeping and not in pain or distress.

"Have a seat," Fes nodded toward barstools around the island. "We'll all have cake, coffee and talk."

"How we get Bree back?" Chazi began.

"Make feel strong?" Perzi expanded on his brother's question.

"No idea, and I'd like that more than anything right now," Ashe sighed. "Cake's excellent, Fes. No offense, Bill."

"None taken," Bill settled on a barstool and accepted a piece of cake. "I've been to Desh's on Tulgalan, remember? I still want to steal the fish recipe."

"We can make it tomorrow if you want. I just need to get the fish."

"Wait, I just had an idea," Trajan gripped Ashe's arm—hard.

"Wow, that must have hurt," Trace walked in, grinning.

"What?" Ashe asked.

"Bring your cake—we'll go out to the groves," Trajan lifted his plate and fork.

"Lead on," Ashe nodded. He and Trajan disappeared.

Ashe's Journal

"You're not joking, are you?" I shook my head at Trajan.

"Look, you're Strength, right? Isn't that what Bree needs? Strength?"

"But how," I almost stuttered the words as it hit me. Breanne—physically, anyway—was vampire. If she took my blood—was it worth the effort?

"What will it hurt? She'll only take a little—she gags otherwise," Trajan pointed out. "Last I heard from Charles and Jayson, you'll never know she's there. Until, well," Trajan didn't finish.

"The climax, you mean?"

"Yeah. Look, boss, you haven't had, uh," he floundered for a moment before giving up.

"Not in a while," I agreed grimly. For me, sex didn't mean much unless I cared about the woman, and there'd been few of those through the years. Yes, I knew how. I'd studied it quite intensely between my seventeenth and thirty-fifth years. Practiced it too—after my twentieth birthday, Trajan and I had been in plenty of bars, from one end of the Alliances to the other. Women always approached us. *Always*.

Both of us, however, had tired of casual sex. We'd begun waiting— hoping—for the one for us to come along. Kalia's face kept appearing in my mind throughout the years. I measured any woman I met against her and found them wanting.

"Look, it won't be a big deal. What if you do need to uh, change your shorts? So what?"

I'll admit, that made me laugh. Trajan was doing it on purpose, too. I felt as if I were sixteen again, and as inexperienced as I'd been back then.

"You mean I'll drop my wad in my pants? Is that what you're saying?" I asked.

Trajan bent over, and it took me a moment to realize he was holding back laughter. Finally, a loud guffaw escaped and he fell to his knees while laughter poured out of him.

Yes, he'd been incredibly stressed when he had no idea whether Breanne would survive. Now that she was back and things were looking up, he was releasing all the tension in booming laughter.

"Bro, I could hear you from two miles away," Trace folded in to stare at his older brother.

"He's releasing some steam," I shrugged at Trace. "Look, we may have an option to help Kay and Breanne. At least I hope it'll work. We just have to convince Breanne when she wakes," I said.

"What's that?" Trace was interested immediately. "Chessman asked about her when I took Frank home."

"Ashe is gonna give Bree some blood." Trajan stood and grinned at his brother.

"Seriously? Sounds like a cool idea. Hope it works," Trace lifted a speculative eyebrow at Ashe. "How long has it been since?"

"We were just discussing that, and the inevitable necessity of changing my underwear," I replied, feigning indifference.

"You could always talk to Aedan, too," Trajan pointed out.

"Yeah. I guess I could talk to Dad," I agreed. "See ya." I folded away.

~

"Son?" He looked up as I approached. Aedan Evans, the only father I would ever know, looked up from the seedling gishi tree he was planting.

"Dad, I need some advice," I said.

"What kind of advice?" He was surprised—I hadn't come to him for advice in two hundred years.

"About the bite."

"Ah. How is she?" he asked, going back to his task and settling dirt around the fragile stem. "Breanne," he added. Everybody at SouthStar knew. It didn't matter—they couldn't pass the barrier anyway. Not without permission and somebody powerful enough to ferry them through. Only three people could do that, and the other two wouldn't do it without my knowledge or consent.

"Better, but really, really weak," I replied.

"So you think to allow her to take from you."

"Yeah. It was a thought and worth a try, since Kay may benefit in the long run."

"Breanne can help Kay?" Dad turned his full attention to me, then.

"Yeah. She says she can, anyway, and there's no reason not to believe her."

"Is there any way?" he began. I knew what he wanted—he wanted to have things as they were before with my mother.

"Dad, I don't know." What I did know—and had never told him (or my mother) was that Breanne had already helped them a great deal. The fact that they hadn't been honest with each other was what eventually drove them apart. I still had hope that they'd set that aside someday.

I felt guilt, too, that Breanne had come to my defense in the past. I felt more than guilt, actually, and wished for perhaps the thousandth time that I'd recognized her when Trajan first brought her to SouthStar. Those things she'd done for me—and my parents—would come about in her future, but I still held hope that she wouldn't be so upset with me that she'd withhold the help she'd given.

That didn't even touch on the fact that she could have helped Kay immediately—if I'd only allowed Trajan to keep her here. So many things had gone awry and I had little reason or explanation for it, other than blaming my own fucking temper.

"Dude?" Sali appeared at my side and watched as my father planted another seedling.

"Sal?" I turned to him.

"How's everything up at the big house?"

"Some things better, some things the same," I shrugged.

"Nothing new with Kay?"

"Not yet, but we may be able to fix that soon. Actually, Breanne may be able to fix that soon. When she gets her strength back."

"I'd like to meet her."

"Come up to the house for dinner. Graegar said she'd be awake by then."

~

Breanne's Journal

I woke next to Bill, who was sitting up and reading on a comp-vid, his feet, covered in socks, stretched out on the bed beside me.

"Feel better?" he asked, setting the comp-vid aside.

"Road kill probably feels better than I do," I wrinkled my nose at him, so he'd know I was teasing.

"At least you look better than road kill," he grinned.

"Reading a book?" I asked.

"Nah. Just keeping up on reports of criminal activity across the Alliances; nothing for you to worry about," he leaned over and kissed me, his mouth lingering on mine for a few seconds before pulling away.

"You can take the man away from the department, but you can't take the department away from the man?" I teased. "Wanting to get back in the thick of it?" I asked, more seriously.

"Bree, Ashe is keeping my body young. SouthStar has that effect on everybody who comes here. If I leave, that goes away and I start aging again, unless I'm with Ashe and he's shielding me."

He was right—Bill looked to be in his early thirties, when he was actually much older. "There's a way to change that," I pointed out.

"I don't want to be vampire," he said.

"That's not the only way," I huffed. "The Saa Thalarr do it all the time. Whoever gets their blood gains immortality."

"Is that how it works?"

"Yeah. Adam Chessman gave me blood, which not only healed me, but gave me the ability to walk in daylight and eat normal food. It's the way that race was created."

"Why did he have to heal you?"

"Well, uh, let's say that my first few weeks as vampire weren't the best," I hedged.

"You walked into the sun?" Bill stared at me in shock. "You attempted suicide?"

"Bill, I thought everybody knew about that. I see that's not the case."

"I knew," Kevis walked into my suite without knocking.

"I think a sharing of information might be in order," Bill growled.

"Bill, I think I know better now," I slapped a hand over my eyes.

"You think so? What was that stunt then, at that stupid church? Tell me that wasn't suicide. And for what?"

I should have known that I'd hurt him—and the others too, by doing what I did. Yes, he'd suffered afterward, when he had no idea whether I'd survived.

"I'm sorry, honey. It was stupid, but I didn't know what else to do."

"Bree, I don't want to yell at you, but, actually, I do want to yell. I don't want to upset you, but I want to yell at somebody or something. I watched you for nine fucking days, with my heart squeezing in my chest because I didn't know if you were still in there." He tapped the top of my head with a finger. "I don't even want to talk about the time I spent on Earth when I thought you were dead."

"Bill." I took his face in my hands. "I'm sorry for putting you through that. If I could make any part of that easier for you, I would."

"I know, sweetheart. I just," He shook his head, as if that might dispel his anger.

"I'll do what I can, as soon as I get my strength back," I ran fingers through his short, dark-brown hair.

"What will you do?" he asked.

"What I'll do for Kay, only on a lesser scale. I don't think you need as much as she does."

"As much what?"

"Love," I said. "I love you, Bill Jennings, no matter what you might think, or how mad you might get."

"Thank goodness for that," he pulled me into a tight hug.

"Are we better now?" Kevis said brightly. I'd forgotten he was there while Bill and I had our small meltdown. There was nothing like having a shared breakdown in front of a psychiatrist, I suppose.

"We're better now," Bill mumbled into my hair. He didn't want to let me go, it seemed, as his arms remained tightly wound around me.

"Good. Less for me to sort out later," Kevis grinned.

"What are you not sorting out?" Trajan walked in, followed by Ashe and another werewolf—Salidar DeLuca. Lowering my shields, I read Sali. He'd once been best friends with Ashe, but things had separated them somewhat.

Ashe was what he was, after all, and Sali had no idea how to deal with much of that. He felt inferior and had spent years studying and learning how to fight in a constant effort to improve himself. It was an attempt to level the playing field and close the distance between himself and Ashe. They remained friends, but might never be as close as they once were.

"A bit of anger from understandable stress and a temporary loss of control," Kevis said. "Nothing world-shattering."

"Bill, I blasted piles of brush to bits," Trajan said. "Worked out some kinks, that way."

"Next time you go, take me with you," Bill sighed. "I tried to take it out on my girl."

"Bill, stop." I leaned away and placed a hand over his mouth. "Let's face it, if Hank were here, he'd have done a whole lot worse."

"We would have to clear smoke for days," Trajan agreed solemnly.

I sagged against Bill. Whether I liked it or not, I had to get back to Earth in the past to do what I could, and that, by default, meant catching up with Hank again. I wasn't looking forward to that.

"What's this about?" Bill noticed the difference immediately.

"Hank's gonna yell," I muttered. Jayson would be right behind him, and likely so would Bill and Trajan—their past selves, anyway.

"It upsets you when that happens, doesn't it? It terrifies you, in fact. Doesn't it?" Kevis the shrink was back.

"I don't want to talk about it." I huddled against Bill again.

"We messed up the last time," Bill whispered.

"How bad was the beating this time?" Kevis asked.

"Kevis, I died. I stood outside my body and knew it was dead. That's how bad it was. Are you gonna talk about my PTSD now?" I turned my eyes on him and blinked.

"Bree, I can't talk about your PTSD. Only you can do that." Kevis sat on the edge of my bed and studied me. Was there concern in his eyes? Yes. Overwhelming concern. I didn't know what to do with that. "It might help if you did talk about it," he added.

"I'm not comfortable with that." I buried my face against Bill's shoulder.

"I know," Kevis soothed. "Maybe someday you'll feel comfortable enough with me to tell me those things. This isn't a job to me, Breanne. Dad and I—we both care about you. We want you happy. If it takes one of these guys to be with you, to hold you while you let this go by talking about it, then so be it. I'll go with whatever works."

"Kevis, that may be a long time in coming," I mumbled.

"Take your time—there's no hurry," he patted my shoulder and stood to stretch. "I believe Ashe has something to say before we go to dinner."

I turned my head and watched as Kevis walked out of my suite. Ashe took Kevis' place on the side of my bed. "Look," he began, "this feels as awkward to me as it will to you," he continued. "But Traje pointed it out to me earlier, and it may be worth a try."

"What?" I asked.

"Well, I'm Strength, so, maybe it would do you some good to get my blood. All I'd ask in return, if the experiment is successful, is for you to help Kay."

"You want me to bite you?" I stared in disbelief. "You know what happens when," I didn't finish.

"I've been advised," Ashe replied dryly. "I'm willing to overlook, well, that's not coming out right."

"You're saying it won't mean anything." What was I supposed to do? Once, I might have been a willing participant, so I could give him pleasure. He wanted nothing of the kind from me. I was merely a means to an end for him, and we were right back where we'd been before—when he'd yelled at Trajan to get me out of the house.

Kay, on the other hand, desperately needed my help. She needed to be in charge, instead of Kalia's fears. I released a weary sigh. "I'll do it," I said. "For Kay."

"That's all I ask." Ashe rose. "Thank you." He walked out without another word.

"When?" I turned to Trajan.

"He says tomorrow morning, after you've rested again. Then we'll see how much good it did."

"Yeah." At that moment, I wanted to mist away. Lick my wounds. Wallow in misery for a while. I didn't have the strength to do it, and therein lay the problem.

"I said everything wrong." Ashe flopped onto the chair behind his desk.

"That seems to be a regular occurrence," Kevis pointed out. He'd waited in the hall outside Breanne's bedroom while Ashe spoke with her. He'd then followed Ashe to his office. "Why do you think Breanne might see this as anything other than a snub, or an effort to use her to get what you want? You may as well have told her she doesn't mean a damn thing to you and get it over with."

"What the hell are you talking about?" Ashe frowned at Kevis. "You appear to have more of your father in you than I originally thought," he added.

"You're not seeing what I'm seeing," Kevis tossed up a hand. "Every time she looks at you, there is fear in her eyes that you'll hurt her. Tell me, Mighty Hand, who can hurt you the worst? Is it the person you don't care about, or the one you do?"

"What the hell are you talking about?" Ashe exploded. "I worry about Kay. That's all I've focused on for months!"

"I know that," Kevis held up a hand. "But you keep beating up Breanne over it, when she likely saw you as something different in the beginning—before you opened your Mighty mouth."

"You're saying she was attracted to me?" Ashe couldn't believe what he was hearing.

"It's likely, and you shredded her. Then, all she kept hearing was that you wanted her back here—to help you. Not the most ideal situation, huh?"

"I suppose not. This complicates everything, doesn't it?" Ashe raked fingers through his hair in frustration.

"Yes, but it was complicated from the beginning."

"True. I don't know how to fix this, Kevis. Or even where to start trying."

"Start by keeping your mouth shut and being respectful. Dad and I have discussed this, and let's face it—so far, the Mighty Heart has done all the heavy lifting. Hasn't she?"

"Yeah. I see your point."

~

Lissa's Journal

"Amara, I never expected to see you here," I began awkwardly. She'd come to my palace—with Edan Desh. I'd invited her into my study the moment I could—they'd shown up for the morning's session with the Council and sat in the public seating area. I was more than grateful there were no executions or sentencing going on.

"Lissa, my feelings toward you have never changed," she said, taking the seat I offered. Edan took the one next to her and sat quietly by her side.

"I'm grateful," I nodded to her.

"I heard something from Kyler," Amara added.

"That Griffin was saved by," I didn't finish.

"Yes. That's what I heard. How is she?"

"Better. Very weak."

"Understandable."

"Yes." I nodded—Amara was a healer, after all.

"Is there a chance I might meet her, sometime?"

"I'll ask," I offered. I had no idea how Breanne might respond, however.

"I don't hate him—your father," Amara sighed. "But."

"Yes," I nodded. "But. Are you happy?" I glanced toward Edan.

"Yes. We have so much in common," Amara smiled at Edan. "Even at the end of the day, when we're both tired, we still talk about work and things we'd like to do."

I understood that perfectly. So many times, I discussed the day's business with whoever ended up in bed with me—before or after sex. It was nice to bounce ideas around—along with bouncing the bed.

"Do you want me to take a message to her?" I asked, meaning Breanne.

"Yes. Tell her that her stepmother will be happy to see her anytime."

"I will," I nodded.

CHAPTER 4

"Our General was not beaten—merely surprised," Acrimus hissed at Calhoun. "We are still awaiting news whether he killed one of the Mighty. It certainly seemed that way before he and I left."

"I sincerely hope she was killed," Calhoun breathed. "Any idea which one she might have been?"

"Not completely, although I have a guess. I'll wait for more information before I reveal my suspicions, however."

"At least we know who she is and what she looks like," Calhoun chuckled. "There's no way for her to hide from us now."

"You are so short-sighted," Acrimus grimaced and shook his head.

Breanne's Journal

The pool really was warm. I was content, allowing Fes to hold me up while four lion snake shapeshifters swam around us—as snakes. Bill thought it was funny—watching Kooper, all twenty feet of him, followed by Chazi, Bekzi and Perzi, who were smaller in length— perhaps thirteen or fourteen feet long. Kooper didn't seem to mind that he had an adoring public swimming in his wake. I wasn't sure what to think, either—that he was the snake who'd been in my bed on several occasions.

That's how he'd gotten information from me—on criminal activity. I'd innocently spilled it to my snaky bed companion, and Kooper wasted no time cashing in on valid information. Briefly, I wondered where you'd have to kick to boot a snake's ass.

Trevor and Trajan were content to lie on lounges alongside the pool, closing their eyes and resting in the shade provided by exotic trees.

"Want to try swimming with me?" Fes breathed against my ear.

"I can barely walk through the water," I leaned back to peer into his eyes.

"Then let's walk. I won't let you drown," he grinned.

"Good," I smiled at him. He leaned in for a kiss before pushing me toward the opposite side of the pool. At least the water buoyed me up while I struggled against liquid resistance.

Eventually I had an audience—I was determined to make my way across the pool and back—more than once. I made three trips before almost sinking below the water. Bill and Fes caught me before my nose hit the surface.

"Better," Trajan said from the side. He'd perked up halfway through my exercises. Trevor, too, had sat up to watch.

"We might even let you have fruit with dinner," Kevis folded in from somewhere and stood at the edge of the pool, his fists on his hips.

"Tease," I mumbled as Bill and Fes lifted my arms so Trevor and Trajan could pull me from the pool.

"Not teasing," Kevis grinned, *Pulling* a cup of tea into his hands. "Sissy," he added.

"What?" I blinked as I was lowered to the tiled patio, almost beside Kevis. I wasn't expecting an insult from Doctor Kevis Halivar, after all.

"Graegar is my half-brother," Kevin chuckled.

I wanted to slap a hand to my forehead. I didn't—mostly because it would take energy I didn't have at the moment. No wonder Kevis knew so much about Larentii lineage. His mother was mated to Renegar, and they were Graegar's parents.

"Graegar has the hots for you," Kevis went on. "So does Barrigar."

"Oh, for crying out loud," I muttered. "What does Conner say?"

"Conner is more than happy. She's known for a while that they'd have another mate, she just didn't know who it was. You're like a celebrity in that household, now."

"That's not embarrassing or anything," I sighed. "Can I sit down, now?" Trajan and Trevor bore most of my weight as it was, and they were just about to get all of it—I was too tired to stand any longer.

"What does your mother say? And Renegar?"

"Bree, stop worrying about that. Dad says he wants to invite you for dinner as soon as you can sit up without assistance," Kevis grinned. "Mom and Ren are more than happy, trust me."

"So everybody knows except me, is that it?"

"Hey, I think they love you already. They just want to see you. Talk to you," Kevis' voice softened. "Nobody wants to scare you or take advantage. This is the Saa Thalarr and the Larentii we're talking about."

"Yeah." Trajan lifted me into his arms, preventing me from hunching my shoulders. There was at least one Larentii who owed me an apology. He wasn't on the guest list.

~

Earth—past

"I hate the desert." Jayson flopped onto a sofa inside the spacious adobe home Bill had managed to acquire in Albuquerque. It would serve as their base of operations while they searched for Vernon Clark. His last verified location had been in Valencia, a small town south of Albuquerque.

"Why?" Opal checked the clip on her gun before slipping it into her waistband.

"Dad used to take us to Palm Springs on vacation, so he could play golf in a celebrity tournament with Ross Gideon. I hate golf."

"So you hate golf and the desert?" Opal lifted a dark eyebrow at Jayson. "And the fact that your dad forced you to go to the same place every year?"

"Sounds whiny, doesn't it?" Jayson turned hazel eyes on Opal. "Even when I was old enough to stay home with Mom and Jamie, because they didn't want to go either, he made us go. To this day, Jamie won't come within miles of Palm Springs."

"So your dad was a little controlling?"

"Yeah. Don't say it," Jayson held up a hand. "I'm well aware of why I like to be in charge."

"Not going down that road," Opal tossed up a hand. "Is there a grocery store nearby? There's nothing in the fridge."

"You want to go?" Hank stalked into the room like a caged panther. "Bill is in his bedroom, answering calls. I think I can get us to the store and back in one piece."

"Let's make a list," Opal nodded. "Damn, I wish Bree was here." Opal pulled out her cell, preparing to tap out items to buy. "Any news?" She tapped a few things into her phone without looking up at Hank.

"Still nothing." Hank blew a curl of smoke.

"I don't know whether to cry or hope," Opal muttered, adding bread and butter to her list.

"Same here, Opal. Same here," Hank agreed. "Bill has just about given up, I think."

"Yeah. He was talking about buying a space in an Oklahoma cemetery. Any idea what that's about?"

"Breanne's sister's grave is there," Hank sighed.

"For real?" Opal looked up and blinked once at Hank.

"Yes. Not many know that."

"I'll keep it to myself, then."

"Where do you think Vernon Clark is?" Jayson asked as he rose to check Opal's growing list. "Add cookies," he pointed at Opal's phone.

"I hope he's still in New Mexico," Hank rumbled. "I really want my hands on him."

"I want to see your hands on him," Opal agreed. "What kind of cookies?"

"Oatmeal and white chocolate chunk," Jayson grinned. "I hope the store has a bakery and a deli," he added. "I like the ones baked at the store."

"Rome, until now, I had my doubts you'd recognize the inside of a grocery store."

"Hey, I used to go with Mom's housekeeper," he grinned. "I love grocery stores. I just don't get a chance to go anymore. Too busy with work."

"And Trina did it for you," Opal sighed. "Fuck."

"Yeah, we miss her," Hank agreed. "But she really is in a better place. We saw that."

"I'm glad we got to see it," Jayson muttered, flopping on the sofa again. "Mom's back in Tahoe and Dan's with her, but I worry that she's still not safe."

"I have my concerns about that as well," Hank agreed. "Not that we can do much about it at the moment."

"Yeah."

"Hey," Trajan wandered in—he'd taken a shower after unloading bags in the New Mexico heat and his black hair was still damp.

"You think Vernon Clark is still in New Mexico?" Opal asked. "And what do you want to add to the grocery list?"

"I think it's possible he's still in the state," Trajan replied. "Winkler seems to think so, too. It's almost a straight shot from Valencia to Juarez on I-25, and if he gets to Juarez, we might as well kiss him goodbye. When are the vamps scheduled to arrive?"

"Tonight, according to Bill," Hank said. "I'm just glad we were able to get this house. You don't find too many around with eight bedrooms plus a guest house."

"Winkler," Trajan coughed into his hand before flashing a grin.

"He knew somebody, didn't he?" Opal turned to the tall werewolf.

"Yeah. This belongs to a werewolf who lives in Chicago. Comes down here for the winter months with his family. He has a large family. He's also related by marriage to the local Packmaster, so there's no problem with the extended visit."

"You guys have to check in?" Jayson asked.

"Usually. Winkler has the Grand Master's permission to park anywhere, though, since we do a lot of investigative work for the werewolf community."

"You do, too—as Winkler's representative?" Jayson asked.

"You catch on quick," Trajan slapped Jayson on the shoulder. "Winkler notified the local Pack—they know I'm here, but they can't disallow the visit."

"Want to go to the store?" Opal asked.

"Yeah. Wolves eat a lot, you know."

Avendor—present

Breanne's Journal

"How are you feeling?"

Adam and Franklin, Merrill's son, had come for dinner. Adam and I hadn't had a chance to talk the night before. I didn't mind—I felt slightly embarrassed that my surrogate sire likely knew of my refusal to allow him to teach me anything else.

"I feel okay—if feeling weaker than a kitten is okay," I sighed. "I barely made it, walking three times across the pool this afternoon."

"You'll come back fast," Adam said. "Faster than a normal person might, anyway." He smiled gently at me. "I hear that Karzac wants to invite you to dinner. We've decided that NorthStar would be the ideal location—Ashe has extended his shield to cover it and EastStar."

"Kevis said that," I nodded, picking at my food.

"Eat, sweetheart. Nobody is here to pressure you or make you feel uncomfortable."

"That still doesn't mean I won't feel that way," I said.

"I understand that," he nodded. "I wanted to see you—tell you that I'm available if you need anything, or to run interference if somebody upsets you." He smiled at that—he was offering to act as a father figure if I needed it, to intercede on my behalf with what looked to be a gathering herd of potential mates.

"That may be the nicest thing anybody has offered to do for me, ever." I smiled at him, but my lower lip trembled slightly. Nobody had ever asked to be my parent before. I had someone stepping up now.

"I contacted Gavin earlier, and we set up an account for you on Le-Ath Veronis. It'll be there, if you need to access it. Trajan has the information, whenever you want something," Adam continued. "Kiarra, Lissa, Kyler and Cleo bought the clothes in your closet. If you don't like any of it, let Lissa know. It was purchased in Casino City."

"How is Teeg doing?" I asked.

"Ah. He's doing well. There was a meeting yesterday, with the renewable energy commission. Things went smoothly." Adam smiled.

"Good. I was a little worried after the stabbing." Adam knew. I knew he knew, and he gave me a slight nod. Tybus was fitting into his new role easier than anyone might have expected.

"I can arrange to invite him to dinner, when you come to NorthStar," Adam offered.

"Would you? I think I'd like to talk with him," I said. "How soon?"

"I think you can go in two days," Kevis spoke up. "Provided everything else proceeds as planned."

"We can make arrangements for that," Adam agreed.

"We have two days to plan," Kiarra smiled at Kyler. "Think we can pull this off?"

"Yeah. No problem," Kyler nodded. "Cleo wants in, too. Daddy wants to bring a contingent from Grey House—they owe Breanne a lot."

"Conner says no way we're leaving her out of this," Kiarra said. "That means Shane will be helping us with the food."

"Will this place hold everybody?" Kyler asked, grinning impishly.

"We'll make sure it holds everybody," Kiarra replied.

Breanne's Journal

"Kevis, why are you here?" I wanted to moan, but he'd just tease me about it. I was already in bed reading, with four lion snake shapeshifters for company. All four were coiled or draped around me, waiting for me to turn out the light.

"I'm here with the finger," he held up an index finger. I blinked at him.

"Huh?" I wasn't getting it.

"It goes like this," Kevis took a step toward my bed. "I hold up my finger like this," he illustrated by holding his hand high, the finger pointed toward the ceiling. "And then let it descend, until it touches your forehead, like this." He poked me in the middle of my forehead. Darkness came immediately.

"I can't believe you pulled that off," Ashe shook his head at Kevis. He'd misted in beside the healer and watched as Kevis placed Breanne in a healing sleep. Both worried she'd get no rest with the bite scheduled in the morning after breakfast.

"I don't believe you'll manage that a second time," Kooper changed to humanoid long enough to blink at Ashe and Kevis. "So savor it while you can." He changed back to lion snake and blinked again at both before lowering his head to rest on Breanne's shoulder.

"Dad always says not to argue with those guys," Kevis stated sagely.

Four lion snakes sniffed in unison.

Breanne's Journal

I didn't wake until after sunrise. Hell, I didn't even wake when Kooper, Chazi, Bekzi and Perzi got out of bed and prepared a bath for me. That meant Kevis had somehow managed to place me in a healing sleep, just as his father could. I was glad to have four lion snakes as guards the night before, or I'd have felt completely vulnerable.

"Get clean," Chazi grinned when he lifted me off the bed.

"You like this, don't you?" My question sounded slightly tart as Chazi carried me into the bathroom. Kooper, Bekzi and Perzi waited inside. I would have help—and an audience—while getting clean.

"We like. Yes."

It's a good thing the bathtub was quite large—I had three reptanoids in it with me within seconds. Kooper just grinned and washed my skin and hair while the others ducked and rolled around me. They were having a good time while I did my best to wash their scales. I swear, if lion snakes can grin, they were grinning.

"Feel better this morning?" Kooper leaned in to kiss me after rinsing my hair.

"Honey, I feel better. Kevis and I may have a discussion, though."

"You got the sleep you needed," Kooper tapped my nose gently.

"Yeah. But he didn't ask first."

"We took care of our girl," Kooper soothed. "Nobody was going to get past us. Trajan's wolf slept outside your door, too."

"Oh, for heaven's sake. On the hard floor?" I stared in disbelief at Kooper.

"Nah, he had a mattress," Kooper grinned. "I heard something and crawled out of bed to check out the noise. Turns out, it was just Traje, flopping the mattress on the floor before turning to wolf. Damn, he's huge."

"Really? I'm looking at somebody who turns into a twenty-foot snake," I pointed out.

"I was trying to be modest," he chuckled.

"Uh-huh. And how about all those times you climbed right into bed with me, letting me think you were just a friendly snake?"

"Oh, baby, those were the best times," Kooper sighed. "You'd be asleep, and I'd wake up and hold you for a few minutes like this before you stirred."

"You, well, *you snake* sounds like a compliment, doesn't it?" I blinked up at him.

"For me it is. Come on, you're clean. Let's get you dry and dressed."

Ashe didn't look up from his plate at breakfast, making me sigh. I was already nervous and he wasn't helping any. If it weren't for the images of Kalia's past invading my mind in unguarded moments, I'd have refused to have contact with Ashe Aedan Evans.

"I feel queasy," I muttered, staring at scrambled eggs and fruit.

"Sweetheart, you don't need to be sick," Bill murmured. "If you can't hold onto, well, it won't do you any good. Eat a little, at least, and Kevis will do what he can to help."

One scrambled egg was all I managed, and Kevis had to put his hands on my belly to keep it down. I wanted to retch and had to put it out of my mind. Trajan carried me to Ashe's suite, which was at the top level of the behemoth he called home, and took up the entire floor.

At any other time, I might have wandered through it and studied the paintings, sculptures and furniture scattered throughout the space. His bedroom was walled off with a door, as was his study, but the rest housed a massive library, with seating areas and artwork scattered throughout. Kings and presidents didn't often have that kind of luxury, I imagined. It certainly competed (nicely) with what Lissa had on Le-Ath Veronis.

"In here." Trajan carried me through the door into Ashe's bedroom, and I gaped at the luxury of it. A massive bed was placed against the inside wall, and opposite that was a wall of windows, overlooking miles of gishi trees. Ashe could see half the grove from his bedroom.

Ashe was already waiting inside—with his father, Aedan Evans. Nervously lowering my shield, I read Aedan. My to-do list got longer in the few seconds it took to learn all about him. Aedan was vampire, and more than a thousand years old. He'd come to make sure I didn't damage his son. Did that rankle and make my stomach rebel? The short answer is yes.

Trajan set me down and helped straighten my clothes while I studied Ashe and Aedan. *Think of Kay,* Trajan told me in mindspeech.

Or close my eyes and think of England? I paraphrased.

"Yeah. Think of England," Trajan said aloud and grinned. "Come on, let's do this." He propelled me gently toward Ashe.

Ashe's Journal

She was shivering. I didn't expect that. With my enhanced hearing, I could hear her breaths tremble. Breanne was terrified of me.

"There's no need to be frightened," I said, discovering that my voice wasn't exactly even.

"I'm supposed to say that to you," she told me, lowering her eyes. "I can't reach properly if you're standing," she added, gesturing with an unsteady hand for me to sit on the side of the bed.

"Better?" I stepped back and sat on the edge of my bed.

"Yeah. Now," she breathed, doing her best to ignore my father, who stood closer than either of us wanted, "I grip the back of your neck firmly, so you can't move. You'll have to help with this, because I'm too weak right now to prevent movement."

"I won't move," I promised. I hadn't noticed before that her eyes were a deep, cobalt-blue.

"Please don't," she said, gripping her lower lip in her teeth to keep it from trembling like the rest of her. "I could tear your skin, and I really don't want that."

"I don't want that either," I said. "Kevis is here, now, just in case."

"Yeah, I got his scent a second ago," Breanne murmured. "Now, I look into your eyes and tell you I won't hurt you," she went on. "And I won't. If it hurts, it'll be unintentional, I assure you."

"You won't hurt me," I insisted.

"Don't be all macho," she quavered. "That's pure stupidity. If it hurts, it hurts. End of story."

I wanted to tell her I understood. I didn't. I had no idea what depths of pain she'd endured in the past. Actually, some of it was quite recent. I hadn't stood my ground and taken a beating from that evil masquerading as a god. Breanne had. Was it to give us time to gather—Wisdom and me? Was it to allow Griffin and Thurlow time to escape without threat of pursuit? I still hadn't determined the answer and frankly, I was afraid to ask what her reasoning was.

"I won't be macho," I answered instead, making my voice as gentle as I could.

"Good. I won't hurt you," she repeated, massaging the back of my neck gently. "Hold still, now," she breathed against my neck before placing a kiss over my artery. That sent an unexpected shiver through me. Dad told me a kiss was expected, but my reaction was unanticipated.

The moment her fangs were in my throat, my body stiffened in the most intense climax I'd ever experienced. She pulled away too soon. Much, much too soon. I wanted it to last. I wanted to savor it. When I came back to myself at her whimper, I discovered my arms were wrapped around her—so tightly I was likely squeezing the breath from her body.

"Shhh," I loosened my grip slightly.

"Bro, I'll take her," Trajan said.

"No. Let me have this moment," I mumbled my reply.

Breanne's Journal

I almost fainted from the intensity of the climax that bled from him back to me, and the energy that came with it. When I came back to myself, his arms were wrapped so tightly around me I couldn't breathe.

"Shhh," he soothed, loosening his arms slightly. Had I made a noise? Obviously I had.

"Bro, I'll take her," Trajan said.

"No, let me have this moment," Ashe's chest rumbled with his reply. I whimpered—I couldn't help it. He didn't get to do this to me—

he couldn't cast me away with one hand and hold onto me now with the other. I couldn't handle that and suddenly I wanted to cry.

"Hey," fingers stroked my face. I shivered.

"Ashe, she's going into shock," Kevis said softly.

"No, no, no," his arms tightened around me again. Kevis' fingers touched my forehead and I was out.

Ashe's Journal

"What happened?" Trajan glared accusingly at me.

"Traje, I can't explain how intense," I raked fingers through my hair. For those moments I'd spent with Breanne, all thoughts of Kay fled my mind and it had been the two of us, connected in an intimate way. I couldn't tell him that—he was in love with her. Hadn't ever had what I'd just experienced, either.

"I've never been bitten by a female vampire," Dad spoke up. We were still inside my bedroom—Kevis and Bill had taken Breanne back to hers. "I can't say how intense that experience might be. I recall the climax I received with the bite lesson very well, but as it was delivered by a male, there was some guilt and shame attached to it."

"You were worried she'd hurt me. I think the opposite just happened," I rubbed the back of my neck in embarrassment.

"Son, she's relatively inexperienced. I just wanted to be present, in case there was additional instruction needed."

"I understand that," I nodded. "But I think we upset her."

"And I understand that," Dad agreed. "Is she all right?"

"Kevis says she's still out but her breathing is normal and her vitals are good," Trajan broke in. He'd had a mental conversation with the healer, apparently.

"Traje, look, we'll sort this out, I promise. I'm just worried how this is going to affect her, going forward."

"Yeah. Me, too, since this was my idea." Trajan stalked out of my bedroom. I watched him go with a sigh.

Earth—past

"Hey, bro," Trajan offered Charles a grin as he and Gavin dumped bags in the foyer.

"Good to see you again," Charles smiled back. "Anything new?"

"Nothing yet. We're waiting on you to help us hunt down Vernon Clark. Last known location was in Valencia, just south of here," Bill said. He, Opal and the others had gathered to greet the vampires when they arrived shortly after midnight, local time.

"I read up on Valencia—has a scattered population of less than three thousand," Charles let the strap of his laptop bag fall from his shoulder as he set the bag down carefully.

"Charles, I'd hire you in a minute if you weren't otherwise employed," Bill grinned. "Are you tired or do you want to get started tonight? I have a couple of addresses to check out."

"We can go, I just want to change and brush my teeth," Charles said.

"I agree. I despise this man, and worry that he may get away from us," Gavin growled.

"Same here, man," Jayson sighed.

"We're rested and ready, so whenever you say, we'll hit the road," Opal nodded.

"Give me five minutes," Charles said.

"I'll take you to your room," Hank offered.

"Thanks."

"I don't like this—it's kinda creepy," Opal shone her flashlight in the bedroom of the empty house. "Power off, cleared out, carpet stinks of blood," she added.

"We need some light in here," Bill agreed, stepping up behind her. "Is there any way to determine whether this is human blood?"

"Most of it is," Gavin growled. "And there is quite a bit of it," he added.

"I keep forgetting you can see a lot better than we can," Bill sighed. "Tell me what you're seeing, here."

The abandoned house was on a dirt road south of Valencia, and barely within the city limits. Bill couldn't tell how long it had been empty, but the air smelled stale and there was a stink of spoiled meat and rot about it.

"I think this floor is," Hank wandered in and bounced cautiously on the carpet. "Yeah. There's something beneath this floor. It's not slab, like the rest of the house."

"I hate to disturb evidence, but let's pull back the carpet," Bill handed his flashlight to Jayson, who'd followed Hank inside the bedroom. "Just be careful doing it. Anybody bring gloves?"

"Is this an investigation or what?" Opal pulled gloves from a pocket.

"We have some," Charles and Gavin both produced gloves from pockets.

Bill, Hank and Jayson stepped back while Gavin and Charles formed claws and carefully cut carpet away from the baseboards. Then, pulling on gloves, they ripped it back, revealing a trap door.

Blood had soaked through the carpet, staining the wooden slats of the door and the boards surrounding it.

"This doesn't look good," Opal muttered, pulling her shirt over her mouth. The stench rising from beneath the trap door was overwhelming.

"Doesn't smell good, either." Hank pulled on a pair of gloves and reached for the metal ring recessed in the wood. "Stand back," he ordered. The others were happy to comply.

CHAPTER 5

*E*arth—past

"What the bloody hell?" Charles had gone down the wooden steps first and stared about him. The room he found was much larger than the bedroom overhead, and extended past the perimeter of the house.

"What is it?" Bill's voice floated down.

"What does Vernon do—for a living? Besides what we see on the Internet?" Charles replied with a question of his own.

"Has no visible means of support," Bill answered. "I always thought his fans and supporters on the Internet kept him in business, so to speak."

"I think he was into other things," Charles muffled. He'd been forced to cover his nose as well. "Who do you suppose wants taxidermic werewolves and shapeshifters?"

"Now that the locals are watching the house, we can come back in the morning and take photographs before clearing out evidence," Bill sighed. A cup of coffee sat in front of him at a local, all-night diner, but it was untouched. All of them still had the stench of rotted meat in their nostrils and they'd only ordered to have an excuse to use the table.

"I get the idea that some of them might not have been completely dead before Vernon started, well, carving," Opal grimaced.

"Agreed. Blood spatter indicates that," Hank said.

"Why else would he need thick shackles and chains?" Jayson muttered. "You don't need to restrain anything that's dead already."

"They were silver, did you notice?" Trajan growled. "Silver won't completely debilitate a wolf, but it'll make him weaker for sure."

"So you think Vernon's into torture? That would fall in line with the stuff we found in the basement of that church," Bill snorted.

"And if somebody's paying for taxidermic wolves and rare shifters," Trajan added.

"That's sick," Opal grumbled, dropping her head in her arms.

"Opal, you okay?" Jayson rubbed her back gently.

"Jayson, if they want rare shifters," Opal lifted her head and blinked dark eyes once at Jayson.

"Yeah. I get it now," he nodded.

"My worry is that Vernon is far away from here," Gavin said.

"That's my worry, too," Bill observed.

"I want to pursue this," Ross Gideon shoved a folder across James Rome, Sr.'s desk.

"What is it?" James opened the folder to study its contents.

"Information on those websites—the ones claiming Breanne Hayworth was a product of our imagination," Ross growled. "I have a couple of names already; I just need your permission to go ahead with it."

"And a little funding, no doubt," James nodded, lifting the top page to read the second. "You think you can track these guys? Looks like the government can't find 'em."

"I found that sheriff in Pecos, didn't I? The feds had no idea on that one."

"True. Look, find a bodyguard. Hell, find two. I'll fund this. If you can make a book out of it, even better. Just don't end up dead somewhere, all right?"

"Any word on the kid?"

James stood abruptly at Ross's question. "No," he snapped. "I got info from SFPD, saying Jayson was never a suspect in that journalist's murder, they just let the media run with it for a while so they could track the real killer. Kathleen still won't talk to me, and word has it she blames me completely for Jayson's disappearance. I guess it's true, since that reporter screwed him and I fired his ass afterward."

"Any trace on credit cards or bank accounts?" Ross asked. "To see where he went?"

"None. The feds froze his accounts, anyway. I don't know where he is or whether he's still alive." James scrubbed his face with a hand and stared through the massive window of his office. "Those people," James turned to tap the folder Ross had given him, "burned down my son's house. They're probably still looking for him. You know which bodyguards to hire."

"I do."

"Ross, I don't care if this gets messy—for the opposition. Just make sure you come out of it clean."

"I've done it before," Ross rose and stretched. "Hundred thousand to start? Those bodyguards don't come cheap."

"Take a hundred fifty. I'll send more when you need it. Just get our money's worth. Find the kid, too, if you can."

"I will." Ross nodded and walked out of James' office.

∼

Le-Ath Veronis—present

Lissa's Journal

"Norian." I barely offered him a nod. Why he'd shown up in my study again, I hadn't a clue.

"Lissa, I know I'm not welcome," he held up a hand to stop me from ordering him out of my palace. "But you need to see this." He set a comp-vid on my desk and tapped it.

"What the fuck?" I stared at image after image in dismay. Hundreds of bodies littered a stone floor. "Where the hell did that happen?"

"Frithia. An entire religion committed suicide. No note or any reason for it. Nothing."

"How?" I tapped the button to enlarge and carefully examine images.

"Poison. A slow-acting one, so these weren't easy deaths."

"I can see that." I could. Faces were contorted in pain. They'd died horribly—all of them. "How many?" I asked.

"Three thousand."

"Are you joking?" I stared at photographs of the dead.

"This religion hasn't existed very long. Their premise is that they believe someone will collect them when they die."

"A lot of religions believe that," I pointed out.

"But this one believes that they will be placed in charge when they arrive at their destination."

"Great. Fucking wonderful," I sighed. "What idiot told them that?"

"That's just it—we can't find him."

"Even better. What's his name? What does he look like?"

"Here." Norian touched the comp-vid again, bringing up an image of a blond male. "We don't have a name," he grumped.

"Doesn't look like much," I observed. "Looks like he's seriously undertall and slightly overweight."

"Both true. But he has charisma, according to a few we've spoken with."

"Yeah? Hitler wasn't much to look at, either."

"Hitler?"

"Norian, I'm getting you a history book from Earth for Christmas."

"Not that idiotic holiday again," he sighed. "Sorry," he held up his hands when I glared at him. "It's perfectly harmless. I agree. I have no problem with it, I promise."

"What are you going to do about this?" I tapped his comp-vid. "Mr. Charisma could be on another planet, plotting out the same scenario."

"That's why I came to you. Will you help me, breah-mul? I really need special assistance with this."

"I'll think about it," I grumbled. If the victims had all been adults, I might not have considered it. I'd seen multiple images of children in those pictures Norian provided, and their deaths had been awful. Whoever was responsible for this deserved to die.

"Let me know soon, Cheah-mul. Frithia wants an answer for this."

"Yeah, Norian. I get that."

Breanne's Journal

"Hey." Trajan brushed hair back from my forehead the moment my eyes opened. Disorientation clouded my mind as I desperately searched for where and when I was. At least I recognized Trajan's face as he leaned over me. A smile curved his lips, and I sighed. Trajan was handsome in anybody's book.

"You have a nice mouth," I reached up to touch it gently with my fingers.

"I want this mouth all over you," the smile turned into a grin and Trajan's dark eyes glinted with mischief.

"That sounds really good," I sighed. "Mostly, though, I want your arms around me." I did. Trajan's arms were thick with muscle, as was the rest of him.

"You do?" Trajan chuckled softly. "They're ready anytime, baby. You just say the word."

"How are we feeling?" Kevis materialized behind Trajan.

"I feel okay, just a little disorientation when I woke," I said, studying his face and tossing the idea of reading him. "How about you, since the question was how are *we* feeling?"

"That was the royal we," Kevis said. "If I can get Wonder Wolf out of the way for a minute, I might check on you for a valid medical opinion."

"I'm a superhero?" Trajan mock-frowned at Kevis.

"Since I can't beat you at checkers, even, that answer is yes," Kevis teased.

"Wow, you play checkers?"

"When I was five," Kevis nodded. "In between reading Freud and Descartes."

"Psychology and Philosophy?" I made a face at Kevis, who leaned in to grasp my wrist in his fingers.

"They were in Dad's library on Earth," Kevis said, releasing my wrist. "Grip my fingers," he held both my hands in his. "Ow," he added, pulling his fingers away as if I'd gripped too hard.

"Sorry," I mumbled. I did feel better—stronger. As if I could actually get out of bed on my own.

"Here," Trajan pulled Kevis' hands into his. I watched in fascination as light formed around them.

"I didn't realize you could do that," Kevis stared at his hands in amazement.

"Ashe," Trajan shrugged modestly.

Trajan and I ended up in the kitchen, where Fes waited to set dinner in front of me. It was late and the others had eaten already. I was served noodles in mushroom sauce, with a salad and a protein drink.

"Fes, that was amazing," I sighed after eating as much as I could.

"That's what I wanted to hear," he grinned before leaning in for a kiss.

"Look who's up." Kooper walked into the kitchen, followed by Bill, the reptanoids, Trevor and Stellan.

"I'm up," I smiled at him and his reptanoid groupies. "How's the snake contingent?"

"Snake contingent good," Chazi offered a cheeky grin. "We learn how to shoot. Kooper and Bill teach."

"And you're good at it, I can tell," I said.

"They're really good," Kooper agreed with a nod before leaning down and planting a kiss on my forehead. "Stellan, too. He's never had to handle a gun, but it doesn't hurt to know how."

"It just takes a touch of power to send the shots to the target," Stellan snickered.

"I didn't let him use power after a while, and he still hit the target," Kooper slapped Stellan on the shoulder. "Trevor intends to teach hand fighting next."

"Sounds cool," I said. "Are you recruiting?" I blinked innocently at Kooper.

"Maybe," he grinned and planted a big kiss on my lips this time. I couldn't say whether I appreciated the audience or not—Kooper let me know with his mouth that kissing wasn't all he wanted, and some of my body parts played traitor and wanted him right back.

"Slow down," Kevis arrived to put a damper on any amorous activity. Kooper pulled away with a smile and a wink—he was promising more later, when Kevis gave the go-ahead.

"Come on, short stuff, let's go talk in the solarium," Trajan rose and pulled me off my barstool.

"It's dark out. Doesn't that defeat the purpose?" I asked, stretching.

"Nah—there are lights throughout the groves—it looks like fairyland at night," Trajan grinned.

Dutifully I followed Trajan, while the others fell in and walked behind. Kooper handed me a comp-vid when we arrived in the solarium, and I studied the image on it. "Genley Reith," I sighed. "Sirenali asshole," I added. "Is that what your boss wants to know?" I blinked at Kooper before shaking my head.

"Yes. I told Norian you'd know who sent this message. I also told him he wasn't in your good graces or anything close. He's not in my good graces, either," Kooper frowned as he sent a reply and pocketed the comp-vid.

"I think that's the general consensus," Kevis muttered.

The General studied Acrimus, making his subordinate squirm beneath the intensity of his gaze. He did it purposely. He didn't want his underlings to guess that he'd been wounded by the Mighty Hand.

He suspected that the Mighty Mind had told the Hand where to deliver the blow, and the Hand had complied quickly. It didn't matter; the General was on his way to recovery, and there were other ways to create mischief for them.

The Mighty Heart was dead—he'd seen that for himself. He took a great deal of satisfaction from that act, although he realized that the remaining two could still harm him. That lesson had been learned swiftly. He would have to devise a way to lure them in singularly, as that might be the best (and quickest) way to dispatch them. Once they were eliminated, everything would be his.

"The mass killing on Frithia was a good beginning," the General began. "We will funnel those who are outraged by that event into other, better-established facilities and take them from within."

"Several are already targeted, Liege," Acrimus bowed his head. "We are working to take them now, while they are vulnerable to us and more apt for our purposes."

"Feed them well, then," the General replied. "Hate and prejudice always go down easier than honesty and respect."

～

Lissa's Journal

"What are you talking about?" Norian stared at me. We'd gone to examine the site on Frithia.

"You said you only found sixteen children. Some are missing, Norian."

"What?" He stared at me.

"Haven't you done a check on the families who were a part of this mess?"

"We're still compiling information," Norian huffed.

"Well, there are scents here and no bodies. Six little girls are missing." I walked around laser outlines printed on the floor, delineating the place where each person died. Scents of six small girls were next to their mother's bodies, but no laser outline marked their space. "I think they were still alive when they were taken, Nori." I blinked at Norian, who stared at me in shock.

"I'll tell my people to concentrate all their efforts on the mothers, then." I'd just thrown a wrench into Norian's investigation, and he was angry that his people hadn't sorted this information already. "All the outbound ships have been checked; nobody got offworld that way," he added.

"I figure our culprit didn't arrive or leave in a conventional manner," I muttered, studying the large temple. "And I haven't caught his scent, anywhere. Do you know where he lived? Any clothes left behind? I need his scent so I can track him. We don't need another scenario like this."

"We?" Norian stared at me in disgust. "You're not the one getting nasty communications from everybody in the Alliance," he growled. "And I, uh, have reliable information that he is Sirenali. His name is Genley Reith, but we have very little besides that. Frithia approved this religion, but they're blaming the ASD for the outcome."

"Did you investigate it beforehand?" I watched Norian carefully— he was upset about this, but possibly for none of the right reasons. I had a guess about how Norian knew the name and race of our culprit now—Kooper was with Breanne, after all.

"Standard questionnaire for a religion already approved by the admitting world," Norian shrugged at my question. "Locals here handled it. We're looking into that, too, just to make sure bribery wasn't involved."

"Or no obsession or compulsion laid, et cetera, et cetera?"

"Breah-mul, you confuse me every time you use one of your blasted idioms," Norian complained.

"I'll have you know, Norian Keef, that et cetera is Latin, from old Earth. If you ask Gavin, he can teach you the whole language. If he doesn't tear your head off, first."

"Should I be worried that he might?"

"If you ask him to teach you anything."

"I'll keep my requests to myself," Norian said dryly.

"Good." I walked away from Norian while attempting to *Look* for six small girls. Their location was blocked. Why was I not surprised? If my hunch were correct, the enemy still thought to manipulate things through others, just as he had all along.

Ashe said he thought some damage was done before the General disappeared, but he couldn't say for sure, or how much damage had been inflicted. Regardless, the enemy thought Breanne was dead, so he'd left before Ashe and the Mighty Mind could do anything else. I'd also asked Connegar how and why all the Larentii had appeared afterward, and he said he couldn't explain it. Not yet, anyway.

"I have a unit assigned to investigate new religions on any world, and Teeg has agreed to do the same. All my agents have the image of the leader here, but so far, no sightings and the investigations are turning up nothing. Teeg and Dee have their agents on alert, but they have nothing to report, either."

I'd tuned Norian out until his last statement, which forced me to turn back to him. He still didn't know (and I wasn't about to tell him), that Tybus was now in charge of the Campiaan Alliance. The fewer who knew the better and it certainly wouldn't do to let the enemy know he'd been successful in killing my son.

"Have you talked to Erland or Ry, then?" I asked. "What about Lendill and Kaldill?"

"I talked to Lendill, and he and his father have been studying the problem, but Kaldill says all information is blocked and he gets next to nothing. Ildevar is more worried than I've ever seen and Kooper decides that now is a good time to use vacation days," Norian huffed.

"Then I'll contact Erland. Are you ready to go home, Norian?" I snapped. Kooper was better off where he was—if he could help Breanne get back on her feet, then that was the best use of his time. We needed her in this fight, and we needed her at full strength. Norian still thought he might ultimately have a hand in this, but any role he played would be a minor one.

"Yes." Norian wasn't pleased by my sudden frostiness.

"Good." I folded us the hell away from Frithia.

~

"Little dragonfly, she isn't an ogre," Karzac smiled lazily at Grace. "I believe she likes comfortable clothing just as much as you do."

"I just want to make a good impression," Grace sighed, tossing a silk outfit onto the bed. "I just don't know what to wear."

"It's a cookout. Jeans or shorts," Devin walked up to Karzac for a kiss.

"It isn't your boys who are seemingly engaged to one of the Mighty," Grace pointed out. "It's Graegar, my Larentii son."

"Remember this is Lissa's half-sister. If she's anything like Lissa, then she'll come comfortably dressed."

"True."

"Besides, we can get Franklin to contact Trace, and he can find out what she's wearing," Devin's dimple showed as she grinned at Grace.

"Why didn't I think of that?" Grace slapped her forehead.

"I think you'll be happily surprised with Breanne," Karzac said.

"Graegar seems happy enough," Grace shook her head. "Oh, wait. I'll ask Conner what she's wearing."

"Here we go again," Devin grinned at Karzac. Karzac leaned in to kiss her a second time.

Breanne's Journal

I rested in the crook of Trevor's arm as I listened to the others talk. I was comfortable, letting them carry the conversation. Bill and Kooper talked about Ranos technology, and the weapons made that employed it. Although only ASD and CSD were supposed to have the weapons, others had managed to get their hands on it, too.

"The new ones all have the identity safety grips," Kooper pointed out. "The weapon is created for you, and only you can fire it. The firing mechanism destructs if anyone else tries to use it."

"Will that still hold true if a wizard or warlock works a shifting spell?" Stellan asked. "Any fourth level and above can do that, and make you look like anybody else."

CONNIE SUTTLE

"Unless you can manipulate DNA, then you have no chance," Kooper explained. "That's how the new safety works."

"That's been in the works for a long time," Bill said. "I've been keeping up with the reports."

"Then you're ahead of half my agents," Kooper grinned. "Of course, my agents can't fry somebody with the power they have, either." He pointed his second statement toward Stellan, who nodded in agreement.

"Fifth-level warlocks are few and far between and generally run in families," Stellan said. "My brothers and I still feel lucky that we're all fifth-levels."

"Teeg is lucky you're all fifth-levels," Trevor pointed out.

"He said that just recently," Stellan acknowledged. "And he gave us a raise and a bonus."

"You deserve it," I said, breaking into the conversation for the first time. Trevor smiled down at me and tightened his arm just a little.

"Sweetheart, how are you feeling?" Bill asked. They'd been waiting for me to say something, I suppose, and there I was, listening to them instead.

"I feel pretty good," I said. "Not up to a marathon, but I might race you to the end of the block and back."

"Do you feel good enough to help Kay tomorrow?"

"I feel good enough to help her tonight," I shrugged.

"Want to try?" Trajan sat on the floor beside me and offered a quick, wolfish grin.

"Yeah. If I'm tired afterward, I can go to bed early."

"All right," Bill stood and gave Fes a fist bump.

"You called?" Ashe appeared in the middle of the room and blinked at Trajan.

"Bree thinks she can help Kay now," Trajan grinned.

"Seriously? That would be awesome!" Ashe high-fived Trajan. "Let's go see her now."

Ashe ferried all of us into Kay's suite, where she sat in a chair, blinking at the wall with the same, blank expression I'd seen before. I made my way past the men in the room and went to her. Keeping my shields up and tight so I wouldn't see the same visions I'd seen the last time, I knelt beside her.

"Kay," I said, taking her hand, "I'm going to let Kalia sleep. She'll still be with you, but you'll be in charge unless you want me to change it back." With that, I gathered my strength and sent her the biggest dose of *Love* that I could.

~

Kay's Journal

I felt as if I'd been asleep forever. It startled me, too, to find so many strangers around me when I woke. Kalia's fears were no longer eating away at my consciousness, and I was aware for the first time in a very long time.

The woman who knelt beside me—I should have been afraid of her. I wasn't. Somehow, I don't think Kalia would be afraid of her, either. She was smiling at me, and that surprised me greatly.

"Thank the stars," someone sighed. I looked up. I knew him—vaguely. He'd done something once—I struggled to grasp the memory.

"I tried to kill myself, didn't I?" I stared at him.

"You did, sweetheart. You're not afraid of me, are you?" he knelt on my other side, and I couldn't decide who to study first—him or the woman. Searching for their lines, I discovered quickly that I couldn't see them.

"You can't see our lines, we're too powerful," she said. "I'm Breanne." She patted my hand before rising to her feet. "This is Ashe. He's been waiting for you for a very long time."

"Ashe?" I turned to him. He smiled crookedly, as if he were afraid I might break or shrink away. Kalia no longer dictated my decisions, so I settled for drinking in his image. Ashe was handsome, with slightly curly, light-brown hair, blue eyes, a strong chin and an amazing smile, even if it was a bit unsure.

"I'll go now, but if you need me," Breanne gave a half-wave and walked away. I realized then that she'd been speaking to me in

English, and I'd answered in kind. Ashe seemed to understand that language, too, and that surprised me.

What also surprised me was that I felt Breanne's absence the moment she walked out of my suite. I almost called out for her to come back—there was something she had that I desperately needed, I just couldn't determine exactly what it was.

"Will I see her again?" My voice quavered, betraying the loss I felt.

"If you want," Ashe said gently, lifting my hand and kissing it. "Whenever you want," he added.

"But," my lower lip trembled, and I was afraid I might cry.

"Hush, Breanne is nearby. Do you want me to get her?"

I wish I could have said no. That would have been a lie. "Please," I begged, my voice a whisper.

"What happened?" Breanne was back in only a few seconds.

"I don't want you to leave," I said. By that time, I was trembling all over.

"Here," she took my hands in hers, and the feeling I got from her was incredible—as if I were drowning in love. I can't describe it better than that. Tears were falling when she took her hands away again, but these were tears of joy. I'd never felt so safe. Or so cared for. As if for a moment, I'd been the most important person in history, past, present and future.

"What is that?" I wiped my tears away with a shaking hand. "That's amazing."

"It's love," Ashe sighed. I stared at him in shock.

Breanne's Journal

I'd given Kay more than I'd ever given anyone, and still she needed a second round. It might take more in the future, too, but that remained to be seen.

Kevis appeared and took over. I was tired after my second wave of sending *Love* to Kay, so I let him take my place at her side.

"Thank you," Kay breathed behind me as I walked toward the door a second time.

"You're welcome," I turned and waved again.

"You all right?" Bill and Trajan were beside me quickly, but Trajan was the one who lifted me in his arms and carried me away from Kay's suite.

"Tired," I sighed. "That took more than I estimated it would."

"Baby, just close your eyes, Trajan and I will get you to bed," Bill soothed. I did close my eyes. I don't remember the getting into bed part. At all.

CHAPTER 6

"*S*he still feels uncomfortable—except around Breanne. Bree has something that does that for her—makes it possible for her to talk," Kevis shook his head at Ashe.

"I got that when she kept asking where Breanne's room was," Ashe sighed.

"At least she slept through the night after we got her in bed," Kevis observed. "It's my guess we may be able to coax her into the kitchen for breakfast, but we may have to have Breanne there, as an enticement."

"Traje?" Ashe said to empty air.

"You rang?" Trajan appeared in a blink.

"How's Bree this morning?"

"Still asleep. Why?" Trajan's brow wrinkled at Ashe's question.

"We may need her to come to breakfast when Kay does. Sort of an enticement, I guess."

"Boss, what does this mean?"

"It means Kay may be more broken than anybody thought, and Breanne may be the anchor Kay is clinging to."

"Bree needs to rest up for tonight," Trajan reminded Ashe. "The cookout, remember?"

"Yeah. Got it." Ashe raked fingers through his hair. "Look, let's get through breakfast, and see where we are."

"Sure."

Breanne's Journal

I guess the thing about multiple mates—or the possibility of multiple mates—is that sometimes, you're just not sure whom you might wake up with.

"How do you feel?" Corent smiled at me. How the hell—*when* the hell had he gotten here?

"Uh, are we naked?" I blinked up at him, trying to get my eyes to focus before realizing his hair was changing from blue to turquoise to nearly green and then back to blue.

"We are. I asked Lissa to send a message last night and Trajan came for me. I undressed both of us," he smiled at me.

"Is this all right?" I chewed on my lip—certain parts of his body had wakened before I had.

"I don't care whether it is," he leaned in to kiss me. "I can be gentle, I'll do all the work and I have some healing skill. I doubt I'll damage you beyond repair."

"Then you get to duke it out with Kevis," I breathed as Corent's hand began to wander.

"I don't duke it out with anyone—I belong to a peaceful race," his fingers found a sensitive spot, making me gasp. "Very appealing," his mouth covered mine as his fingers tingled against my flesh. Who knew the fae could do that kind of—*oh, my God.*

Ashe's Journal

"Breanne will be there," I coaxed. Kay gave me a skeptical look when I asked her to come to breakfast with me.

"Are you sure?"

"You can trust me on this," I wheedled.

"I can't trust anyone," popped right out of her pretty mouth. "Except Breanne. I think I trust her," Kay pouted. Her lips were so perfect in that pout I almost couldn't stop myself from kissing her. Kevis had warned me to take things slow. I was doing my best to follow his advice, but it was so damn difficult.

Kay was speaking to me coherently for the first time ever, and all I wanted to do was hold her, kiss her—and a few other things.

"Come with me this morning, and you can talk to Breanne over breakfast."

"All right. Do I have clothes here?" she looked around, completely lost. She had little memory of her past few months at SouthStar.

"Sweetheart, your clothes are in the closet here," I walked over and tapped on the door leading into the rather large space. "Your bathroom is connected; all you have to do is walk through it."

"You're so tall," she sighed.

"Trajan's taller," I grinned.

"That really tall man?"

"Yes. That really tall man. He'll be there with Breanne and Bill. And a few others, too. Nobody will hurt you, I can promise that."

Kay's Journal

His blue eyes seemed kind enough, and his words sounded true enough, but with my history and Kalia's memories swimming in my head, how could I trust him? Breanne, though—I couldn't explain my feelings on what she'd accomplished for me. If I trusted anyone for the first time, it would be her.

"I'll get dressed," I hunched my shoulders at the thought of going to breakfast with so many there to stare. Most of my life had been spent having meals alone. Kalia's life, on the other hand, had been spent in a fishbowl, with everyone staring and passing critical judgments on even the slightest movements.

"I'll wait out here for you," Ashe promised and settled on the side of my bed. I looked down at the pajamas I wore—they were blue with tiny pinstripes running through them. I sighed and walked toward the closet door.

~

Breanne's Journal

Corent would have spent all morning in the shower with me if he'd thought he might get away with it. I had no idea what to do about that, but there was no hiding the fact that he loved me—he kept saying it and following those words with a kiss.

Did he know that even a kiss from him made me want to crawl all over him and beg for more? It must be the way the fae were made. Thank goodness he was only half-fae—if he were pureblood, I might never get out of bed.

"It is the way we have with our mates," he smiled down at me while toweling me off. "Our true mates," he added. "I have never gotten this before with anyone. I imagined that as a half-fae, it was not my due."

"You appear to be making up for lost time," I muttered, staring at his chest. Corent was well-made, and the work he did in the orchards on Le-Ath Veronis ensured that he had plenty of muscle beneath smooth, golden skin.

"I would breathe you in and hold you inside me if I could," he chuckled, his hair turning a royal blue. I understood that to mean he was happy. Or that there were very few clouds in the sky. It could go either way.

"Now," he said, "I am hearing from Trajan that we are expected at breakfast quickly, so as to not disappoint Kay. We will dress swiftly and arrive on time."

We did arrive on time, and found a crowd waiting. Corent and I barely had time to settle on barstools around the massive island before Kay and Ashe arrived.

Kay immediately came to my side and settled on the empty stool on my right, with Ashe sitting beside her.

"How are you this morning?" I asked. You'd have thought the sun hadn't been turned on until she smiled at me.

"I feel good," she said. "Better than I can remember."

"Good. Are you ready to eat? Fes and Bill are cooking, so whatever you get will be amazing." I reached out and tucked a long, silky strand of black hair behind an ear; it kept trying to cloud her face.

"What are you eating?" Bright, blue eyes blinked into mine.

"Honey, I'm vegetarian. Corent is, too. This is Corent; he's half Green Fae." I introduced Corent to her. "He can grow trees and the best fruit anywhere."

"Is everybody here vegetarian?" She sounded worried.

"Ask those werewolves over there," I grinned at her. She blinked at me in surprise.

"It's nothing to worry about," I sent a bit of *Love* to her. "Nobody here wants to hurt you."

"Werewolves are real?"

"And vampires. Shapeshifters. Fae. Wizards. Warlocks, gods, Elemaiya," I nodded. "Plus lots of other things. You're pure blood Elemaiya, you just don't know it," I added.

"I am?"

"Kalia is, and since this is her body," I floundered for a moment.

"Don't worry, I know she's in there," Kay sighed. "I just don't know how I happened to be in here with her, or how she came to be where she was in the beginning."

"Yeah," I hunched my shoulders uncomfortably. Kalia couldn't recall her parents, or that they'd sold her when she was tiny, for a few credits. I didn't want to upset Kay with that information. It was hard enough for her to deal with the memories she had.

"Look, don't worry about it, all right? We're having breakfast," I said as brightly as I could. Bill set a plate in front of Kay first—bacon, eggs, fruit and a potato pancake.

"Honey, do I get a potato pancake, too?" I smiled at Bill.

"You're the reason we made them," he leaned in for a kiss. "Fes is bringing yours."

"Here you go," Fes set a plate in front of me. I had scrambled eggs, soy sausage, fruit and a potato pancake.

"This looks amazing," I said.

"It amazing," Chazi agreed. He, Perzi, Bekzi, Trace and Kooper were handing out more plates to those around us.

"Did you eat already?" I teased Chazi.

"We eat. We eat again, if we hungry again."

I laughed; he was teasing right back.

"Get kiss?" he grinned at me.

"Yeah." I touched his cheek as he leaned in. I not only got a nice kiss, I got a nose rub, too.

"Bree, we're going to a cookout at NorthStar tonight," Trajan said.

"Huh?"

"We go, too," Chazi said before moving away.

"Perfect," I mumbled. "I hate parties."

Earth—past

"Extraordinary times call for extraordinary measures," Charles sighed as he set a cup of coffee on the kitchen island and studied Trajan. "I gave him blood before he went to bed earlier. We'll see if the effect can be passed on."

"Before now, I'd have said giving Gavin a dose of anything so he could walk in daylight was a scary thing," Trajan pointed out. "But you're right—it's difficult to make this investigation work if he's asleep during the most important parts of it. You think Bree's blood was that powerful?"

"I think her blood is amazing," Charles sighed. "I tasted it, remember?" He lifted his cup and sipped coffee. "Did Bill get any new intel on Mr. Clark, the werewolf and shifter killer?"

"He, Opal, Hank and Jayson are questioning Clark's closest neighbors, to see if they know anything. I hope we have a lead when they get back."

"Any kind of lead would be better than sitting here," Charles grumped.

"I like your accent," Trajan offered Charles a tired grin. Except Gavin, none of them had gotten any sleep.

"It evolved over the past three centuries," Charles said. "It used to be an 'orrible mess."

"I definitely like the newer version," Trajan snickered.

"If I still talked like that, Wlodek would order me beheaded, I think. My sire taught me right away how to speak properly."

"What did you do—before?" Trajan asked.

"I was an acrobat—in a circus," Charles smiled mischievously.

"Seriously? Maybe you ought to ask Hank to teach you Krav Maga. As a vampire, you'd be more than lethal."

"I read about it, just never had the opportunity to practice it," Charles agreed. "I know all the investigative techniques the Assassins and Enforcers use, too; I've just never been in the field, so to speak. Until now."

"Do you like it?"

"I like the mystery and discovery of it, I just hadn't considered the seriousness of the situation before," Charles sighed. "I was always on the other end, disseminating information and making arrangements. It's quite different on this side of things."

"And the fact that we don't have Bree and Trina really sucks," Trajan muttered. "If I weren't so tired, I'd go hit something."

"I believe the uncertainty over Bree is more damaging than anything else," Charles pointed out.

"I hear that," Trajan growled.

"We're back," Opal walked into the kitchen and sat beside Charles with a sigh.

"Get anything?" Trajan asked. "Want coffee?"

"I just want orange juice and a bed," Opal grumped. "Bill, Hank and Jayson will be in here in a minute. They're unloading the van."

"What are they unloading?"

"Contraband, seized from one of Vernon's neighbors. It's a taxidermic shifter. A small one." Opal snorted in disgust. "Looks like some of the werewolf scent we got from the site may have been Vernon's helpers and not his victims," she added.

"That pisses me off," Trajan rose, his voice a rumbled snarl.

"A bunny?" Charles stared when the mounted flop-eared rabbit was carried in by Hank. "That's somebody's relative," he added after getting the scent.

"For sure, and since the shifters aren't organized and generally keep to themselves, there's no registry or anything to track down family," Opal shook her head. "This is awful."

"It irritates me that a citizen was murdered, and there's not a damn thing we can do about it," Bill said.

"We can track down Vernon Clark and make him dead," Jayson pointed out.

"I think that's our mission," Charles agreed.

Avendor—present

Breanne's Journal

Kevis was doing a session. Well, forcing a session was a better description. Kay wanted to talk to me; Kevis wanted both of us to talk to *him*. Or spill our guts to him.

"Breanne, why don't you start?" The doctor was definitely in.

We sat in Ashe's solarium, with windows all around the turreted space and plants scattered throughout, making the space inviting. Comfortable chairs and sofas were also placed strategically so a magnificent view of the groves could be had from almost any angle.

By we, I meant Kay, Kevis, Ashe, Corent, Trevor, Bill and me. Trajan and Kooper were teaching the reptanoids hand-fighting techniques somewhere in the groves.

"All anybody has to do is read that awful book," I pointed out.

"What awful book?" Kay turned to me.

"This awful book." I used up some of my precious reserve of strength and *Pulled* a copy of *Torture in Texas* into my hand. "I know you can read this, I just warn against it. And looking at the photographs," I added.

"Oh, no. That was you?" Kay shuddered as I showed her the cover. "I couldn't read it—before. It just looked too horrible."

"I don't recommend doing it now, since you have Kalia's memories, too," I said. "Why don't you talk about things on Earth?"

"I died in a bank robbery," Kay shivered. "And then I woke up in Kalia's head. It was awful."

"Breanne said it was," Kevis agreed. "Can you tell us what was happening, or is it too painful?"

"It makes me sick," Kay said. "There was so much blood." She and I had some things in common, and none of it was pretty or comfortable to discuss in a crowd.

"Kay, may I sit with you?" Ashe asked.

"If Breanne will sit with me, too," she quavered. "This is so upsetting, and I'm terrified Kalia will wake and I'll be lost again."

"Kay needs you beside her," Kevis nodded to me.

"Then I'm coming with Breanne," Bill muttered. "She needs somebody, too."

"I won't argue that point, but there's limited space on Kay's sofa."

"I can fix that," Ashe said and held out a hand. The sofa became long enough for six people—instead of three. Bill rose, walked to my chair and took my hand. Once all four of us were settled comfortably on the sofa, Kevis began again.

"Kay, can you tell us now?" he asked gently.

"Iversti Foculis wouldn't leave Kalia alone," Kay's voice trembled as she began her story. "He wanted to make sure everybody recognized her as his property."

"Tell me about Kalia's husband," Ashe insisted, once Kevis declared the session over for the day and Fes managed to entice Kalia into the kitchen for a bowl of gishi fruit ice cream. I wanted ice cream, too, but Ashe wanted information.

"He only wanted her because he knew he could sell her. Iversti was the first—and only buyer," I said.

"If he weren't dead already," Ashe's fists clenched.

"Honey, you'd have to stand in line. My targets now are Rezil Foculis, Hordace Cayetes, those women who trained Kalia and Q'And and Q'Ind Ribalo."

"All of them are involved?"

"Yeah. Start *Looking*, dude. At least some of that information isn't tied up with a Sirenali's curse, and the rest of it I can read from Kay."

"Generally I don't do that, since there's so much temptation to interfere and potentially expose myself," Ashe gazed out the huge windows of the solarium. "But we're allowed to protect our mates, or do what we feel we must to counteract the enemy."

"I think all those people I just mentioned fall into both categories," I pointed out dryly. "I know we're supposed to do quick and painless deaths, but those women deserve to be crucified. As soon as I'm able, I'm *Changing What Was* and removing those scars she has," I added. "She deserves so much better than she's gotten."

"Bree, I know that about you, too. I wish that weren't the case. Really."

"Ashe, I wish I knew what it was like to have parents." I walked as steadily as I could out of the solarium.

The mountain lion was a ghost, as was the girl at his side. Both stared at me with unblinking curiosity. I'd misted into the groves to get away from the house for a while—and all the people in it.

"Elizabeth, Philip," I nodded to each.

"Can you see us?" the girl asked. She'd died young and her ghost still looked like the young, pretty girl she'd been. Philip, an Elemaiyan shapeshifter, had died as his alter ego, and couldn't change back while he remained where he was.

"I can see and hear you," I said. "Philip, you only have to think what you want to say—I'll understand."

"Ashe asks us now and then if we'd like to move on. We like it here," Elizabeth said. "We just wish we had our bodies back."

"What would you do, if you did have them back?" I asked.

"Make up for lost time," Elizabeth snorted. "And not like you think," she held up a hand. "I know what we were; we both do," she flung out a transparent arm to include the mountain lion. "We've learned a lot since we died. It's just that we can't talk to anyone except Ashe. Until you came along, anyway."

"Who are you talking to?"

Turning, I saw two people walking toward me. Wynn and her mate, Ace. Ace recognized me—he'd seen me in Dallas around four hundred years in the past.

"They thought you died," Ace nodded to me.

"I thought I did, too," I agreed. "How are you, Ace? Wynn, nice to meet you," I added.

"She can read just about anybody," Ace said quietly to Wynn.

"Don't worry; I keep a shield up most of the time. It's just not comfortable if I don't," I reassured the woman who transformed into a rare, unicorn shapeshifter. She and the white werewolf were a good pairing and very well suited to one another.

"Sali said you were unusual," Wynn said. "You probably know already how your talent might upset people."

"I know that very well," I agreed. "And trust me; I stopped making judgments long ago. It's just too tiring."

She laughed, and that's what I'd hoped for.

"Are you going back?" Ace asked. I knew what he meant—he meant Earth in the past.

"As soon as I have enough strength to get there," I nodded. "I intend to go back disguised, too, so nobody will recognize me. They think they have me on their radar, since they've seen me and know my name. That's just idiotic to think I'd do that again."

"You can use my image," Wynn smiled. "Nobody except the people here would recognize me. That way, you'd only have to come up with an alias."

"Really?" I studied Wynn for a moment. She was beautiful, with white-blond hair and blue eyes. "Would you mind if I shortened the hair—maybe to here?" I touched the top of my shoulder.

"No problem," Wynn dimpled. "That way, I'd feel as if I were helping the cause."

"You would be," I nodded at her. "More than you know. I was talking to Elizabeth and Philip, by the way. You have anything you want to say while I'm here?" I turned back to my ghostly companions.

"Tell Wynn I love her boots," Elizabeth said.

"Elizabeth says she loves your boots," I relayed the message.

"Really? I had to order them, and sizes are always iffy when you order," she replied. "It's so much trouble to ask Ashe to take us away from here, so we'll be safe."

"Someday, if I have anything to say about it, that won't be a problem," I told Wynn. "Philip, Elizabeth, if I live over all this, we'll talk about fixing your problem, too."

"She's in the groves; I just heard from Ace," Trajan growled.

"She had to be somewhere—she can't leave SouthStar," Bill said. "It would be nice if she'd tell us she's going walkabout, though."

"She has many things to consider, and worries about them—and us," Corent said. "I agree that it would be nice for her to tell us where she is, but so many things weigh on her and that's adding one more task to an already lengthy list."

"It worries me that she's in so much danger," Fes said.

"She's planning to go back; you know that, don't you?" Trajan said. "I can't go back with her, because I'm there already. At least Trajan one-point-oh is back there."

"Bill one-point-oh, too," Bill nodded.

"As am I," Trevor sighed.

"I'm not," Kooper began.

"We not, either," Chazi, Bekzi and Perzi chorused.

"I'm not there, but what might a cook do?" Fes tossed up a hand.

"I'm not there, either, but I could hinder her instead of helping," Corent agreed.

"I'm going if I have anything to say about it," Stellan huffed. "If she won't take me, I'll ask one of the Larentii to do it. I think Graegar or Barrigar would be willing."

"How soon?" Chazi asked. "We ready."

"She still isn't very strong," Trajan said. "Who wants to help me track her down, so I can take her through some exercises?"

I'd only walked a quarter mile after misting away from Wynn and the others before the mate contingent showed up. Trajan hauled me up one-handed and folded me back to his dojo. He let me know how grumpy he was over my disappearance by forcing me to do push-ups and lift weights.

"Better than I thought," Trajan said when I found myself on the mat again, my back pressed against the heavy canvas.

"Thank goodness something's not pissing you off," I muttered up at him.

"You think I'm pissed?" Trajan tapped his chest in disbelief. "Baby doll, you haven't seen me pissed."

"This isn't going well," I slapped a hand over my eyes. Trevor, the unflappable, eternally reserved vampire, snickered nearby.

"Come on," Trajan held out a hand.

"Really?" I misted myself upright. "You haven't seen me pissed either, mister." I stalked away, leaving him and the others staring after me.

"Breanne, they're worried." Kevis sat on the side of my bed. I was still in a snit and sat with my back against the massive headboard, staring at the wall and closet door straight ahead.

"Look, I don't need any head fixing at the moment," I snapped.

"My mother is worried about meeting you," Kevis said, surprising me.

"What?" I turned and stared at him. He was now staring at my closet door, his green-gold eyes troubled and a frown wrinkling his forehead.

"She's sort of afraid, actually. She heard that you can read people, and she's worried about her past."

"Because she was mistreated when she was small, too." I made it a statement and not a question.

"She won't even talk to me about most of it—I have some information from Brock, but that's it."

"Look, tell her I'll keep my shields up. I sure wouldn't want anybody picking through my memories," I sighed. "There's no need for her to be uncomfortable. I think I'm uncomfortable enough for both of us."

"There's no need for that. Graegar and Barrigar will be there, plus a lot of other Larentii, if I know them at all. I think all the Saa Thalarr are coming, but they're just regular people. Besides, you'll have your mates there, and I sure wouldn't want to get Trajan, Stellan, Trevor or Kooper riled up," Kevis turned to offer a smile. "Or the reptanoids, either. Or Bill. Or Fes or Corent. I don't know exactly what Corent might do, but bad fruit for a hundred years might be in the offing."

"Kevis, stop, you're making me laugh," I snickered.

"My work here is done," he said and rose. "Dress comfy. Like for a pool party." Kevis folded out of my bedroom while I considered what to wear.

Navy walking shorts, a white tank top and sandals. That's what I found in the closet. "This better be good enough," I mumbled, hoping all the other women wouldn't be wearing sundresses and hats.

"That looks nice," Bill walked into my bedroom, the reptanoids right behind him. "Ashe is ready to take us. He's bringing Kay, and she only agreed to go because you are."

"I hope he's ready to hold her hand," I said. "Doesn't he see that this may be too much for her?"

"I think all the healers will gather around her and trust me, a healing sleep can be placed if necessary. I'm hoping she'll feel comfortable soon."

"I'm hoping I'll feel comfortable soon," I muttered. "I'm as ready as I can be. Lead the way."

~

Ashe's Journal

"Sweetheart, they won't bite. They just want to make you feel welcome," I said as Karzac, Joey, Franklin and several other healers walked toward us. Kay practically quaked at my side while Breanne, standing nearby, went pale. I was beginning to realize how much courage Bree actually had, to be afraid and struggle every moment to overcome it.

Breanne, I whispered into her mind. *Nobody here will hurt you.*

~

Breanne's Journal

"Mom, Aunt Devin, this is Breanne." Kevis sounded proud as he introduced me to his mother and his aunt.

"Hello," I smiled and worked to recall my manners.

"She's shaking, Kevis," Grace announced as she took my offered hand.

"She does that, Mom. I gave you a copy of the book," he sighed.

"I couldn't look past the first few pages," Grace admitted.

"I had a meltdown after looking at the photographs. I didn't know they were taken," I admitted. "I was unconscious at the time."

"The one who took those photographs committed suicide, so he wouldn't embarrass his family," Bill stepped up beside me and took my hand. "Hello, I'm Bill Jennings, and I had an investigation run on the former Sheriff after the book was released," he added.

"The Director of the Joint NSA and Homeland Security Bill Jennings?" Grace asked. "You did a lot of good work. Nice to meet you." She shook his hand enthusiastically.

"I had a lot of help, some of it from Bree," Bill smiled modestly.

"I'm going back as soon as I'm able, to help you again," I stood on tiptoe to kiss Bill.

"Sweetheart, I couldn't ask for anything better," he smiled when I pulled away.

"We come. Kooper, too," Chazi announced, appearing at my side and offering Bill and me glasses of wine. "We sit?" he pointed to a circle of comfortable chairs beneath a banana tree near the huge pool complex.

"Where are our manners? Of course we should sit," Devin laughed. "Come on, we have so much to talk about."

Kay ended up with us. Lisster, a shapeshifting leopard, came to lounge at Devin's feet. Dragon, co-First of the Saa Thalarr with Grace, sat between her and Devin. Ashe sat with Kay and happily held her hand.

Secretly I fed Kay a bit of *Love* to steady her, and soon she was smiling and speaking occasionally as the conversation turned to Earth of the past—all those present were familiar with the subject.

Bill and all three reptanoids crowded around me; Chazi, Bekzi and Perzi soaked up the conversation (and attention) happily. Food and more wine were placed in our hands as we laughed and talked.

"Enjoying yourself?" Graegar managed to increase the space inside the circle so he and Barrigar could fit.

"Hi, honey," I touched his blue face—he was quite handsome, as was Barrigar behind him.

"Hey, where's my seat?" Conner appeared, making Barrigar smile. He raised a hand and formed a chair from nothing for Conner.

"We were just discussing Earth politics," Devin gave Conner a huge smile.

"Here," Graegar lifted me from my chair, then seated himself before pulling me onto his lap. It gave Barrigar enough space to do the same with Conner. "Now, I find Earth politics fascinating," he said. "Tell me about them from your perspective."

"They're filled with posturing, lies and misdirection, not to mention photographs of sensitive body parts," Bill laughed.

"Did you have to take care of any of that?" I turned to Bill, almost biting my lip to keep from laughing.

"Only a time or two," he grinned at me.

"Our tax dollars at work, covering up willies," I grinned back. Dragon laughed.

Earth—past

"Mr. Gideon, we'll be happy to work for you again," werewolf brothers Rafe and Braden Reynolds nodded at Ross. "You got cash, like always?"

"Yeah. Fifty grand to start, and there's more if this ends up taking more time," Ross said. Ross had no idea they were werewolves; he merely knew they were effective at tracking anyone. Both lived in the Phoenix area, and that's where Ross had gone to meet with them.

"Who's the target?" Braden asked.

"Vernon Clark, to start," Ross replied. "Know who he is?"

"Yeah. We've heard of him," Rafe and Braden exchanged a glance before accepting the small briefcase of money Ross offered. "We've heard of him, all right."

CHAPTER 7

A *vendor—present*
     Breanne's Journal

"Tybus, I only wanted to make sure you were all right," I said. We'd stolen away from the crowd at the cookout, so we could talk for a few minutes.

Tybus held a drink in his hand and looked exactly like Teeg San Gerxon. So much so, in fact, that he lounged comfortably against the windowsill while we talked.

"I am fine," he assured me with a nod. "While at times I might prefer to be wandering the gardens that surround San Gerxon Palace, I have more than enough to keep me busy. I am grateful for Gavril's memories, and I usually let them dictate what I do."

"Don't let them interfere all the time," I said. "You need space—and time—for yourself, remember?"

"The running of an Alliance keeps me busy and away from the memories I have of the past century," he pointed out. "That is not a bad thing, I assure you."

"I understand that," I nodded to him.

"I know," he said simply, with a shrug. "It's too bad we can't wish those things away."

"Don't worry," I sighed. "If I ever see Acrimus again, I know to kill him immediately."

～

Sometimes, being vampire is more trouble than it's worth. I now had dozens of new names floating in my head, and I was too tired to consider any of them. The cookout had gone very well; Kay even had a good time, Ashe was more than happy and I was getting itchy about the past.

Something was happening, I just knew it, and I still didn't feel strong enough to go back. I figured Trajan would laugh if I asked him to transport me, too, so I didn't. Regardless, I wanted to discuss this with somebody, and that ended up being with the entire male population at the big house when we got back to SouthStar.

"I'm getting itchy about it," I told Ashe when he asked. I didn't want a pat on the head and an order to go to bed, either.

"I am, too," he admitted. "I don't like it, either. Something has happened to alter the timeline dramatically; otherwise this wouldn't be bothering both of us so much."

"You can't get information on any of this?" Bill asked. He was worried, I could tell, because he was still there—in the past.

"This isn't fucked up or anything," Trajan raked a hand through his hair. He was frustrated; it was easy enough to see. Trevor was as well, he just settled for allowing no expression to mar his features.

"Bree, how about biting me again?" Ashe asked, his blue eyes begging for something that I couldn't define. "Kevis says you didn't take much before. What if you take a decent amount this time and get a night's rest? If you feel stronger in the morning, I'll send you, Kooper, Stellan and the reptanoids back. I'm hoping that with the added manpower and abilities, you'll be able to get this sorted."

"Wynn said I could borrow her likeness," I said. "So I won't look the same. I just need to come up with another name and get proper ID."

"What about Tamara Bray?" Bill asked.

"Her." I nodded. Tamara was Joyce Christian's first victim. I figured

Bill in the past wouldn't have much trouble getting me ID under that name. It seemed appropriate, somehow, that I might carry her name, at least for a little while. "That sounds good, Bill."

"Bree, are you ready, then?" Ashe asked. Kay had already gone to bed—it was late when we returned to SouthStar.

"I suppose." I couldn't help sighing. It hadn't gone well for me the first time. Now I was facing the same thing again.

"Trajan and I will be there with you," Bill assured me.

"Good," I sighed again.

~

Ashe's Journal

If it weren't for Kay, I would go back with Breanne. It irritated me that Kay had come to me when she did, and that trouble seemed to appear just as I was attempting to form a bond with her after Breanne brought her back to consciousness. I didn't want to abandon her early on, and I didn't want to upset Breanne more than I already had.

I sent mindspeech to Trajan, asking him to bring Bree back to my bedroom. I intended to make it easier for her this time, and if I were honest with myself, I was looking forward to it. Kevis had seen it when I hadn't—that she'd felt something between us at the beginning.

I couldn't push her now, or profess any feelings. It was too early, and she wouldn't believe me anyway. There had to be a way through this mess I'd made, I just didn't know what it was. At that moment, I realized how my dad felt. He'd done what he thought best, and it still hurt everyone involved.

~

Breanne's Journal

I wasn't looking forward to this. The last time, I'd ended up unconscious and I'd spent too much of my time in that state, lately. At least I walked in under my own power this time, and Ashe's blood was likely responsible for that.

He was already sitting on the bed, waiting. Since I couldn't read him and he had no expression on his face, I had no idea what he was thinking. Aedan Evans wasn't with him this time, and that brought on a relieved sigh.

"You look like you're being led to an execution," Ashe held out a hand. How was I supposed to respond to that?

Bill's hand went to the back of my neck and he massaged it gently, attempting to get me to relax. It wasn't working.

"Bree, it helped last time. Let me help again, all right?"

"Add power to her taking," Renegar appeared at Ashe's side. They were obviously good friends—very good friends.

"You mean infuse the blood with my power?" Ashe turned to the Larentii.

"Yes." Renegar smiled. "Graegar and Kalenegar suggested it, and it makes sense. While anyone else might be destroyed, one of the Mighty should take no harm."

"If Kalenegar suggested it by himself, I'd walk out of here now," I fumed. Just the mention of his name upset me. Sure, everybody said he was contrite, but that didn't make up for what he'd done to me.

"He knows this," Ren nodded solemnly. "Graegar consulted the other Wise Ones first, and then contacted Kal. The suggestion was agreed upon by all."

"I won't hurt you, I promise," Ashe said.

"I'm supposed to say that to you," I pointed out. Was I grateful my voice didn't quaver? Yes.

"I think we can dispense with the formality; you didn't hurt me last time," Ashe grinned. "Now sit here beside me and let's do this."

"I will assist," Renegar offered. "You may bite, I will hold him steady," Ren smiled. His smile was like sun shining through clouds.

"Are you sure?" I blinked at the Larentii. Trajan and Bill stepped back when Ren appeared—they were used to him while I wasn't, and they trusted him, that was easy to see.

"Father, perhaps you should allow us," Graegar and Barrigar appeared beside us.

"Yes, perhaps that would be best," Renegar agreed and pulled back.

At that point, I had no idea what was going on. I was about to find out.

~

Ashe's Journal

The Larentii have energy sex. Yes, they can do it the other way, too, but I was about to discover why energy sex was the preferred method.

Renegar had offered initially, but the moment Graegar appeared, I realized that Breanne might feel uncomfortable getting any kind of climax with her mate's father involved.

The Larentii don't see things that way—they only see it as a pleasure to be shared since no intimate contact is required. Parents didn't ever share with their children, but past a certain age, Larentii felt comfortable sharing with any other Larentii, male or female. The more Larentii involved, the more intense the result. Or so I'd heard. I was about to experience this myself—for the first time.

Larentii don't share with humanoids as a rule—most humanoids would disintegrate from the wash of power. The humanoid would have to hold power of his or her own to survive the climax.

"I'm ready," I nodded to Graegar and Barrigar. I'd known Graegar since he was an infant—Renegar had brought him to me not long after his birth. He and his Protector were Breanne's mates, and that was why I allowed this now.

"Bree, are you ready?" I asked.

~

Breanne's Journal

I wasn't ready, but I said I was anyway.

"Lean in, dearest, and place the kiss," Graegar urged while Barrigar gently rubbed my back with large, blue fingers.

I did as Graegar instructed, leaning in and breathing Ashe's scent before kissing his neck over the artery. He sighed. Whether it reflected impatience or anticipation, I had no idea.

"I won't hurt you," I whispered against his skin before sinking my fangs into his flesh.

You'd have thought Avendor's sun had gone nova with the flash of light and burst of power that burned through us, followed by such an intense climax that I imagined it might kill a normal person.

Was it pleasurable? I can't begin to describe how pleasurable it was —how euphoric it made me feel. Could it become addicting? My last thought before disengaging and fainting was that I might already be addicted.

~

"How is my little butterfly? Was her first experience with energy sex a good one?" Barrigar cradled me in his arms and smiled down at me.

"See, she liked it—her eyes are still clouded with pleasure," Graegar's face appeared beside us. "Dearest, that is how Larentii prefer to have sex," he added.

"Can we do it again?" I croaked.

"Already asking," Barrigar chuckled. "Ashe said the same—when he regained consciousness."

"All involved generally lose consciousness," Graegar informed me with a smile. "My father made sure you and Ashe were disengaged and safe before you fainted."

"Then I owe him," I said. "I was afraid I'd tear Ashe's skin if I fainted before pulling my fangs away."

"Father says you are welcome," Graegar leaned in and kissed me. "You taste like sunlight and a hummingbird's flight," he said. "We are more than happy with our mate."

"Where are we?" I thought to ask. We were in sunlight, wherever we were. It had been late at night on Avendor when we'd had our group orgasm, so someone had moved us.

"We are on the Larentii homeworld," Graegar explained. "On the side facing the sun, of course. Larentii must feed after they wake following energy sex. The act, while pleasurable, can be somewhat draining."

"I can understand why," I agreed, grinning at Graegar.

"You should eat when we return to SouthStar, and then rest. Barrigar and I will transport you and the others to the appropriate time. Remember, too, that if you have need, you only have to send mindspeech. Someone will come."

"Thank you; that means a lot," I said.

Earth—past

"What the hell?" Trajan stared at the tall, red-haired, blue-skinned Larentii. Trajan didn't often come across anyone taller than he, but this one was nearly ten feet tall and quite muscular.

"Hello, my name is Kalenegar, but you may call me Kal if you insist on shortening my name," Kalenegar replied. "Breanne will be joining you shortly; therefore, I will be here as well. You must accustom yourself to this now."

"Dude, this is just," Jayson was shocked. Hank crossed arms over his chest and examined the new arrival skeptically.

"Vhirilaszh," Hank finally nodded. "If you expect to stay, then you will contribute when appropriate and fit in with the rest of us."

"As if I hadn't already considered that," Kal huffed. In a blink, he was as tall as Trajan, with latte-colored skin. His hair he kept red and shoulder-length, however, and swept it back with a careless hand.

"Wow. I saw what Bree did with Jayson, but that's impressive," Opal muttered.

"Breanne has learned much from my race," Kal replied. "Although none of it from me."

"Would you like to talk about that?" Smoke curled from Hank's nostrils.

"Not at this moment," Kal replied stiffly. "I am here to help protect Breanne when she arrives. She will not arrive alone."

"Who is coming with her?" Bill asked.

"Four lion snake shapeshifters and a warlock," Kal replied. "She will be disguised, so I suggest all of you make allowances. She cannot be seen as herself outside our presence."

"What will she look like?" Charles asked.

"I understand that this is how she will appear when she arrives." Kalenegar formed a three-dimensional holographic image that greatly resembled Wynn O'Neill.

"Direct opposite, almost," Jayson breathed. "Pale hair, a little taller, but still pretty."

"She needs proper identification. I have taken the liberty," Kal held out his hand and documents appeared, including a driver's license and a passport. "Director Jennings, you may present these to her when she arrives."

"Tamara Bray?" Bill's forehead furrowed. "That's the girl Joyce Christian," he began.

"Cruelly tortured and killed?" Kal asked. "Yes. Breanne felt the identity was appropriate."

"When will she get here? We've had no word, were worried she was dead and suddenly you appear," Gavin growled.

"Vampire, you are fortunate that you received what you have when you did," Kal observed. "Walking in daylight is a gift; I suggest you appreciate it. I can negate that if you annoy me."

"Larentii, I suggest you hold your judgments in reserve," smoke poured from Hank.

"As you wish," Kal nodded respectfully to Hank.

"Where will we put everybody?" Opal shook her head.

"That will not be a problem," Kal held out his hands and light formed around them.

～

Avendor—present
Breanne's Journal
"Yeah, I like this length," I fingered the platinum hair and nodded at

my image in the mirror. Ashe knew Wynn best, so he'd done the honors, making me look like her, only with shorter hair.

"Wynn is beautiful, but I think I like Bree better," Ashe smiled over my head.

"Can't do anything about that now—too many bad guys know my name and number," I sighed.

"Bree, I don't want to be called again—for the same reason," Ashe said. "If you need help, call me first, all right?"

"Okay." I dropped my eyes. So many things went through my mind, and none of them were comforting. I felt better now, but there was no way I could stand against the General again. No way.

"We're packed and ready," Kooper announced as he, the reptanoids and Stellan walked into my bedroom. "Bree, is that really you?" He and Chazi came closer to inspect Ashe's work.

"Yeah. My voice hasn't changed," I blew out a sigh. "I don't even recognize myself anymore."

"At least you're taller and I won't have to lean down so far," he grinned and bent toward me for a kiss. "Taste the same, too. Like honey."

"I've altered your clothing—it'll all fit," Graegar stepped out of my closet with Barrigar close behind. "And it's packed in three trunks, with your shoes."

"Thanks. I didn't know what to take," I shrugged.

"It's all in there; there is no need to fret," Barrigar offered a sunny smile.

"You're amazing, you know that?"

"It never hurts to hear those words," Barrigar chuckled.

"I've yet to meet a modest Larentii," Ashe laughed.

Earth—past
Breanne's Journal
Graegar and Barrigar dropped Kooper, Stellan, our luggage, the reptanoids and me outside a huge house in New Mexico.

"This looks like a compound," I stared at the walled adobe behemoth in disbelief.

"It is, in a way," Graegar smiled.

"What am I going to tell them?" I hunched my shoulders. Was I uncomfortable? You bet. Hank would surely yell, and I wasn't strong enough emotionally to deal with that. I also didn't need him, Kooper and Stellan getting into an argument about it, and I had no idea what Chazi, Perzi and Bekzi might do, other than attempt to protect me against a High Demon who was impervious to poison.

"We will come with you," Barrigar sounded determined, suddenly.

"I hope it helps," I said and walked toward the gate leading into the almost-fortress.

"They have arrived and will be at the front door in seconds," Kalenegar announced. "I have received mindspeech from Graegar."

"You yell and I swear I'll smack you," Opal glared at Hank.

"I have no plans to yell," Hank's voice was stiff.

"I want to," Jayson muttered. "I was scared shitless."

"I will strike you dumb," Kalenegar warned.

Breanne's Journal

Why bother ringing the doorbell, when you have Larentii? The double front doors opened wide with barely any effort on Graegar's part as we approached, and people spilled out of the house. Bill. Hank. Jayson. Charles. Gavin.

Gavin? What the hell? *He was standing in daylight.*

"Dearest, it seems the benefits of receiving your blood may be transferable," Graegar whispered as I stared at my vampire sire.

"That's comforting," I mumbled, suddenly feeling shaky and short of breath. Did I think that shock the last one? I shouldn't have. Kalenegar stepped out of the house behind Gavin. Yes, he'd disguised himself as a humanoid, but there was no mistaking the long, red hair and cobalt-blue eyes.

"Sweetheart, you're hyperventilating," Bill quickened his steps and held out a hand. I went to my knees, my body struggling to draw in air, my arms pulled tight across my chest.

"I'll handle this," Hank shouldered his way through the crowd. His fingers touched my forehead and I was out.

"We upset her, that's why," Charles pointed out.

"Not upset Bree," Chazi snapped.

"Who the hell are you?" Jayson demanded. Chazi's eyes went strange. Jayson backed up a step.

"Everybody calm down." Hank was tight muscles and controlled anger as he led Barrigar to his bedroom—Barrigar carried Breanne, who was still unconscious.

"Trust me, you don't want to tangle with any of them," Hank growled at Jayson. "I think the warlock is considering turning you into a lizard."

"Or worse," Stellan grumped.

"Can he do that?" Jayson turned to Bill. Bill shrugged.

"Stellan Starr is a fifth-level Karathian Warlock. A lizard would be simple for him to achieve," Graegar informed Jayson.

"Good to know," Jayson breathed and backed away another step—from reptanoid and warlock.

Breanne's Journal

My shoulder was uncovered and cold while the rest of me felt deliciously warm. Barely conscious, I struggled to pull the cover over chilled skin.

"Avilepha, my wings don't work that way." A chuckle accompanied the statement. Cracking my eyes open cautiously, I stared at Hank—in smaller Thifilathi. One wing cradled me below; the second covered me above. Except for the exposed shoulder. Focusing on what lay beyond Hank's head, I realized I blinked at the stars in a New Mexico night.

"Hank, where are we?" I attempted to make myself smaller to fit all of me under the tip of his warm, buttery-soft leather wing.

"On top of a mesa," he smiled down at me.

"Where are your arms?"

"Behind my head." They were—he lowered them to show me. "I've been holding you for hours while you slept, and decided to let my wings carry the burden for a few minutes while I stretched muscles. Of course you chose this moment to wake."

"You're not going to yell?"

"Bree, I know that frightens you. I will reserve my yelling for when it might do the most good—and you are better able to handle it."

"Why are we on top of a mesa?"

"Because Graegar and Barrigar wanted to speak with Kalenegar, and I didn't want any of that to disturb your rest. So I pulled you out of the house."

"Do Larentii yell?"

"Not per se, no. I believe it may have been more in the line of advice—and warnings."

"Warnings?"

"I know how he treated you while under the influence of a mind cloud. That undue influence is the only thing saving his ass and his power, in my opinion. He is more than contrite now, and is going overboard in his desire to protect you. I believe Graegar and Barrigar told him the same thing—to pace himself and not be a nuisance."

"Hank, have you ever had energy sex?" That just popped out of my mouth—and out of the blue.

"No. Have you?" A slow smile curved his lips—he knew what it was.

"Yeah. You definitely need to get in on that."

"I'll be happy to volunteer. If I understand correctly, the Larentii may include anyone in what they term *the backwash of pleasure*."

"Well, we'll have to discuss that with them, I guess."

"I suppose we will." Hank's smile widened.

"Hank?"

"What, love?"

"I missed you."

"Hala avilepha, you have no idea how much I missed you. We should go back now, before Kalenegar attempts to find us."

"Great. Nothing like a grumpy Larentii," I muttered.

They were all waiting for us to return when Hank landed us in a huge kitchen. It was barely ten at night and we hadn't kept them up past their bedtime. At least I didn't think so.

"We've been discussing Vernon Clark—without you," Trajan lifted an eyebrow at me. This was the original Trajan, who couldn't fold or move things with a thought. I couldn't tell him that awaited in the future, either. My life was complicated enough without adding the time factor to it, so I had to watch my steps—and my words—with Trajan, Bill and Gavin.

"Any new leads?" Hank asked, setting me gently on the tiled floor.

"We have rumors that he may have been in Silver City," Bill replied.

"That means he's getting closer to the border," Hank nodded. "If the information is correct."

"Rhett and Dalroy are sniffing out the lead right now—Gavin asked to have them assigned to the night shift," Bill said.

"Rhett and Dalroy are vampires who often work for the Council," Gavin informed us. "They will contact me should they find anything."

"Are we ready to go if we hear from them?" Opal pointed her gaze in my direction.

"Yeah. I got some unplanned sleep, so I'm awake now," I said. "Hank may be pooped, though."

"I am fine," Hank released a thin stream of smoke.

"No problem, then," I tossed up my hands and moved away from him. As if on cue, Gavin's cellphone rang.

"Gavin here," he answered curtly. I heard the conversation clearly, when the vampire on the other end said Vernon Clark might be in Tyrone, a small town south of Silver City.

~

"This must have been something in the day," Ross Gideon studied the interior of the abandoned mansion, built by Bertram Goodhue in the early 1900s. The town had been originally constructed with the intention of making it the most beautiful mining town in the world. The mines failed quickly, leaving abandoned Spanish-style mansions in its wake. The current town of Tyrone was located nearby.

"This part is a ghost town, now," Rafe Reynolds offered Ross a wolfish grin.

"You say your contact is meeting us here?" Ross asked.

"That's what he said. He told us he had a lead on our target, but wanted to see us—and the money—first," Braden Reynolds echoed his brother's grin.

"Did he indicate what kind of information he had?" Ross asked. "On Clark and Jayson Rome?"

"Nothing on the Rome case. Knows a lot about the Clark thing, though," Rafe replied. "He should be here soon—just relax and wait."

~

Breanne's Journal

"Gavin, we have him in our sights—he's heading to the old ghost town portion of Tyrone," the vampire reported over Gavin's cell. Kalenegar, who still hadn't spoken to me directly, transported all of us to a café in Tyrone to await further word from Gavin's contacts.

"How many with him?" Gavin barked.

"At least three others—that's all we can see through the van's windows."

"They are unaware that you are following?"

"Or they fail to care."

"Any idea why they're visiting the ghost town portion so late at night?" Charles asked.

"Charles, is that you?" the vampire asked.

"I requested a little field time," Charles almost smiled. "How are you, Dalroy?"

"The same. As is Rhett. We have no idea why our target is going to the old portion. Perhaps a meeting?"

"That doesn't sound good," Bill muttered.

"Can you meet us out here quickly? We have to stop our vehicle now and follow on foot. We're too close to the old mercantile building."

"We'll be there shortly," Charles said. Gavin ended the call.

"I will transport," Kalenegar said.

"I will turn everybody to mist, first," I said. "That way you can set us down in that old building and nobody will notice."

"I'll leave a replica of us here at the table, so nobody will know," Stellan offered. "Our likenesses will even engage in small talk and answer the waitress' questions appropriately," he added.

"You can do that?" Opal stared at Stellan with respect.

"Easily," Stellan nodded.

"Do it," Bill said. "Now."

"This'll be easy. Probably the easiest thing we've done in a while," Shafer Priest, Vernon Clark's acting second-in-command grinned at Vernon. Vernon sat in the van's passenger seat while Shafer drove toward the old mercantile building in Tyrone's ghost town.

Shafer's three sons—all half human, sat in the back, rifles loaded and lying across their laps. They couldn't turn but they were marksmen—their father, a werewolf—had taught them well.

"Pruitt would have come with us, but his wife just had a kid. Wouldn't look right," Shafer swerved to miss a pothole in the graveled road.

"You think we can hold this guy long enough to bleed Rome

Enterprises for as much as we can get, and then kill him nice and slow?" Vernon grinned at Shafer.

"Yeah. I hear Rome is pretty fond of this one. Plays a lot of golf with him. It was lucky his investigator is working another job, or we'd have to kill him right off."

"Would it be a bad thing if we sent body parts of Bob Sullivan, private investigator, along with the ransom note for Ross Gideon?" Vernon laughed.

"You know, you're right," Shafer acknowledged. "How much do we hurt Gideon before we send the note?"

"Oh, we'll see," Vernon pulled a knife from the sheath strapped to his belt. "I sharpened this yesterday. I'd like to check the edge on it."

Breanne's Journal

What the hell? Jayson sent mindspeech to all of us as Kal set our invisible collective mist on the floor of an old, Spanish-style building that once housed a department store.

Ross Gideon—one of two people who'd turned my life into more hell than necessary, stood nearby with two werewolves. The wolves were brothers, and I felt Trajan's anger immediately. Why hadn't I given him mindspeech?

Without any alternative, I lowered my shields and read Ross Gideon. He was confused; I could see that clearly. He also trusted the two with him—they'd worked for him before. He just didn't know they were werewolves, and he also didn't know they were connected to Vernon Clark. An obsession lay on the werewolves, too, but as usual, I couldn't get information on that.

Jayson, I sent, *Gideon doesn't know those two sold him out. He's about to be kidnapped and a ransom note will be given to your father before they kill him.*

I hate to save the old fucker's skin, Jayson growled.

I feel the same, but I get the idea that Vernon's on the way, and he may have company, I returned.

We have to do this, as much as I'd like to see Gideon squirm, Bill joined our silent conversation. *These won't move until Vernon shows up, I think. Vernon will likely make a grand entrance, just to make Gideon scream. From what we've seen of Vernon's work, he likes that sort of thing.*

What about the vampires tailing them? I asked.

They'll likely hold back until all the rats are in the trap, Hank offered.

What's the plan, then? Opal asked.

I want as many taken alive as possible, Bill said.

Gotcha.

"Rhett, I smell werewolf," Dalroy said softly. The wind was in their favor, sending the scents of those exiting the van toward Dalroy and Rhett, while carrying sound away. The desert became cold at night and the winds came up. Dalroy was grateful for that piece of luck.

"The others are human or half human, I think," Rhett informed his vampire sire.

"Agreed. Want to wait until they get inside to run in after them?" Dalroy flashed a grin at Rhett.

"Yeah. Sounds good."

"Calhoun, Vernon Clark is in danger," Wildrif spoke quickly into his cellphone. "I have had a vision and his death is coming—I feel it. I caught sight of two vampires in the vision before it was cut off. Too much of that is happening lately, and I have no explanation for it."

"Where's Vernon?" Calhoun barked from his end of the conversation.

"New Mexico. Tyrone. The old ghost town."

"Never mind, I have it," Calhoun snapped before the call ended.

Hank's Journal

I felt him before he arrived—he believed only vampires waited to endanger this enterprise. He was of the lesser gods; that wasn't difficult to discern.

Maintain your mist, I instructed Breanne. *I will assist the vampires outside. Another is coming to join these, and he is more dangerous than all the others.*

You're joking.

Always skeptical, my Breanne. It was so difficult for her to trust. To believe anyone. Had I been in her place, I might feel exactly the same.

No. Keep your shields up. Ask Stellan to place some as well. This one will detect his, not yours, and as he will not recognize the warlock's shields because yours will interfere with identification, he will be puzzled. That may give you enough time to pull Gideon into your mist and fold the hell away. Do this, Breanne. For me. The two vampires and I will take care of this crowd.

Hank, she began, worry saturating her mindspeech.

Bree, do this.

All right, but you better be safe.

I will be safe. I love you. I am skipping away from your mist to collect the vampires outside. Take Gideon. Go back to the café and allow Stellan to keep my image there at the table.

Okay.

That's my girl. I skipped away from Breanne's mist, aiming for two vampires outside.

Breanne's Journal

Hank didn't tell me what—or who—he felt coming. That worried me. Actually, it terrified me. It seemed, too, that he'd become more formal in his speech patterns once I learned he was High Demon. Sure, he still sounded like Hank at times, but it was almost as if he were letting some disguise slide away.

Shoving away those thoughts, I focused on what he'd asked me to do. *Stellan,* I sent, *can you put up a shield around us? Hank says it'll confuse our targets.*

Putting up shields now, Stellan immediately obliged.

Now it was a waiting game.

CHAPTER 8

reanne's Journal
So many things happened at once, and I almost lost the opportunity to pull asshole writer Ross Gideon away when the power surge hit the building with a resounding boom. The building shook on its foundation and I screamed mentally at the shock of it before coming back to reality and snatching Ross Gideon away.

Yes, I wanted to stay and make sure Hank was safe. I couldn't. I did as he asked and folded the hell back to the café, Ross Gideon squirming in my mist.

Hank's Journal
You will take the others, I will handle the power wielder, I instructed the vampires. Rhett and Dalroy stared, how could they not? I appeared in my smaller Thifilathi and laid a god's version of compulsion.

When I set you down inside, take the werewolves first, I added. *I will neutralize the weapons as quickly as possible. Once you have finished with your assignment, take your vehicle and meet Gavin at the Tyrone Café.*

I watched with them as Vernon Clark and four others entered the building. Bill wanted them taken alive, but they were too dangerous. Breanne would know they carried obsessions, just as I now did. I'd learned much from her when I'd pulled information away with our first kiss. Only her most powerful mates might accomplish that, and two others besides me held her heart and the talent to do it.

When the god came close and hit the building with a precursor of his power and a loud boom, I folded the vampires inside the building.

~

Abort your mission, you fool! Acrimus shouted mindspeech at Calhoun. *You are in more danger than Vernon Clark. He is expendable and easily replaced. Turn back now. I command it!*

~

Breanne's Journal

"Gideon, I'd like to take you apart right here," Bill hissed in Ross' face. The fact that Bill held Ross' jacket collar in his fist didn't help matters much—at least from Ross' perspective. Jayson stood beside Bill, and I knew he wanted to disassemble the quaking author as well.

"Director Jennings?" Ross almost stuttered as he gazed into Bill's angry eyes.

"Yes, fucking Director Jennings," Bill snarled. "Do you have any idea what we saved you from?"

"Wh-what?" Ross did stutter that time.

"Vernon Clark was about to walk into that building, bringing four armed men with him," Bill said. "You were a dead man, right after they got as much ransom money as they could from Rome Sr. Vernon Clark likes to flay his victims, did you know that?"

"What?" Ross attempted to pull away. If Kalenegar hadn't shielded us, the café patrons would have seen (and heard) our little party, instead of the illusion of us still sitting at a long, back table.

"We found evidence that he likes to practice taxidermy, and not all of it was on animals," Opal stepped up.

115

"Oh, my God," Ross started shaking harder.

"Your bodyguards have worked with Mr. Clark in the past," I said.

"Who the hell are you?" Ross turned in my direction. Yes, I was still in disguise. He had no idea who I might be.

"It doesn't matter who she is," Bill jerked Ross' attention back to him. "She saved your fucking life—that's all you need to know."

"Look, I was only trying to get information on the youngest Rome boy," Ross whined.

"Sure you were," Jayson broke in. "The old man sent you right out to hunt him down, shortly after he was fired." Jayson, still looking like Matt Michaels, crossed arms over his chest.

"Look, he was worried about the kid," Ross insisted. "And he was pissed that Clark likely had something to do with the kid's disappearance."

"And he didn't like that Vernon was calling him a liar," Bill said. "Vernon claimed Breanne Hayworth was a hoax, and Rome didn't like it. Did he?"

"Hell, I didn't like it. You have no idea what I had to go through to get that research."

"You have no idea what Breanne Hayworth went through, so you could have a best-seller." Bill tossed Ross Gideon backward. Trajan reached out and caught him before he fell.

"Look, I didn't feel good about that," Ross claimed as Trajan (not gently) set him upright. "Just like Rome had second thoughts when the kid disappeared."

"It amazes me that you're calling a thirty-year-old a kid," Jayson growled. "And the old man doesn't feel, so don't give me that bullshit."

"Who the hell are you?" Ross asked again.

"Somebody who wants to punch you in the face," Jayson said.

"Jayson, hold off on that for now, and you'll have to wait in line anyway," Bill said. "Look, we need to take our seats and pretend we were here all along. We'll act friendly until Hank gets back, and then we'll leave. I think I can find something to charge Mr. Gideon with so we can hold him for a while. We don't need to worry about his ass. We've got enough to worry over, trying to keep our own safe."

Hank's Journal

I have no idea what frightened the approaching power wielder, but something did, causing him to turn away from his target. The vampires did their job—quite well, in fact. Three werewolves were decapitated swiftly, almost before they realized they were under attack.

The rifles wouldn't fire—I saw to that. It only takes a bit of power to destroy a weapon from the inside, and three humans died while attempting to shoot the blurs that were two vampires.

Vernon Clark stared—he hadn't expected an attack such as this. He still couldn't believe that Ross Gideon disappeared before his eyes. He'd counted on a huge ransom from James Rome, which would never happen without the intended victim.

I appeared before Vernon Clark in my smaller Thifilathi, making him squeak in alarm. For anyone who believed that demons might be real and prepared to carry you to a fiery lake for eternal damnation, a High Demon could fill that visual role nicely.

That's when the godling became spooked. He shouldn't be frightened of a High Demon, and would recognize me as such immediately. Why he fled before he arrived, I may never know. I was prepared to allow him to think he might destroy me; instead, he vanished without a trace.

That left Vernon Clark with me. He swallowed hard as I stepped toward him, flanked by two vampires who still sported fangs and claws. In his mind, the devil and his minions had arrived to collect his soul and I wasn't about to disillusion him.

"While I'd love to torture you, for Breanne Hayworth's sake," I held up a hand, "I will remain true to my kind." Vernon Clark's sparks flew toward the ceiling, winking out before arriving at their destination.

Breanne's Journal

"They're all dead. Ask Breanne why I had to do it." I heard Hank's voice clearly as he spoke to Bill over his cell.

We still sat at the table at the café, and Bill turned a puzzled look in my direction.

Obsession, I sent. Bill nodded.

"The vamps are driving in—I'll meet them outside the café. We'll be there in a minute," Hank added before hanging up.

Just as he said, Hank and two vampires—Dalroy and Rhett—walked through the café door seconds later. Gavin rose to greet the vampires, Charles right beside him. Dalroy and Rhett showed little signs of wear, with only a smudge or two on their clothing to indicate they'd fought werewolves—and won.

"Baby," Hank came to me first and leaned in to kiss me before sitting at my side.

"What happened?" I asked softly.

"Killed those you saw. The bigger fish got away. Got scared or something and barely showed up before getting the hell out again."

"You do look scary, honey, at times."

"That wouldn't have worked with this one. Something's going on and I don't like it."

"Yeah. This isn't scary or anything," I shivered. Hank put an arm around me and asked Trajan to order coffee for the table.

Calhoun whistled as he studied the identical twins. At least they seemed identical. He knew there were differences. He knew, too, that Acrimus had a hand in this, and that one of the twins was a clone of the original.

"The Khos'Mirai," Calhoun nodded. "Brilliant. That's how you knew to call me back," he nodded his deference to Acrimus.

"I saw Vernon Clark's death, just as the quarter-blood seer did, and knew danger lay in your path," the clone shrugged indifferently. "Thank you for restoring me to my brother."

"I am grateful for this interference," Saxom agreed. "We will do what we can to assist in the defeat of the enemy."

~

Le-Ath Veronis—present

Lissa's Journal

"I need Kooper back, plus ten more like him," Norian grumbled as he paced inside my office. The Frithia thing was wearing him down, as he had no news and no leads. Both Alliances fretted over the lack of information, and this tragedy, following so closely on the heels of killing sandstorms, had everybody on edge and looking for disaster around every corner.

I'll admit, I was on edge, too. I'd heard from Ashe—Breanne had gone right back into the mess that had caused her death the last time, and here Norian was, asking to get Kooper back.

"Nori, this is madness. I know you need Kooper. How are you going to convince him that leaving Bree is a good idea?"

"He has a job," Norian grumbled.

"And he'd quit in a nanosecond if you threatened him with that," I snapped. "Look, I hear there's a crowd around her as it is, and that in itself may paint a bigger target on all of them. Let me come with you and talk to him. Frankly, I think this Frithia thing is connected and we need to come at this from every stinking angle we can think of."

"Can I borrow Trevor?" Norian turned begging eyes on me. "He and Kooper work well together. You think I might get one of Teeg's warlocks?"

"Look, I'll tell Trevor he can do this if he wants, but I warn you, he's still pissed at what you did to Breanne."

"Then I'll let Kooper ask," Norian tossed up a hand.

"If you can convince Kooper to come back," I pointed out. "Stellan is with Kooper right now, and they have three reptanoids with them."

"You think I could borrow them, too?" Norian's voice filled with hope.

"I think if they agreed to leave Breanne, that she and Reah would beat you into the ground if you mistreated them."

"You have so little faith in me," Norian grumbled.

"You haven't done anything to make me feel otherwise," I snapped.

$$\sim$$

Earth—past

Breanne's Journal

Hank and I transported Bill, Jayson and Opal to D.C. so we could deliver Ross Gideon to waiting agents. Bill wanted him held for a few days, and asked that Ross be questioned on his dealings with Rafe and Braden Reynolds.

Ross would be housed appropriately and kept from wandering away, but he wouldn't be behind bars. At least Bill said no communication between James Rome, Sr. and Ross. Bill planned to tell Mr. Rome personally that his son was safe and in an undisclosed location, as was Ross Gideon.

"What an asshole," Jayson huffed as we watched Ross Gideon being led away. I just shook my head at the bizarre events of the evening. Ross had not only cost me my privacy, he'd landed me on a hit list and caused Jayson to lose his job.

"Where's Kathleen?" I turned to Jayson after Ross and his guards disappeared down a long hallway inside a D.C. federal building.

"Back in Tahoe with Dan, her bodyguard," Jayson said. "I don't like it, but she says she doesn't feel comfortable anywhere, nowadays, so it's just as good as any other place."

"This is so much crap," I muttered.

"Ready to go back?" Bill asked.

"Yeah."

"Baby, I'll get this," Hank dropped a hand on my shoulder before skipping all of us back to New Mexico.

$$\sim$$

Hank's hands are amazing. He was simply smoothing hair away from my forehead as he gazed down at me, and it felt wonderful. No surprise—I'd ended up in his bed, my trunks shoved against the wall of his bedroom.

"How do you feel?" His breath was warm against my neck as he placed a kiss there.

"Not too bad, but still a little tired. Like I'm stretched too thin," I replied, closing my eyes.

"Don't push it, baby," he whispered before kissing my collarbone. "If you felt better, I'd skip us to the hot tub."

"Uh-huh. Actually, hot water sounds good."

"Does it?" Fingers trailed down the side of my face as he smiled lazily at me. "Ready?" My squeal of surprise was lost as he skipped me to a section of the compound I hadn't seen before.

"Look who's here." Jayson, Trajan and Kooper were all sitting in bubbling water when Hank landed me there, sans clothing. How he managed that I may never know, and at first I kept my hands moving to cover things up. I then recalled it wouldn't do a damn bit of good anyway and dropped my hands.

"Hi. Kooper. Trajan. Stellan." I settled between Trajan and Hank, wedging myself between two heavily muscled arms. At least the water covered me above my breasts, with only a clear spot showing between bubbling froth now and then.

"Well," I said after a while when nobody said anything, "Kooper, Trajan, do you want mindspeech?"

"Yeah," Trajan drawled. "I was feeling left out. Of lots of things."

"Oh, boy." I covered my face with a hand. "You think I don't feel bad about that?" I dropped my hand and turned to him. Trajan's eyes look like black velvet when he's happy and obsidian when he's pissed. They were somewhere in between at the moment.

"You know what I'd like more than anything?" I said when Trajan didn't speak. "I'd like to be somewhere far away from here with all of you and the others who care for me. I'd prefer not to worry about anything more pressing than what we'll have for breakfast when we get up in the morning. I want to sit with all of you and let you tell me what you like and what you don't. Where you want to go or be, and what you'd like to do. Since I can't read you, I don't know those things like I would with everybody else. Right now, the universe is hanging over my head, and that weight could drop any minute. Do I want to wake up with you in the morning?" I blinked at Trajan. "Yeah. I do. I want to crawl all over that fine body of yours and ask you what you want. The truth is, I wake up most days too tired and worried to consider it. I'm sorry about that. I hope it changes, someday."

"Baby doll, I didn't mean it to come out like that," Trajan lifted me onto his lap.

"I know." I settled my head against his shoulder with a sigh before gathering the necessary power to give him mindspeech. I gave it to Kooper and the reptanoids too, while I was at it.

We can talk in private, now, I informed him.

Wow, Trajan's smile came through in his silent reply. *Have I told you how much I love you, or how often I have to jerk off in the shower?* He added.

Okay, the first part was nice. The last was a little over the top, I replied.

You're coming to bed with a werewolf tonight, Trajan informed me and stood with me in his arms. I squeaked when he nodded at the others and nearly vaulted out of the hot tub. Werewolves are definitely not modest. Trajan hauled me down the hall toward his bedroom, both of us naked and dripping, and one of us displaying an erection at least the size of a northeastern U.S. state.

Did it matter that we got the sheets damp? Not to Trajan. Werewolves are all about touch, scent and taste. He was all over me, nipping, licking, tasting, kissing, and then fucking. Lots of fucking. Did he wake up the entire house, howling afterward? Yeah. I'm surprised somebody didn't come in and shoot him for disturbing their sleep.

Baby? Trajan's mindspeech permeated my sleep.

"Hmm?" It was all I could do to get a sleepy mumble out. My eyes were glued shut and refused to open. All I wanted to do was curl into a ball against Trajan's warmth and go back to sleep. For a week.

"I'm sorry I wore you out," Trajan breathed against my neck before kissing a tender spot. "We have to get up. I just heard from Hank. People are disappearing from Kansas and Oklahoma."

~

"Your pet, Vernon Clark, died last night," Acrimus informed V'ili. V'ili sat inside the office cleared out for him, naked and in his natural form.

"I feel it whenever an obsession I create drops away." One of V'ili's claws slid down Janine's face, leaving a thin trail of blood behind. She whimpered from her position at his feet and leaned closer against his leg. "This was news I already had. Do we know who might be responsible?"

"Vernon had a meeting with Ross Gideon set up, through the Reynolds brothers. Ross went hunting for Vernon, thinking the Reynolds brothers would take care of him. He had no idea they were werewolf. It appears, however, that Ross had other allies. He has disappeared and the stink of High Demon is all over the building in New Mexico, with the ash from burned werewolves and half-breeds scattered across the floor."

"Likely the same High Demon who appeared in Tahoe to destroy my chimera," V'ili growled, his voice garbled by anger and sharpened teeth. "I had no idea a High Demon would consent to serve any of these," he indicated Janine with a contemptuous glance.

"I had no idea any High Demon would condescend to helping these," Acrimus agreed. "It was so convenient—and simple—to wean them away from their duties."

"Convenient that our god slept and neglected his obligations," V'ili offered Acrimus a toothy grin.

"Decidedly convenient, but he was never strong enough to hold the Dark Realm anyway. It has been easy, chipping away at the foundations built in the beginning. All are teetering now, and will readily accept the General's offer to rebuild and rule when the others are destroyed."

"He has already destroyed one," V'ili purred. "Only two remain."

"True."

"Have you seen how well our slaves are performing? My pool is filled and our dungeon is nearly finished," V'ili added. "We will celebrate its construction with sacrifices."

"We won't need all those slaves afterward, anyway," Acrimus agreed.

~

Breanne's Journal

Breanne? Lissa's mindspeech sounded tentative, as if she were worried that I wouldn't reply.

Is everything all right? I sent back.

Yes and no, she replied. *We have a situation on Frithia and Norian, asshole snake that he is, needs Kooper back. He could use Stellan, too, in addition to—in his words, anyway—as many reptanoids and other talented helpers as he can get. He's already commandeered Trevor to help, plus anybody else he can convince to come.*

Yeah, I *Looked*. I couldn't get to the actual event—all I could get to was the furor in the media about the mass suicide. *This is connected*, I said immediately, *to what we're working on, here. Sirenali are involved, or I'd get a better picture of all this*, I explained.

I was hoping you'd be able to tell me something, Lissa said. *And I detected scents from bodies—live bodies—that were taken away.*

Who?

Little girls.

Fuck, I said. *Any leads?*

This one, Lissa sent a mental image of one I'd seen already—Genley Reith, the Sirenali Norian had asked about.

This is awful, I said. *Has anybody explained to you about Kay—Kalia?*

Ashe told me what he knew, but that was a while back, Lissa said.

There are new developments, I returned. *It's likely the ones involved in selling her as a child sex slave are involved in this, too, right with the Sirenali. That doesn't sit well with me. If the ASD needs help tracking some of those assholes, I'll send Kooper, Stellan and a few others. Can you come here, or do I need to come to you? I asked.*

Can you get away? I don't want to mess anything up by showing up back there again. I hear memories had to be altered the last time.

Yeah. Look, I just have to tell people I'll be gone for a few, and I'll bring Norian's helpers with me. I hope Norian won't be there with you, because frankly, I want to hit him really, really hard.

I can bring him in if you want. I wouldn't mind watching you punch him.

No time for that now. Give me a minute and I'll be there.

Thanks.

"Bree, where were you just then?" Bill studied me as I sat at the table, a forkful of cheese omelet halfway to my mouth.

"Having a conversation. Look, I need to be gone for a little bit. I can't explain exactly where, but I need to take Stellan, Kooper, Chazi, Bekzi and Perzi with me."

"I'm going," Hank announced. I watched as a thin stream of smoke punctuated his statement.

"Fine, but that's it. I can't take any others," I pointed out. "This is a sensitive situation, okay?"

"As long as Hank is with you," Charles sighed. "Are there any biscuits left?"

～

"Lissa's palace?" Stellan and Kooper both knew where we were when we arrived outside my sister's private study. So did the reptanoids— they'd all been here before.

Hank remained silent while I knocked softly on Lissa's half-open door.

"Come in," she said.

～

Lissa's Journal

I hid my surprise when Li'Neruh Rath arrived with Breanne. Belen had knelt to him and asked him to make a command when I'd seen him before. He knew I remembered. *Keep your silence*, he ordered. *I will give information to her when the time is right.*

Could I have ignored that command? No way in hell. I recalled Merrill's compulsion when I'd first met him centuries ago, when I'd been susceptible to compulsion for my first year as a vampire. Back then, Merrill's instruction had felt like thunder and lightning. This was more like the silky feel of polished titanium, holding back the heart of a million nuclear explosions. *As you command*, I lowered my eyes respectfully.

Breanne's Journal

"So we have a battle on more than one front," Kooper said. He didn't like it that Norian wanted him back. He liked it less that he'd have to leave me. Stellan felt the same and had already voiced his opinion, but Norian had gone to Tybus, and Tybus had given permission for Stellan to be approached for this assignment.

Chazi, Perzi and Bekzi were torn between staying with me and going with Kooper, who'd won their loyalty early on.

"Go with Kooper," I sighed. "I'll miss you, but you may be needed more where he's going. You may have to help track down Hordace Cayetes, and he has Rezil Foculis plus Q'And and Q'Ind Ribalo with him. They all need to be dead and I figure you might be able to get to him when somebody else won't."

"What about those women—the ones who likely have six little girls, now?" Lissa turned back to me.

"I really want to make them dead myself, but I think Reah needs to help on that. Can Aurelius and a few of hers tackle that?"

"Farzi and Nenzi go," Chazi nodded. "They help."

"I imagine she can put a few people together," Lissa pointed out dryly.

"There's something I want from Norian," I said. "Because he owes me. For this," I indicated my bunch, "and for what he did before."

"Agreed. I don't care what it is," Lissa nodded.

"Good. I want Ranos pistols and rifles for the folks I left behind. And for Hank," I nodded at him. "The kind that accepts their DNA and won't fire for anybody else. The kind that'll self-destruct if anybody messes with them to see how they work."

"I can arrange that," Lissa agreed grimly. "If Norian won't do it, I'll go to Ildevar myself."

~

"Don't let anyone else open these and pull them out of their protective sleeve," Kooper warned. "They've only been handled by robots up to this point."

I stared at the boxes and crates of weapons to be transported to Earth's past. We even had two rocket launchers, and I considered that Hank and Trajan might be the ones to handle those. The cost of the weapons was outrageous, but we needed them. I wasn't going to quibble over it.

"Thanks," I told Kooper.

"Just stay safe," he leaned down to kiss me. "You can send mindspeech, too, when you're not busy. Or drop in. I won't mind." He grinned.

"I'll consider it," I offered him a smile. "Gotta go. Thanks, Lissa." I gave her a hug before Hank and I folded away from Le-Ath Veronis, leaving part of my heart behind with Stellan, Kooper and three reptanoids.

~

Earth—past

Hank's Journal

I had no idea she'd ask for Ranos technology. I wasn't going to argue, however. The weapons would prove useful and the technology was safe. Keef certainly owed her, and I looked forward to teaching the others how to use the weapons.

Bill waited, too, for us to transport him to Kansas City. Something was going on in the area—it wasn't only the homeless missing this time. I couldn't get to the reason, and Breanne likely wouldn't either, which spelled Sirenali involvement. I'd gotten a brief message from Kifirin, too, after I'd sent him on a sensitive mission.

Years ago, Lissa, with assistance and a bit of a power loan from the Mighty Hand, sealed a void against time. The void in question housed the Khos'Mirai when he still lived. That seal remained unbroken, which meant the original Khos'Mirai was still dead. It didn't preclude the possibility that one of his clones might have been pulled away from death without Lissa's knowledge.

Many of our enemies outranked Lissa. Greatly. It would only take one Khos'Mirai clone to escape her notice in the past and our troubles would increase tenfold. Breanne might have read those things in Lissa, but since she may have read an inaccurate account of that debacle in her sister, she could possess faulty information.

"His name was Moxas," I said, the moment we landed in the huge compound kitchen in New Mexico. Moxas was Saxom's identical twin in every way except one; there could only be one naturally-born Khos'Mirai.

"Moxas?" Crates and boxes landed around us, crowding the kitchen and causing Bill and the others to rise from the table. Breanne looked up at me, expecting an accounting of my statement.

"Nothing, avilepha. We must show the others what we have for them, and then travel to Kansas City."

Breanne's Journal

He'd said *his name was Moxas*. I had no idea what that meant, and Hank was still as unreadable as he ever was. Regardless, we had an interested crowd the moment Hank explained Ranos technology. We even had weapons for Gavin and Charles, and I learned that both understood how to shoot. Who knew?

"Open them carefully, because once you touch, nobody else will be able to use these," Hank pulled his rifle from its crate and checked the charge. "They fire red blasts of power, and those will generally destroy whatever they hit, depending on the weapon and the size of the target."

"It only needs our touch to recognize our DNA?" Opal handled her new pistol, fingering the grip and trigger reverently.

"And it will destroy almost anything," Hank nodded. "Pistols work best for smaller targets, rifles for something bigger. You can bring down a huge building with a Ranos rocket launcher."

"If you shoot somebody, be ready for them to splatter everywhere," I warned. "These aren't for wounding or firing warning shots."

"What's the range?" Jayson examined his pistol carefully.

"Pistols accurate up to a hundred yards, rifles much farther, with the scope. Solar charged," Hank added. "No wall plugs needed. Just sunlight."

"I'll be damned," Bill whispered. "This is amazing."

"Like I said, if somebody else tries to use them, they won't work. Somebody tries to take them apart, they self-destruct. Probably taking the tampering idiot with them," Hank rumbled.

"Good to know," Charles grinned.

We had the whole upper floor of a hotel in Kansas City, Missouri. Some of the rooms were empty, but Bill had commandeered it, since it required an appropriate key card to get to the top floor. Only Bill's contingent now had that ability. Except for housekeeping and hotel employees, anyway.

The suite Hank and I shared opened on one side into Trajan's suite, and into Bill's on the other. Charles, Jayson, Kalenegar and Gavin occupied the rooms opposite ours. We'd left the corner suite for Opal, who liked the extra window space just fine.

Dalroy and Rhett were taking over the compound in New Mexico, and would be watching for Obediah Tanner, Winkler's and Bill's would-be assassin wrangler, to come home. Winkler planned to send an extra werewolf or two to help.

"We're scheduled to meet with some locals in two hours," Bill said, once we got luggage unloaded and stowed. "Let's have lunch first, before we figure out what they know."

"It's raining, baby," Hank pulled my arm through the sleeve of a sweater. "It's September outside," he reminded me. Kansas City in September was cooler during the day than New Mexico in September.

"Oh. Yeah." I let him guide my other arm into the opposite sweater sleeve.

"There." He straightened the shawl collar before pulling me into a hug. "I'm still getting used to the platinum hair," he breathed against my temple.

"Me, too," I mumbled against his chest. I was tired—after spending the night with Trajan. Werewolves seemed to be made of steel or something. Trajan almost bounced wherever he went today.

"You're getting some sleep tonight," Hank informed me.

"Good," I yawned.

Lunch was at a small bistro near the hotel that offered better vegetarian selections. We could have sat outside under an awning, but it was still raining and the temperature was in the low fifties.

"Veggie chili is good," I sighed, crunching into a cracker provided by our waiter.

"Can you tell us where you went, and where Kooper and Stellan are?" Jayson asked.

"No, but they're working on a similar project now."

"They're on another planet, working on a similar project," Hank said, lifting his iced tea glass and draining it.

"So other places are being attacked," Opal said, watching me carefully with her unblinking, dark eyes.

"Yeah." I thought of Reah, whom I'd only seen in passing. She had children. I knew she was the one to send after Song and Serenade. Those two women—their names made them sound so nice. Peaceful, even. They were anything but. They purchased pretty children—girls and boys, for next to nothing and then cruelly taught them to be sex slaves for pedophiles.

Hordace Cayetes was their best customer, but they had many on multiple worlds, in and outside both Alliances.

"What are you thinking about, sweetheart?" Bill brought me back to the present.

"Sadly, I was thinking about pedophiles and the scum of the worlds," I sighed, staring at my hands.

"Don't ask," Hank held up a hand to keep Bill from pursuing the subject.

∾

Hank's Journal

She helped someone recently who was raised and trained as a sex slave, Hank sent mindspeech to Bill. *Bree saw those images from the woman, according to Kooper and Stellan, and now that shit won't leave her alone.*

What's going on? Trajan broke in on the conversation.

Almost before he was done, I heard from Jayson and Opal, too. I explained mentally what Breanne's statement meant as I cut into a slice of apple pie.

That happens here, or close enough, Opal snorted. *Parents or grandparents sell their kids to brothels in some countries. It's sickening.*

The worlds are in a terrible place, Kalenegar broke in. He'd sat quietly at the table, refusing to pretend to eat. At least he'd fed from the sunlight in New Mexico before traveling with us to Kansas City.

I get the feeling we're standing at a crossroads, Bill said.

We are, Kalenegar replied.

CHAPTER 9

Breanne's Journal

We sat around a long, boardroom table while an FBI agent explained that there'd been more than three hundred unexplained disappearances from Kansas, Missouri, Oklahoma and Arkansas in the past month.

"Many of them," Special Agent Quin Folsom explained, "are maintenance workers, plumbers, construction workers, electricians and such." He tapped a key on his laptop, which changed the image on the screen behind him. They'd broken down the missing into blocks of employment-related categories.

"So they're cherry-picking?" Trajan asked.

"It looks that way. They tend to disappear either on their way to work or going home afterward. People are starting to panic."

"They're building something," Bill sighed.

"Bill, do we have information on who built that church in the Dallas area?" I asked.

"I checked; all standard construction permits and a local company, but the list of legitimate employees doesn't match how fast that structure went up."

"No sign of where they're building?" Gavin broke in.

"Nowhere in this area. We have agents checking, but no building permits have been requested or filed in any of the affected states."

"Because they're hiding it, more than likely," Hank snorted. I was surprised that there was no smoke connected to his statement.

"And with the ones we're dealing with, it could be anywhere, or even in more than one place," I said. "Are people still disappearing? Have others come up missing elsewhere? What about foreign countries?"

"We're attempting to contact a few places, but let's face it, some countries are in such upheaval, nobody would realize something like this if a few disappeared here and there. We'll have to track this—or attempt to track it—by the types of skilled workers missing," Agent Folsom said.

"My concern is that evidence of any construction may be shielded," Kalenegar offered.

"What?" Agent Folsom's disbelief was evident as he turned toward Kal.

"He knows what he's talking about," Bill sighed. "Were you at the meeting in D.C.?"

"No, but I was briefed. I have a problem believing some of the reported events," he began.

"They're all true," Bill said. "We're not dealing with locals, for the most part."

"There really are chimeras and sirens?"

"Chimeras and *Sirenali*," Kalenegar corrected stiffly. I could tell he didn't appreciate anyone questioning his honesty. "In addition to other—races and such."

It's okay; he just doesn't know what to think. He's not used to anything other than humanoid, I sent to Kal. Well, it was time to see if I still pissed him off in any way.

I understand that, but this doubtfulness wastes time, which is in short supply, Kal replied.

My love, you look tired, filtered into my brain. I'd heard that before, and just as before, that unfamiliar mental voice didn't come again.

~

"What now?" Hank asked as we piled into the van to drive back to our hotel. Bill asked for a vehicle so we wouldn't attract attention by appearing and disappearing. We didn't need to be caught because somebody might be watching for such anomalies. At least Agent Folsom didn't have an obsession—I checked him and everybody else we met at the local FBI office.

"We'll need dinner eventually, and we need information," Bill grumbled. All of us were tired—we'd had a really long night rescuing Ross Gideon, and then I'd had to give up nearly half my crew for another mission on Frithia and other parts unknown.

We were stuck in rush-hour traffic getting away from the downtown area, so it took nearly an hour to get back to the hotel.

"I say room service and bed," Jayson suggested as we trooped past the front desk.

"Second," Opal raised a hand.

"I'm too tired to eat," I mumbled.

"I'll keep you awake long enough to eat," Hank sighed.

"Right." I was too tired to nod.

We rode the elevator in silence and Hank pulled out his key card to open the door. Ashe and Kay waited for us inside.

~

Ashe's Journal

Breanne looked as if she were ready to drop, and the one she had with her—it was Kifirin's superior, Li'Neruh Rath. He'd been there when Breanne was attacked by the General. Now I knew why—they were together.

She doesn't know, smoke filtered from Li'Neruh's nostrils as he gazed steadily at me with dark eyes and a deep frown. *I'd prefer telling her myself, when the time is right.*

Tread carefully, I returned. *She's still pissed at me because I yelled at her.*

That is of no consequence; she needs rest.

Kay needs Bree, I offered a mental sigh with my sending.

Kay can watch Breanne sleep, his mindspeech contained a growl. *After she eats.*

Look, I know she's tired, but just a few words for Kay while she's eating will do wonders, I pointed out.

I hope you're not suggesting that we stay in the same room, Li'Neruh snapped.

No, nothing of the kind, I began when Breanne took matters out of our hands and handled it herself.

Breanne's Journal

I could tell Kay was shaky, and as tired as I was, I didn't want things to get worse for her. "Kay, what's wrong?" I held out a hand to her.

"I feel really shaky," she hugged herself.

"There's no need for that. Come give me a hug," I offered, holding my arms open. She came immediately, so I used up what little strength I had to give her as much *Love* as I could.

"She's just worn out, sweetheart," I heard Ashe say when my eyes blinked open. "Bree's been through a lot."

"But nobody will tell me what that was," Kay grumped. "And I want to know. I love Bree. She's my friend. Don't you think I ought to know?"

"Kay," my voice sounded rough. I found myself lying on the king-sized bed that Hank intended to share with me. "Honey, you really don't need to hear all that. It's upsetting. For me and for you. Okay?"

"Will you tell me someday?"

"If you're ready for it. Kevis will have to say when that is."

"Fine. I feel better now. Can we stay? Can I help you with anything?"

"Bree," Hank settled on the bed beside me and stroked my face with a finger, "I ordered food for all of us. Do you feel up to sitting so we can eat?"

"Yeah. Will you help me up?"

"I'll let you lean against me," he offered.

"That'll be nice. Did you order a glass of milk for me?"

"I did, and a fruit and cheese plate, plus a salad. They're not big on vegetarian in the restaurant downstairs."

"No surprise," I sighed. "Did you get something for Kay and Mr. Grumpy, too?"

"If you mean Kay and Ashe, then yes, I also ordered for them—after they studied the menu."

"I wish we had a big house again, and Fes here to cook for us," I mumbled, closing my eyes when Hank pulled me against him.

"Baby, go back to sleep. I'll wake you when the food is here."

Kay's Journal

Nobody would tell me anything, but my guess was that Breanne had a terrible past, just as Kalia and I did, and I still hadn't had enough courage to read the book about her. I did and didn't want to know what it was about. Kalia's past was horrible enough, and I worried that her fears would take us over again, so I decided to let the subject go for now.

I felt bad, too, that I'd taken all of Bree's strength just to feel better—and I did feel better. I always did after she touched me and performed her magic. I was even beginning to feel better about Ashe, too; he was always good to me and somehow, I knew he always would be.

Without Kalia's fears weighing me down, I was certainly warming up to Ashe. He hadn't attempted to kiss me or anything, but he'd touched my hands or my shoulders occasionally and always asked what I wanted or how I felt.

That's how we'd ended up where we were—on Earth in the past. He'd explained it once we arrived at the hotel; Bill described where he was in the past, and that's where Bree was as well.

"Is there anything we can do for her?" I whispered and tugged on Ashe's sleeve.

"Sweetheart, she needs rest. Lots of rest."

A knock sounded on the door, causing me to jump and Bree to wake with a terrified shriek.

Breanne's Journal

"Hank's here, baby," Hank kept me from jumping off the bed, I was so startled by the knock from room service. His cheek was pressed against mine and his arms were locked around me, as if he were afraid I'd disappear.

"I'm okay," I croaked, and revealed the lie by shivering against him. He answered by tightening his arms slightly and kissing my temple. Across the room, I heard Ashe rise to answer the door. He even tipped the waiter, which made me wonder about the exchange rate on Campiaan Alliance credits and U.S. dollars.

"Ready to eat?" Hank breathed against my hair.

"Yeah."

What followed was a bizarre sort of picnic on our bed. Ashe had a burger with fries, which made him smile and me shake my head. Hamburger restaurants didn't exist in either Alliance, shockingly enough.

He'd ordered a burger for Kay, too, because part of her hadn't had one in a long time, and the other part had never had one. Hank, on the other hand, ordered a steak with all the trimmings.

"Want this?" Hank offered his dinner roll to me. "It didn't touch the meat," he grinned.

"Do you have butter?" Both items were handed over. Hank rubbed my shoulders while I spread a pat of butter on half the roll and ate it.

"We'll find some protein drinks tomorrow," Hank promised after I finished as much of my food as I could.

"Protein drinks?" Kay blinked at me.

"I have a hard time getting enough protein," I replied.

"Gotcha," she smiled. Truly, when Kay/Kalia smiles, it is a wondrous event. I've never seen anyone so beautiful, and a smile from her was worth more than gold because it was so rare. With a sigh, I hoped Reah would be successful tracking Song and Serenade, because those two deserved to die.

"Hey, what's green and goes up and down," I grinned back at Kay.

"No idea," a dimple appeared in her cheek.

"A frog in an elevator," I said. She laughed. It was like music, that laugh, and it made Ashe smile. The rumble at my side surprised me, though. Hank was chuckling at that stupid, ancient joke.

"Are we staying?" Kay looked hopefully at Ashe.

"If you want to," he nodded.

"I want to."

"Ashe," I warned.

"I know Bill is here. How about this?" He changed his appearance until he resembled someone I didn't recognize with olive skin, black, slightly curly hair, dark eyes and well-shaped, sensuous lips.

"Who is that?" I asked.

"Somebody we used to call Old Harold. Bill and Trajan never saw him, so I think this disguise is safe."

"You don't look old," Kay offered shyly. He didn't—he looked quite young, with possible Greek ancestry.

"Old Harold was a vampire, sweetheart. Somebody killed him before Bill met him."

"I know you told me not to be afraid of most vampires," Kay began.

"I'm a vampire," I volunteered. "You're not afraid of me, are you?"

"No." Kay lowered her eyes and shook her head. "I won't ever be afraid of you."

"Great. Where are you and Ashe spending the night, again?"

"Bill has the entire floor rented, so pick a room," Hank yawned. "Opal is in the one at the end, and the ones across the hall are taken."

"Opal is here, too?" Ashe sounded shocked.

"You know Opal?"

"Yeah. What the hell is she doing here? That doesn't fit with how I met her in the future."

"Something is fucking with the timeline," Hank snorted. "Haven't you figured that out, yet? Opal is one of Bill's Special Agents. Seems to be good at it. Has an excellent working knowledge of weapons, too."

"This really is screwed up, isn't it?" Ashe raked fingers through dark, curly hair and shook his head.

"More than you know," Hank agreed.

Ashe's Journal

I chose a room with two queen beds—Kay likely wouldn't appreciate sleeping with me. I still worried about sleeping in a bed across from her and wondered if she'd be unable to sleep with me in the same room. What actually happened surprised me.

"Hank really loves Bree. Doesn't he?" Kay settled gracefully on the end of my bed.

"He does. It's easy to see how much he loves her."

"I really liked it when he told her he was there, after the knock scared her awake."

"You liked that?"

"Yes. And he was so careful with her. Did you see that, too?"

"I did." I didn't know where this was leading, but my hopes were beginning to rise.

"Do other men do that?" she asked innocently.

"Other men do that," I said softly. "May I show you what it's like?"

"I think it would only be like that with someone who loved me," Kay began.

"Sweetheart, I have loved you for a very long time," I responded. "Come here. Let me show you how much you mean to me."

"But," she rose uncertainly, blinking at me with bright-blue eyes that held a tiny amount of trepidation.

I walked to her, instead, and wrapped my arms about her. "Ashe is here, sweetheart," I mumbled against her hair. "You're safe. I'll always keep you safe."

"Really?" She blinked up at me.

"Really." I leaned in and kissed her gently.

Breanne's Journal

I slept in Hank's arms; he was seemingly afraid I might disappear. I didn't, and slept like a rock once I fell asleep.

"Baby mine, are you gonna wake up, now?" Hank brushed his lips over mine. I woke to find his face hovering over mine and a sliver of morning light peeking between hotel curtains.

"I guess." I stretched beneath Hank and moaned a yawn. "What time is it?"

"Nearly nine. Bill let us sleep late. He was up earlier, talking with the Prez and a bunch of other folks on a conference call."

"Hank, he has to be exhausted," I forced my eyes to open wider.

"I know, but he's not as bad off as you. Come on, I've gotten mindspeech from half a dozen people already, asking if you're ready to go to breakfast."

"You could go without me," I pointed out.

"Nope. You're coming now, in your pajamas if you don't get dressed in the next five minutes. You can shower after we eat. Bill has a couple of leads to follow—one in Arkansas and the other in Colorado."

"All right." Hank took my arm and pulled me to a sitting position. It took a few seconds to work up enough courage to slide off the bed —I just wanted to huddle beneath the blanket and sleep again.

Ten minutes later (I insisted on brushing my teeth) we walked into the hotel café downstairs and found the others waiting for us. Ashe, still in disguise, and Kay were there as well.

"I hear we have help," Bill cut his eyes toward Ashe and Kay.

"Big help," Hank nodded. "They're perfect to chip in."

I struggled not to stare—Ashe stood behind Kay, his arms wrapped around her. She seemed perfectly happy to allow the contact. Deliberately, I refused to read her.

"I'm Ashe—Ashe DeLeon," he held out his hand and shook with Bill and the others. "This is Kay, who is extremely shy and looking for new friends."

"Ashe can do most of the things I can do—without the fangs," I said. "Kay is very talented; you just wouldn't know it by looking at her."

That is the most beautiful woman I've ever seen, Jayson breathed in my mind. *But you're the one I want.*

Jayson, you need to tread carefully where Kay is concerned. No kink around her. She was sold as a sex slave at age nine, and she's fucked up because of that and the fact that parts of her are covered in scars where one asshole sadist carved her up while she was chained to a wall.

Are you fucking kidding? he sent back.

Nope. She doesn't need to know what you or Hank are into, I added.

Got it. Haven't been much in the mood lately, anyway. Not since I was outed on the Internet.

Understood.

"Bree, how tired are you?" Bill asked while we ate.

"Tired but the coffee is helping," I lifted my cup and saluted him. "How about you?"

"I'm tired, too, but I got info from the FBI this morning. There are a couple of sites to check where construction is happening without permits. I need you and Hank to provide transport, if you don't mind."

"No problem," I shrugged. "Where do you want to go first?"

"Arkansas, then Colorado," he said. "I have addresses."

"We'll get you there," Hank said.

~

Frithia—present

Lissa's Journal

Norian had Kooper, Stellan, Trevor, three reptanoid brothers and me with him when we walked into the cavernous, empty building. Norian had gotten a tip that our target, Genley Reith, had purchased the building under an alias. The plan was to move his growing congregation to the new location, but they'd turned up dead before that could happen. Obviously, something had changed or orders had come from above, aborting the move.

"We found out about this because he defaulted on the loan," Norian took in the high, vaulted ceilings overhead, the half-built stone altar at the front and construction materials littering the floor.

"It looks as if he were planning to recruit more followers, but got spooked," Trevor observed dryly.

"I was thinking the same thing," I agreed. "Who knows what that was? Norian, do we have any information to go on? Was anything left behind?"

"Nothing has been touched; we're the first ones here," Norian blew out a sigh. "Let's split into teams and investigate. Kooper, take Chazi, Bekzi and Perzi with you to the basement. Trevor, Stellan, see what you can find here in the sanctuary and Lissa and I will check the rooms at the back."

I wasn't sure I wanted to be paired with Norian, but there was no help for it. I followed him through a narrow doorway behind the altar, and into a labyrinth of office spaces and classrooms.

The walls were new—the space had clearly been used for something else before. "Nori, what was this building before it was sold to Reith?" I asked.

"Warehouse. Actually, Tory owned it for a short while—it belonged to Schuul Enterprises, before Reah exposed them. The building has changed hands three times since then, last time bought as an investment and a few improvements made before Reith took it."

"My son owned this?" I shook my head. Truth really was stranger than fiction.

"It has changed hands three times in the last ten turns, so he didn't own it long. Come on; show me that famous nose and itchy goose bumps. Tell me what we're looking for," Norian coaxed.

"What if there's nothing here?" I countered. "It would be really stupid to leave anything lying around."

"Unless your boss told you to kill everybody and then get the hell out of—Dodge, wasn't it?" Norian wiggled an eyebrow at me, attempting to make me smile.

"Nori, you have a convenient memory, you know that?" I shook my head at him and followed him to the next room. We walked through nine rooms before we came to it, and if I hadn't been with Norian, he'd have walked right into it.

A gate, as incongruous as its existence was, lay inside the ninth room and only one of the Elemaiya or the powerful might see it. None of the Elemaiya were left who might travel through a gate unless—I grabbed Norian's arms and pinched him with barely-formed claws.

"Norian, you almost walked into a trap," I warned him. "You and anybody else who came to investigate this place."

"What are you talking about?" Norian grimaced. I realized then that I'd drawn blood.

"Sorry," I mumbled, taking my hand away. I'd closed all the gates to the Elemaiya, yet here one stood, ready and waiting to transport anyone through it. How could I tell? It was different. Warped. Any creature could disappear through this gate and appear who knows where on the other end. I figured there was a specific destination wired to this unusual gate, and that someone would be waiting on the other end—to welcome allies or to kill enemies.

"Nori, we have to seal off this room, and then we have to call a meeting and discuss this," I said, attempting to keep the quaver out of my voice. This was terrifying on so many levels, and I couldn't even begin to calculate what harm multiple gates such as this might do.

The horrifying part of all this was that there were precious few who might recognize a gate. Too many might disappear before anyone thought to stay away from something they couldn't see or comprehend.

It all made sense, though. I was a Nameless One. So many others were more powerful, and some of them still worked the wrong side of the fence.

∼

Le-Ath Veronis—present

Lissa's Journal

"You closed the gates," Merrill said.

"Only to the Elemaiya, but this isn't a normal gate. This one has either been manufactured recently, or changed to suit the enemy's purpose. We already know there are more powerful beings than I on the other side who might do that," I said. "This gate is wrong—anybody can go through it. That means it has been set as a trap for the unwary or as a gateway to get an enemy from one place to another if they don't have the ability to fold space."

Norian and I had taken our crew away from Frithia after I sealed off the room with power. At least nobody from the outside could get in. I just worried about what might get out after transporting into that building.

"Do you think there are more of these gates?" Merrill asked.

"It makes sense," I sighed. "And who knows how many are out there? Norian, have there been reports of disappearances from the areas surrounding that building?" I turned to him.

"Many," Norian consulted his comp-vid.

"Besides the powerful, who might recognize these gates?" Rigo asked.

"Only the Elemaiya and a few others could do it in the past," I said. "And I've prevented the Elemaiya from gating," I added.

"Along with taking away their immortality," Drake observed.

"Even though they can no longer gate, can they still recognize one if they see it?" Drew chimed in.

"Good question," I blinked at him. "Very good question. How do we find out? All the Elemaiya are at SouthStar, now. At least all the ones I know about."

"Will they be allowed to leave?" Kiarra asked. She, Adam and Merrill had come together when I sent a call to Merrill to help sort out this mess.

"They'll start aging again if they do," I pointed out. "SouthStar is a haven to those who live there."

"I'll send mindspeech to Ashe," Merrill began.

Be prepared to send it across time, I sent mindspeech. *He isn't there, right now.*

Can you contact him, then? Hidden gates are nothing but a minefield, and if the enemy built one, then there are likely many others, just as you say. Norian needs to get with the CSD and start gathering information on similar disappearances across both Alliances. Somebody needs to coordinate this, too.

Any suggestions?

What is Torevik doing? I can pair him with Lynx or someone else. He's bored anyway. Lynx, that is.

Saa Thalarr can see gates?

Yes. Your ah, father taught us.

Fuck. I forgot about Griffin. He could be so much help right now, and he's hiding and licking his wounds. Bree should have left him dead.

My darling, do not say that. She knew best—Griffin had to be saved in that time period, no matter how you might think otherwise. You do not know all things connected to him.

I'll defer to your judgment for now, because you know him better than I do, I replied. *You didn't see the mangled mess left of my sister after the General was finished with her, though.*

No, I didn't, a mental sigh accompanied Merrill's sending. *I'm merely glad the Larentii came.*

That makes two of us, I declared. *I'm still surprised she came back to her body. Do you think the Elemaiya will consent to be our gate hunters? They probably won't do it for me, anyway, since I'm the one who stripped them of their power and immortality.*

I'll ask, or get someone else to do it, Merrill said. *Franklin has done plenty for Kay, so he may be the one to ask Ashe.*

I don't care who asks, just as long as we get some help, I said. *And the sooner the better. We need somebody with every investigative team Norian sends out, and the same goes for those Tybus sends out.*

Agreed. Let's work on contacting Ashe and see where that gets us.

Yeah. Thanks, honey.

~

Earth—past

Ashe's Journal

Merrill? I was surprised to hear from him, especially where and when I was.

We have a problem, he began.

What problem?

The enemy has constructed gates that anyone can travel through. Lissa found one on Frithia, and it's connected to the Sirenali who's behind that mass suicide there. She figures it was a trap, set to capture anyone who inadvertently wandered through it.

This isn't good, I sent. *Most people won't see them and can go right through with no warning.*

Exactly what we're thinking. Most people won't see them. We figure the Elemaiya will recognize them, however.

Merrill was right, and I figured he and Lissa had already discussed this at length before contacting me about the Elemaiya living at SouthStar. While they might not be willing to help Lissa for obvious reasons, if I or someone else they respected asked, that answer could change.

I know several who will likely help, no questions asked, I said. *Because Breanne will save them by taking them through a gate and landing them on Avendor with me in the future.*

The half-Elemaiyan children, Merrill acknowledged.

Edward is with Reah, or I'd ask him as well. I'll speak with Breanne about this and we'll get the ball rolling. Tell Lissa I'll contact you when I know more.

Thank you, Merrill said.

This is more than frightening, I said. *I have word from another source, too, that one who shouldn't be resurrected may have been.*

You're not talking about Saxom, are you?

Not Saxom. His brother, Moxas. The Khos'Mirai. If not the original, then one of his clones, which is just as dangerous.

This is so much worse than I ever imagined, Merrill replied. *I'll take this information to Lissa, but she is worried enough as it is.*

Understood.

Le-Ath Veronis—present

Lissa's Journal

Merrill came to deliver the news himself, without bothering to send mindspeech. I was glad he did.

"Ashe is willing to ask the Elemaiya to help us," he said. "He believes the half-Elemaiyan children from Earth will volunteer, regardless."

"That's wonderful," I said.

"He said he'd let me know when he has a definite answer from the others," Merrill said.

"You don't look happy that some of them might help us," I said.

"That's not the unhappy part," Merrill stated. "Ashe also said he had information on another possible resurrection."

"Oh, no," I muttered, watching his face. Merrill seemed unusually pale to me.

"He says that Moxas may be among the living again. And if not the original, one of his clones."

At first, I didn't recognize the name. Never knew he had a name, actually. The moment Merrill said the word clones, however, I knew. "The Khos'Mirai?" My breaths stilled and I stared at Merrill in alarm.

CHAPTER 10

*E*arth—*past*
Breanne's Journal

I only knew of the Khos'Mirai from reading Lissa. A tragic character, but still capable of creating so much harm. His talents spelled trouble for our side, no doubt about that.

Ashe asked for a brief meeting with Hank and me after he'd gotten the news, so Hank and I were attempting to digest what the Khos'Mirai's reappearance might mean in the long term.

"I believe it is a clone," Hank said. "Nevertheless, the trouble will likely be the same. He can see many things, and we may be helpless to block many of his visions. We have no Sirenali on our side, while they seem to have them in abundance."

"You don't think there were ever any good Sirenali?" I turned to Hank.

"They attacked the Larentii homeworld, in an attempt to control Larentii. Imagine what that act might have accomplished—had they commandeered the most powerful race ever created by the Three."

"That is so messed up," Ashe shook his head. "I suppose it's a good thing Larentii are immune to them."

"Can Larentii see gates?" I asked.

"What?" Ashe stared at me.

"Well, it makes sense, doesn't it? That they might see them?"

"Kalenegar?" Hank said to empty air. Kal appeared in a blink.

"Can Larentii see gates—similar to the ones the Elemaiya used to travel through?" Hank asked.

"Of course, but they are such an inelegant method of traveling," Kal said. "We knew where all of them were located—Nefrigar had them mapped for the archives. The gates are seldom used, now, so the information is for historical reference only."

"Can we get to this information—those maps?" Hank asked.

"Yes," Kal said cautiously. "Why?"

"Because a gate has been located on Frithia, and it's open for anyone to walk through," Ashe said. "We believe the enemy's agents may be waiting on the other end of it, to ensnare or kill the ones who accidentally stumble into it. We want to know if it's a new gate or if the enemy warped an existing gate."

"Nefrigar?" Kalenegar said to empty air. I blinked when another Larentii appeared. This one was mated to Reah. I knew that when I read him.

"Ah. I never thought to see two at once," Nefrigar nodded respectfully to me and to Ashe.

"May we borrow copies of the old maps to the Elemaiyan gates?" Kal said.

"Of course—I have several copies," Nefrigar said. "Which format?"

"Paper will do," Kal said dryly.

"As you wish it." Nefrigar held out a large, blue hand and a huge book appeared there. "These are written in Alliance common, so those from this planet will not be able to decipher them."

"Good enough," Ashe accepted the book from Nefrigar. "Thank you. I'll send this back when we're done."

"Even if you cannot return it, it is nothing but a copy. We have the originals still in the archives."

"Is Frithia in here?" Ashe asked, opening the huge book. The cover was thick, rigid cloth, in black with a gold spine. The language on the spine was in the Larentii language, and the title proclaimed the book

Maps of Elemaiyan Gates, a Pictorial Reference, with Illustrations and References in Alliance Common.

"Here," Nefrigar held out a hand and pages flipped until they fell open in one particular place.

"Do we know where the gate was found?" I asked, rising to look at the map, which indicated two gates.

"Merrill said here, in the capital city," Ashe replied, placing a finger over a portion of the map. Neither of the previous gates was in that place; that was easy enough to see.

"They're creating new ones instead of changing old ones, then," Kal said. "That requires a great deal of power. Even the Larentii do not do this."

"Kifirin borrowed power from his parent, one of the Al'Riyu, to create the Dark Realm and everything in it, including the gates from world to world," Hank breathed smoke. "It was not discovered until later that the gates connecting the Light Realm to the Dark were also created. That means it requires the power of the Al'Riyu or above to create gates."

"Well, I know what I stared down, and he was definitely stronger than that," I huffed.

"Very true," Ashe agreed.

"Are there any Larentii willing to help the ASD and CSD?" I asked Nefrigar.

"Only if one or more of the Three ask or command," Nefrigar inclined his head to me.

"I'm asking some of the Elemaiya to cooperate, so we should only need a few. Do I ask you or should I approach Ferrigar?"

"You may ask me," Nefrigar smiled. "I am connected with Ferrigar at this moment, so your message will be transferred to him through me."

"How many should we ask for?" Ashe turned to me.

"Let's ask for five volunteers," I said.

"Sounds good," Ashe agreed.

"Ferrigar says that he will call for volunteers, but he is likely to get many more than five," Nefrigar's smile widened.

"Tell him we'll keep the extras in reserve, in case they're needed," Ashe said. "And thank you. Very much. This will make our work easier."

"Ferrigar says he is happy to accommodate the Three."

~

Le-Ath Veronis—present
Lissa's Journal
Reemagar and Connegar appeared in my study together. "We have news," Connegar began.

"Ferrigar has given permission for a few Larentii to assist the ASD and CSD in recognizing gates during their investigations. Ashe is also approaching some of the Elemaiya to do the same."

"How many?" I stood—this was almost unprecedented—that the Larentii might help in mundane, humanoid affairs. Well, almost mundane. Anything that might involve the God Wars was certainly not so mundane.

"Ashe asked for five to start," Connegar said. "Ferrigar asked for five volunteers. He received many more than that, but he chose those who have the most experience dealing with humanoids."

"Do I know any of them?" I asked.

"I am one," Reemagar smiled broadly. "Lenigar is another, as is Jerigar. Nefrigar's oldest sons have also been chosen—Serrigar and Valegar."

"Does Norian know yet?" I asked.

"Ferrigar requests that you pass this news to him. Ashe will let you know which of the Elemaiya have volunteered."

Norian? I sent mindspeech immediately.

Breah-mul? He sounded surprised to hear from me.

Nori, the Larentii and a few Elemaiya will be helping your investigation teams—they'll be able to recognize the gates so your agents don't fall into them, I said.

Deah-mul, what if we send something through the gate we found already?

Norian responded. *I've been studying this. Wouldn't it be prudent to try to send a sensor or spybot through?*

Let me ask Reemagar if we can borrow some of their technology. They're famous for their microscopic cameras, and none of them ever shows up on anybody's radar.

Are you joking? You think they might do that? Norian's mindspeech sounded breathless with excitement.

"Reemagar," I said to my Larentii mate.

"I have already sent the message to Ferrigar," he smiled brightly. "Ferrigar gives his permission, provided the Larentii remain in charge of their technology."

"Suits me, I'll just tell Norian that," I smiled back.

Norian, they say as long as the Larentii volunteers have control over their technology, we can use it.

Cheah-mul, that is outstanding! Norian crowed in mindspeech.

Nori, you don't order the Larentii. Keep that in mind. You ask, and ask politely. Okay?

I know; he deflated just a little. *How many do I get, and how many does Jett Riffler get?*

Jett Riffler was Director of the CSD, and he'd have to be brought into the loop as well. Jett was Avendoran, and I had a feeling that Ashe had been instrumental in getting him hired as the Director. He'd been in charge of the Avendoran CSD office for five years before his promotion after his predecessor retired.

I'm hoping that Ashe can come up with five as well, so you'll have some Larentii and some Elemaiya. I'll ask your five to meet you here, and I'll contact Teeg to inform Jett. It irked me whenever I was forced to refer to Tybus as Teeg, but there was no other way around it. To everyone else, he *was* Teeg.

Let me know when you've spoken with Teeg. I'll contact Jett, too, Norian said. *We need to coordinate teams.* He sounded worried after I told him to look for unusual disappearances.

Nori, we're all worried. I don't have any knowledge of how these gates are created to begin with, or whether they have to be in the appropriate place to create one. I sure as hell don't want one in the middle of my palace.

I never thought about that, he replied, his sending thoughtful. *Keep me informed; I have to talk to Lendill about this.*

I shut down our mental conversation with a sigh and turned back to Connegar and Reemagar. "We have to visit Tybus and Jett Riffler," I sighed.

~

Tybus smiled when I walked into his private study flanked by two Larentii. Jett was there, waiting with him.

"Queen Lissa, how are you?" Tybus rose and offered his hand. I took it and managed to control most of my trembling. *Daughter, do not be afraid*, he sent mindspeech. "I hear you have welcome news for us," he continued aloud and released my hand. "Please, sit. Is there anything we might offer you? Food or drink?"

Yes, I'd been informed that he was my father in his previous life. I did and didn't find that comforting. Honestly, Tybus seemed more at ease with the concept than I did.

"Wine?" I asked. It was almost the dinner hour, and a little wine might not hurt. Connegar was transporting me home, after all.

In less than five minutes, I had a glass of chilled white wine in my hand while I explained, with help from my Larentii, what the plan was.

"I'm putting teams together now. It appears that we need five. Norian is researching unusual disappearances, as well as any new religions. I'll ask my agents to question their priests and leaders," Jett said. "If our volunteers can see these invisible gates, I will be most grateful for their help."

Jett was perhaps six feet tall, with dark skin and a black ink tattoo covering the left side of his face. It resembled images of animals, leaves and vines, marking him as a member of the Southern indigenous race of Avendor—the Fi'Gu.

Much like the Falchani, the more elaborate the tattoo on a Fi'Gu, the more important the man or woman. Jett had an extremely elaborate tattoo, which likely ran down the entire left side of his body.

The tattoo indicated the respect due the person wearing it. The right side was never tattooed—they left it bare in deference to their gods.

"The Larentii will be pleased to work with you, Ku'Ri," Connegar nodded to Jett.

"I should have known the Larentii would recognize me as such," Jett smiled.

Ku'Ri is Warrior Chief to the Fi'Gu, Reemagar silently supplied.

He's the Chief of the Fi'Gu? I responded in surprise.

There are two. The Ku'Ri and the Ku'La. The Ku'La is the Chief of Law for the Fi'Gu. You should see her—she is amazing.

I'll bet she is, I acknowledged.

"How soon will your teams be placed in the field?" Tybus asked Jett.

"Tomorrow. I've already briefed them. There will be two of my agents, plus a volunteer on each team. We're going through potential targets now, so we'll have a plan in place by tomorrow morning."

"We will be most pleased to work with you," Serrigar and Valegar appeared inside Tybus' study and nodded respectfully to Jett.

"You know where my office is?" Jett grinned.

"We do."

"Meet me there at eight bells, local time, then."

"We will." Serrigar and Valegar disappeared as easily as they'd appeared.

"This will be an amazing and welcome experiment," Jett observed.

Avendor—present

Breanne's Journal

Ashe bent time to find out whether any Elemaiya might be willing to work with the ASD and CSD. The ones who answered his call didn't surprise me in the least.

Macy, Luanne, Keith, Philip and Elizabeth waited for us inside Ashe's massive study. Philip and Elizabeth were still ghosts, but that was about to change—provided I had the strength to do it.

"Elizabeth, are you willing? Philip, what about you?" I turned to the ghostly mountain lion.

"I am," Elizabeth replied.

I certainly am ready, Philip's words were accompanied by a growl. *Ashe has explained the God Wars to us in the past. I wish to serve with him.*

"Ashe?" I turned to him.

"Do it, but let me get Traje and Bill in here, first. If you fall, they'll catch you."

~

Kay's Journal

Ashe left me in the kitchen, where one of the shapeshifter women worked to prepare lunch. I knew this was an unusual occurrence but Bill, who normally cooked for everyone inside the big house, was doing research with Trajan for Ashe. I wasn't sure what research it was and didn't want to pry.

After all, I was seeing plenty back on Earth, and that's where we'd return once Bree and Ashe finished their errand here.

At least Kalia's fear of women no longer held sway as I watched Adele Evans prepare lasagna. "I didn't know what Ashe was—who he was—when he was born," Adele said abruptly.

"You're his mother?" I was amazed my voice didn't tremble or squeak when I spoke.

"Yes. For the most part. You'll have to ask him about the rest—it's very confusing."

"You think he'll answer my questions?" I watched as she placed a layer of cooked lasagna noodles in the bottom of the large pan before ladling sauce over them.

"I think he'll do just about anything you ask, including moving the planet," Adele replied.

"He can do that?"

"Hon, Ashe is one of the Three. I don't know what might be beyond them."

155

~

Breanne's Journal

Ashe had already assured me that his shield would block my energy pattern if I *Changed What Was* at SouthStar. I figured the attempt would drain me, but it needed to be done.

The half-Elemaiya waited expectantly while I considered what I had to do for them. "I'll try to restore your immortality, while I'm at it," I nodded to Macy, Luanne and Keith. "You'll be like you were before, if I can pull this off."

The same goes for you, I sent to Elizabeth and Philip, whose ghosts also waited. This was a test—to see whether they deserved to keep physical bodies. Ashe had spoken with them already about it.

"Don't worry," Ashe held out a hand, "Nothing will happen to you if she's not successful; you'll just remain as you are."

"You ready?" I nodded to Trajan and Bill, who stood on either side of me.

"Yeah," Trajan said.

"Same here," Bill agreed. I pulled as much power as I could to me and began.

~

Ashe's Journal

I'd only seen her like this once before, and that's when she'd kept me from joining the rogue gods. She shone so brightly inside my study I had to shield the eyes of everyone else present. They might have been blinded, otherwise.

I felt grateful, too, that she didn't collapse until she finished. Without even *Looking*, I knew she'd been successful. I stared at the physical bodies of Philip and Elizabeth, corporeal again for the first time in centuries.

Bree was unconscious in Trajan's arms, while Bill washed her face with a cold, wet cloth, attempting to wake her. Kevis appeared and checked her vitals while I rose from my chair and walked toward

Elizabeth and Philip. Philip hadn't been humanoid in a very long time.

"Is this real?" he held out his arms and stared at his feet—both of which were bare. Actually, all of him was bare, but like most shifters, he didn't seem to care. Without a word, I *Pulled* clothing in and tossed it his way.

"What do you think?" I asked as he snagged the pants with one hand.

"I think this is awesome," he grinned at me. Macy giggled while Philip shoved legs into trousers and fastened them with hands that shook with excitement.

"Are we?" Keith began.

"You are. You sure as hell are," I said, grinning like a lunatic. "You're immortal. Breanne did it."

"She's the one who brought us through," Luanne breathed.

"Yeah. Only it hasn't happened yet," I attempted to explain.

"What?" Elizabeth stared at me.

"Never mind. Nothing to worry about. Trajan, how is she?"

"She's drained, but that's no surprise," Kevis answered instead. "I suggest you let her sleep for a while and then bend time to get her back. Remember what I said about heavy lifting?"

"I remember," I sighed. "Luanne, are you in charge?"

"I guess," she shrugged.

"Then Trajan will get all of you to Le-Ath Veronis tomorrow. Queen Lissa will see that you get to your respective assignments after that. You all have mindspeech; send to her, Trajan or me if there are problems or you find anything. I especially want to know if you find any rogue-engineered gates. Okay?"

"We will," Luanne nodded. "Tell her—Breanne—thank you. From all of us."

"I'll tell her," I said.

"Wisdom," the Ear nodded to the Mighty Mind.

"Where are the others?" Wisdom asked.

"Coming. Even the Mouth is coming," the Ear replied.

"Good."

"Is the time near?" the Ear asked.

"Yes and no," Wisdom replied.

Le-Ath Veronis—present

Lissa's Journal

"Nori, you'll have Reemagar, Lenigar and Jerigar, plus Keith Caldwell and Macy Hill," I said. "Jett is getting Serrigar, Valegar, Luanne Jansen, Elizabeth Frasier and Philip Raymond." Norian had folded to my study when I informed him that I had the information he needed on the volunteers.

"I'm heading one of the teams, just as Jett is manning one of his. Which of those five do you suggest I work with?"

"Norian, at times I think Reemagar believes you're nuts, so that's probably not an option."

"Well, that means all Larentii probably feel the same way. I'll take what was her name again?"

"Macy Hill. Don't push her, Nori, or I swear I'll smack you myself."

"I'll let Kooper have Reemagar, if that's all right, and Lendill can take Lenigar. I'll figure out the other two before tomorrow. Who's bringing the volunteers to my office?"

"Ashe asked me to take the Elemaiya where they need to go, so I'll bring them. The Larentii can get themselves around."

"Isn't it rather ironic, that he asked you to transport the Elemaiya?"

"These were never affected by my edict. At least not by much. They were at SouthStar all this time," I huffed. "Besides, I'm a quarter Elemaiyan, or have you forgotten?"

"I haven't forgotten," Norian grumped. "Breah-mul, are we ever going to be together again?"

"Norian, tell me again why we're not together now," I snapped.

Breanne's Journal

Kevis was leaning over me when I woke. Wearily I slapped a hand over my face. "How long?" I mumbled.

"Seven hours. Not bad," he grinned. "Mom asked how you were. She wants you to visit again when there aren't so many around."

"Kevis, I'd love to visit your mother." I removed my hand and blinked at him. "I have so much crap to do," I shook my head at him.

"I know," he soothed. "I sent a message to Grae and Barry, too. They asked to be updated."

"Does he mind if you call him Grae?"

"No. Barry doesn't mind, either." Kevis' green-gold eyes held laughter. "If you speak their name sincerely, that's all they're concerned about."

"Okaaay," I said.

"Come on, you can trust me, I'm a doctor," Kevis snickered. Yeah, that made me laugh.

"Ready to go back?" Ashe asked when he appeared inside my bathroom. Kevis had helped me up and left me alone to brush my teeth.

"I'm hungry," I muttered. "Sorry."

"I know, there's no need to apologize. What do you want?"

"A hummus sandwich," I said.

"I'll take you," he offered. "Kay may want something, too. We ate four hours ago and she napped afterward, so we should be ready to help Bill when we get back."

"All right," I shrugged. Night had fallen on SouthStar, and I knew Trajan and Bill had gone to bed where I was. Trajan and Bill in the past were waiting to start their workday.

Earth—past

Hank's Journal

I knew they'd been gone several hours, although only a few minutes of time passed on Earth. Breanne still looked exhausted. Ashe explained that she'd *Changed What Was* for five half-Elemaiyans. Two of those five had been ghosts. They lived, now, thanks to Bree.

"Baby," I pulled her against me, "You feeling all right?"

"Yeah." She hunched her shoulders.

"Come on, I'll be transportation today," I said. I nodded to Trajan and Kalenegar—they'd help keep an eye on her. I just hoped we'd get through the rest of the day without her dropping.

~

Breanne's Journal

If I were honest, I only wanted to snuggle against Hank and sleep again. We had to go to Arkansas, first, and then to Colorado. Charles approached when Hank let me go and placed a latte in my hand.

"Thanks," I offered him a smile and sipped the coffee drink. "Mmm, real sugar and half-and-half," I sighed blissfully. "You are awesome," I nodded at Charles.

"At times," he grinned at me.

"Ready?" Bill turned to Hank.

"Ready," Hank nodded. He skipped us to Arkansas.

~

"You some of them from the government?" The man held a rifle, the barrel (thankfully) pointed downward as we stood outside a gate leading into mostly wilderness. Tall grasses grew around the barbed-wire fence and at least three parakeet-sized grasshoppers jumped out of our way when we walked up.

"I'm from the government," Bill pulled out his ID.

"You're not gettin' in," the man declared.

"You will not only let us in, you will politely show us around," Gavin growled.

"Yep. Come on in. We're buildin' a retreat for like-minded folks," The man stood aside and waved us through the gate.

I think that means the huntin', shootin' kind, Jayson's voice filtered into my mind. I smothered my snicker against Hank's shoulder.

With the gun now draped lazily over his shoulder, the man, dressed in denim pants, a sleeveless checkered shirt and frayed baseball cap, led us past the construction. Buildings were going up, and wooden frames were everywhere. The sound of saws and hammering echoed throughout the peaceful woodland.

After dropping my shields and reading the workers, I knew none of them were obsessed. They'd volunteered for the work and none had been taken unwillingly from anywhere else.

No building permit aside, I sent to Bill and the others, *all these people want to be here.*

I detect no underground construction, Kal offered.

They'll get flooded in the spring, Ashe added. *They're building too close to that creek.*

Three strikes, Bill's sending was dry. *This isn't our target.*

"We've seen enough, thank you," Bill called out. "Good luck with your facility," he added.

The man stood and watched as we headed toward the gate. Hank skipped us away the moment we were out of sight.

"The apocalypse is upon us," the woman in Colorado spoke gruffly. "Our operation is secret. How did you find our hidden compound?" Another gate stood before us, on grassy public land with a lake and mountains in the distance.

"Spy satellites," Jayson lied with a grin.

"I knew something was going on. Are there aliens with you?"

"Yes. Definitely," Bill agreed. "Why?"

"They're taking over," the woman whispered. "Didn't you know? Why did you let them come along?"

"I am an alien to you," Kal stepped forward. "I mean no harm, but there are others who are not so benign."

Kal, she's crazy, I sent.

I know this, but as they say in your culture, even a broken clock is right twice a day.

He was correct up to a point, only it was rogue gods attempting a takeover and employing a few aliens to aid in their cause.

"We will examine your construction, to make sure it will withstand alien scans," Jayson said. How he said that with a straight face, I'll never know.

Without anyone laying compulsion, the woman let us through the gate.

These buildings weren't wood—they resembled concrete bunkers. We walked between square, cinderblock constructions and around scattered piles of roofing material. Only a few workers labored here, and the ones I read had other jobs; they were doing this on their days off.

Some underground construction, but it is small, Kal reported. *I believe it is to be used for emergency purposes only.*

No obsessions, I added.

This is on public land, Bill snorted mentally. *It'll have to be torn down.*

I'm not telling her that, Jayson said.

We'll let her live her fantasy for a little while longer, Bill agreed. *However, this leaves us where we started—with no leads.*

Frithia—present

Lissa's Journal

"Are you sure?" Norian had to lean his head back to study Connegar's face.

"While I have no experience with the enemy, these have always worked in the past," Connegar replied.

I couldn't see them at all, even by *Looking*. I have no idea how the Larentii had created this magic, but they had. Connegar held a small sphere in his hand, which, according to him, held six microscopic cameras. They'd operate at his command and would send sound and images back to a monitor the Larentii had installed in Norian's office.

Connegar intended to release the cameras into the gate, and I'd come to Frithia to mist Norian inside the walled-up room. He'd decided to do this the night before the investigative teams were set to go to work, just to see if we could detect anything.

"Then let them go," Norian nodded at Connegar and stepped aside. The sphere in Connegar's hand melted away as he turned toward the gate. I had to watch him—I couldn't see anything.

"They are traveling," Connegar said. "Now we go back to Le-Ath Veronis and wait."

"Are Drake and Drew set up to watch the monitors?" Norian asked.

"Yeah."

"Then get us out of here."

"We haven't been away from SouthStar since we got here," Macy picked at her meal.

"I know, Mace, and these aren't the most ideal circumstances," Luanne nodded. "Let's just hope we can help. Maybe this is the reason we survived, when so many others didn't."

"I think about them sometimes—the ones who died. We never got to meet them."

"I know."

CHAPTER 11

*E*arth—*past*
    Breanne's Journal

"At least we know where they're not," Dan Kelsey raked fingers through his hair in frustration. Bill asked Hank to transport us from Colorado to D.C., to meet with the FBI Director. We'd been ushered into a private meeting the moment we arrived.

"I'll have the squatters removed in Colorado next week," Dan added with a sigh.

"We're back where we started," Bill agreed. "Nothing new coming in?"

"Not really. I've got people checking out foreign countries, but there's nothing showing up there, either."

"No reports of burning buildings that were difficult to put out?" Hank asked.

"Not recently, or the fires were attributed to rational causes," Dan shook his head. "Just the disappearances, as previously reported, and the theory that they're building something."

"Lying low and plotting," Bill muttered.

"The traps are waiting, General," Acrimus bowed respectfully. "Any sensory devices sent through will merely show blackness. They will send their investigators anyway, without knowing that the gate will expand once they pass a certain point, sucking them inside." Acrimus attempted a laugh. It sounded like a cough.

"It was a wise move to place the first as a non-expandable gate," the General nodded to Acrimus. "They will approach the others just the same and spring the trap. We will have them, and you may do whatever you wish with them once they are transported through."

"Oh, I have plans," Acrimus gloated. "I certainly have plans."

Le-Ath Veronis—present

Lissa's Journal

"There's nothing. At least we can't see anything, and Connegar says the cameras will pick up even the tiniest speck of light," Drew said. He and Drake sat before the Larentii-supplied monitor, watching a black screen.

"Are you sure it's working?" I asked, staring at the monitor.

"Yeah, it was checked before Connegar gathered the cameras for Frithia. It worked fine."

"This isn't good," I muttered. "What if they're doing this on purpose?"

"That's what I think," Drake agreed. "They've blocked light around the exit point, leaving us in the dark."

"So we won't know what's waiting on the other side," I blew out a sigh. "I guess it's a good thing we have people assigned to those teams who can see the gates."

"I don't think it's a good idea to get too close," Drew muttered.

"Yeah, but how close is too close?" I asked. None of us had an answer.

Earth—past

Breanne's Journal

I didn't think the day would end so soon, or with no information. We had nothing. Taking out Vernon Clark had seemed so simple. Now, my skin itched and I felt as if we were walking into a trap.

"Kay, you look tired," I reached out to give her a hug. She'd followed Ashe during our trips and never said a word.

"So do you," she pointed out.

"Did you see anything unusual today?" I asked. "In anybody's aura?"

"Just the mental impairment of the woman in Colorado," Kay sighed. "She's not dangerous, she's just afraid."

"I saw pretty much the same when I read her," I agreed.

"Are we hungry?" Opal walked up to us and asked. We'd arrived back at the hotel, and the others were discussing places to eat.

"An army marches on its stomach," I nodded. "I'd really like something better than French fries and a salad," I added.

"How about the West Coast?" Bill asked. "I haven't had time to talk with Jayson's dad, so we can eat and pay Rome Enterprises a visit."

"Ross still in the hoosegow?" I asked.

"For all practical purposes," Bill nodded. "I handed him over to Dan Kelsey. Dan's investigating a few things. Looks like Ross may have used less than legal channels to get in and out of the country a few times," Bill chuckled.

"Bill, Jayson," I said. Something had been worrying me for a while, and I wanted to take care of it before something else came along and drove it from my mind.

"Huh?" Jayson turned to me.

"I want to move your mom," I said.

"Bree?" Hank lifted an eyebrow.

"To Le-Ath Veronis," I shrugged. "I think she'll be as safe there as anywhere."

"What's that—Lee what?" Jayson asked.

"Don't worry about it, Rome. Bree's right. Too many know where your mother might be and let's face it; we don't need a kidnapping as a distraction."

"Her bodyguard has family in California, so we can send him home with pay," Jayson sighed.

"Great. We'll do it," I said.

"Mom will have the final say," Jayson pointed out.

"Agreed," I nodded.

~

Before it was over, we'd stopped to pick up Kathleen so she could have dinner with us in Los Angeles. She was overjoyed to see Jayson, and kept hugging him while we waited for a large enough table at an upscale restaurant.

"Bree, is that really you?" Kathleen whispered across the table after we were seated.

"Yeah," I nodded.

"I recognize your voice, but this—you look beautiful, but you're so beautiful already."

"Necessary evil," Hank sighed. "Too many recognize her the other way."

"I understand that all too well." She studied Jayson before lifting her menu.

~

Kathleen insisted on visiting James Rome, Sr. after our meal. We'd discussed taking her elsewhere, and instead of Le-Ath Veronis, Ashe ended up offering SouthStar as a refuge. Kathleen accepted. Kay seemed to like Kathleen very much, so I doubted there'd be any friction later.

Bill, Kathleen, Hank, Jayson and I rode the elevator to the top of the Rome Enterprises building. Kathleen shocked everybody by her appearance and that, in itself, paved our way to the penthouse.

We were shown directly into James Rome's office by a shaking assistant, who asked Kathleen immediately if she needed anything. Kathleen declined. Once the office door was closed behind us, I dropped Jayson's and my disguises. Let James Rome Sr. stew in that sauce for a while.

"Kathleen, what are you doing here and why?" James Rome began. He stared at Jayson—and then at me.

"I came to tell you I want a divorce," Kathleen snapped. "Jayson's here to show you he's all right without your stupid job, Breanne is here to call you a pig, and Director Jennings is here to tell you that Ross is being held by the FBI for collaborating with known criminals in less than legal dealings."

"That is not true," the elder Rome blustered. "Ross has never involved himself."

"With Rafe and Braden Reynolds?" Bill asked. "I can assure you they're involved in criminal activities. In fact, they were ready to sell Ross back to you—in pieces. You see, they've been on Vernon Clark's payroll for a while. They only worked for Ross—and you—because you paid cash."

"Now see here," James huffed.

"Don't pretend to be outraged, James. Director Jennings is right," Kathleen said. "If some of his agents hadn't arrived when they did, Ross would probably be dead and you'd likely be out a lot of money for his ransom."

"That can't be true," James Rome sat heavily behind his desk, the soft leather creaking slightly beneath his tall frame.

"It's true, Dad. I've seen the evidence myself," Jayson said. "Rafe and Braden are dead, as is Vernon Clark and four others who tried to kidnap Ross."

"I don't believe this," James rubbed his forehead.

"It doesn't matter whether you believe it or not," Hank said. "Ross Gideon is currently being held by the FBI, and they aren't allowing him to communicate with anyone for several days. If I were you, when you hear from him, I'd watch what you do from this point forward. I'm sure your name came up a few times during the questioning."

∾

"I'm glad that's over," Kathleen declared when we left the Rome building behind and met up with the others at Kathleen's house in Tahoe. I'd restored Jayson's and my disguise, and now we were ready to transport Kathleen to SouthStar.

"You'll be fine, Mom," Jayson reassured her. Someone, likely Ashe, had placed all her clothing in trunks for the trip.

"Who's coming to see me off?" her voice quavered.

"I'll come," I said.

"I will," Hank nodded.

"This is beautiful," Kathleen declared when Ashe landed us in a suite on the first floor of his palace. "What are those trees?"

"Gishi trees. The fruit is the best you'll ever eat," Ashe said. "I've alerted a few to your presence. Don't be surprised when you see them," he added. "We need to go back soon."

"All right. Bree, give me a hug," Kathleen smiled a trembling smile. I did. I hugged her and sent her *Love*. She wiped tears away afterward. Ashe transported us away before I started blubbering myself.

"Kathleen?" Trajan and Bill stole into her suite. "Ashe said you were here."

"What? Director Jennings?" Kathleen stared at him and at Trajan.

"Don't worry, you're about four hundred years in the future," Bill grinned. "After you spend a month here, you'll look twenty-five, guaranteed."

"Are you joking?" Kathleen stared at Bill, who did look much younger now than he had only a few minutes earlier.

"Not at all," Bill laughed. "Come on, we'll find a glass of wine for you and we'll talk."

"Here's where she is." Ashe pulled a comp-vid from his pocket and showed Jayson an image of Kathleen, with wide windows behind her and gishi groves beyond that.

"That's amazing," Jayson breathed.

"SouthStar is amazing," I agreed. "The best place for her, actually."

Le-Ath Veronis—present
Lissa's Journal

As requested, I ferried five half-Elemaiya to their assignments. Jett nodded respectfully to me when I appeared in his office with Luanne, Philip and Elizabeth. Serrigar and Valegar were already there, waiting.

"I have unexpected allies," Jett smiled and nodded toward Lynx, who'd arrived with Tiger, another retired Saa Thalarr. "I was having difficulty putting a fifth team together, when they appeared and made my life easier."

"So, two big cats," I nodded to both.

"Can't hurt," Lynx shrugged with an attractive, careless grin. He was mated to Conner, and I could see why. Tiger, on the other hand, was mated to a still-active Saa Thalarr—Mavrillek, a hellcat. I'd never seen him change; I'd only heard rumors of how dangerous he was. Not something you wanted to meet if he were in an angry mood, that's for sure.

Tiger was six feet tall, and Lynx was barely an inch or two taller. I imagined that Tiger and her mate would be vicious if they fought together.

"I'm Luanne," Luanne held out her hand. Jett took it with a nod. "This is Philip, and this is Elizabeth."

"I'll leave you now, let me know if you need anything," I said.

"We will be fine," Jett assured me.

I folded away.

Earth—past

Breanne's Journal

"I'm glad that's taken care of," I sighed as I leaned against Hank.

"I'm glad you're not worrying about it anymore," Hank nuzzled my neck.

"Yeah."

"Bree?"

"What?"

"I want to fuck you. Fuck you good. Fuck you until you fall asleep in my arms," Hank mumbled, pulling me backward onto the bed. "Just relax and let me make you come."

"I was hoping I'd get to see you naked," I said.

"Baby, I'll walk around naked if it makes you happy," he grinned. "I'll be even happier inserting tab A into slot B." He pulled my top over my head and with nimble fingers, unbuttoned my jeans.

"Honey, that joke's older than I am," I said while he pulled my jeans away and pushed my underwear off.

"But not older than I am," he leaned in to kiss me while he undid my bra and sent it flying across the room. "First, we get you nice and wet," he grinned before sliding down my body and placing his mouth on me.

"I hate Gorly," Norian muttered as he walked through the building. The ASD had gotten information regarding missing transients in the area, and most of the disappearances centered around the abandoned temple.

Gorly was the poor sister-planet to Norly, which supplied precious metals for comp-vid construction and other manufacturing. Gorly was lucky to keep its population fed and often created problems with riots and disturbances. RAA and the ASD had been called in many times to help calm the population.

Norian wondered, for perhaps the sixth time, why he hadn't

demanded that Kooper lend one of the reptanoids to him. They'd all gone with Kooper, and there was no mistaking the hero worship in their eyes as they followed the Vice-Director around.

Instead, Norian had ended up with Steeg, a rookie agent, and a shy woman who walked carefully through debris littering the old temple. He'd have been foolish not to recognize it from the start—Solar Red had once gathered there. They'd left quickly, once the religion was outlawed in the Alliance.

"Perfect place for a gate—or an ambush," Norian sighed. He wished Lissa were with him, but she'd had a Council meeting. He'd thought about asking her to cancel it or allow someone else to take it. Rigo could handle it easily, or Aryn.

"Mr. Keef?" Macy's voice drifted toward him.

"Macy?" Norian turned toward her.

"There's a gate, near that altar." Macy pointed toward the back of the temple, barely fifty feet ahead.

"I see footprints," Norian said, "leading toward it." The trouble was, those footprints in thick dust disappeared only a few feet ahead.

"Where do you see the gate?" Norian turned back to Macy. "Where does it begin?"

"Just a short distance in front of the altar," she said. "But," she sounded uncertain.

"But?" Norian sounded impatient.

"Something's not right," she began. "I think we should leave."

"I need images," Norian pulled a comp-vid from his pocket and prepared to take photographs. "Tell Steeg to get in here; he can help." The hapless rookie had been set to guarding the entrance while Norian and Macy explored the temple.

"All right," Macy turned toward the wide entrance to retrieve Steeg when Norian's shout made her turn in shock and terror.

"Help me!" Norian shouted as something invisible dragged him toward the gate.

Macy shouted for the one person she could think of in a crisis —Ashe Evans.

With a flash of light, Ashe appeared in the old temple, only to watch as Norian, with a final shout, was swallowed by the gate.

∾

"Ready?" Acrimus grimaced at Yaredolak. "If I don't find them suitable for my purposes, it's fun to watch them die after you bite them."

Yaredolak—Reedy to those who knew him best, waited in serpent form for the hapless humanoid to be spit out on this side of the gate. If Acrimus commanded, he would attack. He was more than surprised at what landed instead. Coiled and hissing quickly, Reedy stared at another lion snake shapeshifter.

∾

Norian struck first, but his bite had no effect upon another lion snake. Reedy sunk his fangs into Norian's side, but Norian twisted away and bit Reedy a second time. They seemed evenly matched and the fight might have gone on for a while, but Acrimus had seen enough. Raising a hand, he separated the atoms that made up Norian Keef's body, allowing the sparks of life to wink out until nothing remained.

∾

Le-Ath Veronis—present
  Lissa's Journal
The moment Norian died, I knew. My heart squeezed in my chest until I couldn't breathe. Drake, Drew, Gavin and Rigo were at my side quickly, and the Council meeting erupted into speculative whispers.

"Norian's dead," I wept and dropped to my knees.

As Gavin lifted me into his arms and carried me toward the door, a numb detachment settled over me as I heard Rigo calling a recess behind us.

∾

"Call all the investigative teams back. All of them," Kooper shouted into his comp-vid. "Contact San Gerxon as well. Tell him Director Keef was taken through a gate and died. We have to analyze this and find a way to destroy these things before others are killed."

$\sim$

"Jett, call your teams back," Tybus ordered. "Director Keef has been killed by a gate on Gorly. We need to study this further before we approach any others."

"On it," Jett replied. "Making calls now."

$\sim$

"What happened, Macy?" Ashe's voice sounded weary.

Macy could barely speak through her sobs. "I told him we should leave," she wiped tears from her cheeks with a shaking hand. "I told him something wasn't right."

"Norian has never been known for listening to advice," Ashe sighed. "Macy, it wasn't your fault."

$\sim$

Earth—past

Breanne's Journal

"Norian's dead." I flung clothing on with barely a thought for what it might look like. Hank and I had just gotten to sleep when the knowledge hit me like lightning. Ashe had already gone—he'd gotten a cry for help from Macy.

"I know he's dead," Hank buried his head in his hands. "I'll come with you. Do you want to go to your sister first, or find Ashe?"

"Let's see Ashe, first. Lissa will have at least a dozen mates around her." I jerked my sweater off the floor and blinked at Hank.

"Yeah." Hank stood and pulled his shirt off a chair. "I'll ask Bill and Kalenegar to look after Kay."

"Thanks. Ready?"

"I'll take us," Hank said. He did.

Kooper, Chazi, Bekzi, Perzi and Stellan stood behind Ashe. They were surrounded by three Larentii and several of Norian's agents.

"I have a shield covering the gate," Ashe mumbled. His arm was around Macy, who wept against his shoulder.

"Bree?" Kooper pulled me into a tight embrace the moment I touched his arm. "Norian's dead."

"I know." Not only would the ASD have to find a new Director, Ildevar Wyyld would have to find a new heir. That didn't include Lissa's grief over losing a mate, albeit a nearly estranged one. I had mixed feelings about his death. I only hoped that he hadn't suffered when he died.

"Let's go to Le-Ath Veronis," Ashe said. "We'll sort this out there."

"Bree," Lissa held her arms out when I appeared inside her suite with Ashe, Hank and the others. Without hesitating, I went to her and sent as much *Love* as I could. This death followed closely on the heels of Gavril's and was another heavy blow against Lissa's already battered emotions.

While I was embracing Lissa, Ildevar Wyyld appeared with his elvish seer, Willem Drifft.

"Lissa," Ildevar knelt beside us and reached out to touch her cheek.

"What are we going to do?" Lissa turned a tear-filled gaze to the Founder of the Reth Alliance.

"We will keep walking forward, no matter how heavy our steps," Ildevar sighed. He was in pain, too, so I sent him *Love* as well.

"She doesn't usually look like that," Drake explained to Ildevar. "She's in disguise to throw the rogue gods off her trail."

"She's the one who saved my life twice?"

"Yes. She's Lissa's half-sister," Drew said.

"This is unusual—and disconcerting, to see the one I want on the day my heir dies," Ildevar rubbed his forehead.

"You need to ask Lissa about her—when you're both in a better place," Drake suggested.

"We need to decide whether to send the investigative teams out again, looking for rogue-engineered gates," Ildevar turned deep blue eyes on Drake. "Has a meeting been arranged?"

"It's scheduled in the library in two hours," Drew nodded. "Lissa says she'll come. Bree is trying to put her back together now."

"I don't know what that woman did for me, but it feels as if my heart was cradled in pure love for a moment. I feel better, although Norian's death still grieves me."

"I think that's the way it works," Drake said. "It's something Breanne can do."

Breanne's Journal

The meeting was to be held in Lissa's library. Ashe had left Lissa's suite earlier to discuss things with Hank and some of Lissa's mates, leaving me, Gavin and Roff with her. Macy, poor thing, had gone with Ashe. I think Jerigar was doing his best to comfort her, too, and that wasn't a bad idea.

"You ready?" I asked Lissa, brushing a few stray tendrils of hair back.

"Yes. I suppose." Lissa was so pretty, and I knew she looked much like her mother, who'd died horribly when Lissa was young.

"Your mother would be so proud of you," I said.

"You think so?" Lissa's lower lip trembled.

"Yeah. Let's ask for some tea when we get to the library."

"That sounds good. Have we ever had tea together?"

"I don't think so," I replied.

"You keep refusing dinner invitations, too."

"I know."

"I'll let Cheedas know," Roff said.

"I'll escort you to the library," Gavin offered.

"Gavin, fold us there, please," Lissa said.

"I will, cara."

"I will display the images," Reemagar offered, once everyone was seated comfortably in Lissa's library. I sat beside Lissa, and Gavin sat on her other side. We both held one of her hands in ours.

The information didn't shock me, because I'd already read it from Macy. She'd tried to warn him, and he'd kept walking anyway. What we couldn't get was anything past the moment he was sucked into the gate.

"He died quickly," Ashe muttered. "I've extrapolated the time, and his death occurred less than a minute later."

Lissa gripped my fingers tighter, so I sent an extra dose of *Love* to her.

Bree, are you all right? Hank's voice filtered into my mind.

I'm okay, I replied. Yes, I was still tired, but that was a constant, nowadays.

"I believe we should still search for these gates—we know how dangerous they will be to the population," Serrigar said. He'd transported Jett Riffler and the teams from the CSD to Lissa's library after a message was sent to Tybus, requesting their presence at the meeting.

"Serrigar speaks for all Larentii," Lenigar agreed.

"I want to keep looking, too." Macy's voice was shaky when she stood, but she seemed determined enough. She'd recognized the danger of the gate somehow, and Norian had ignored her warning.

"We'd barely started our investigations when we were alerted," Jett offered. "After seeing the images, I concur with the Larentii. I feel we should keep looking, as this threat needs to be exposed and people warned to stay away."

"This is like sweeping for mines in a minefield," Lissa muttered beside me.

"I was thinking that, too," I agreed. "I just hope their little trick of expanding gates to suck in unsuspecting victims doesn't fluctuate much as far as distance goes."

"Macy," Lissa said, "How did you feel—what alerted you that the gate was dangerous?"

"I felt it," she replied. "It was wrong, and I knew Mr. Keef shouldn't walk any farther."

"And yet he did." A tear coursed down Lissa's cheek. I dried it with a bit of power.

"I sensed the power of it when I joined the others, there," Reemagar agreed. "I felt it was too dangerous to approach."

"So the Larentii and the Elemaiya can both sense the power it gives off," Kooper said. "The rest of us are blind to this, it seems."

"It appears that those who are blind to it, as you say, should stay with the Larentii or Elemaiya volunteers and keep back when warned," Ashe said. "Do we still have targeted areas to investigate?"

"Several," Jett acknowledged. "It is my hope that we lose no others to these abominations."

"So they're going out again tomorrow," Lissa sighed as she was offered a plate of food by a kitchen comesula. I was finally sitting at the official dining table in Lissa's palace, and under less than ideal circumstances.

Others had shown up as well and surprisingly, many of them were Saa Thalarr. Grace and Devin had come, escorted by Dragon and his twin brother, Crane. Kyler and Cleo arrived, accompanied by Glendes, Shadow and Harvel Grey.

Conner came, too, with Graegar and Barrigar. Those three sat near me, just past Hank, who hadn't said much but kept an eye on me, just the same.

Last of all, a contingent from Kifirin arrived and that's when the trouble started. Jaydevik Rath, King of Kifirin, with his wife, Queen Glindarok, bowed to Hank. "High Lord," Jaydevik said as he inclined his head in respect. My breath stopped.

CHAPTER 12

Le-Ath Veronis—present
Breanne's Journal

"Breanne, I had an assignment that I couldn't ignore," Hank said. "I had no idea who or what you were when you dropped into my lap. I couldn't deny the attraction, but I worried that you were mortal and that created a paradox."

"Hank, I'm not mad," I held up a hand. "I just wish I'd been smarter. Evidence was there, I just wasn't seeing it."

"Then come back to the table and eat," Hank said. "The others are discussing why we left and making outrageous conjectures."

"I kind of feel sick," I said, staring through the window of my old suite at the eternal twilight that covered Lissia.

"I know. I wish I weren't responsible," he said.

"What level are you?" I asked.

"Ko'Ahmari. The highest echelon of Ko'Ahmari."

"It would take someone that powerful to bring the Dark Realm in line," I sighed.

"I believe the one behind this assignment knew that," Hank agreed.

"Are you really—well, into all that stuff?" I asked.

"Breanne, that was part of the assignment. Some of it I like. Some of it, well, I only participated because the human I was with wanted it. I supplied what was needed and wanted, just as I said on several occasions. I know how much that upsets you."

"You don't need," I began.

"Breanne, I will never harm you. I mean it. I will admit I approached sex with trepidation in the beginning. You know how much I like it now," he grinned at me.

"Uh-huh."

"Baby, I love you. I hope you know how much I love you. This is Hank talking, not Li'Neruh Rath. I'm the guy who leaves his work behind when he's alone with his girl."

"Great. We've wasted so much time," I hugged myself tightly.

"No, baby. We've gotten to know each other without all the god crap messing it up. I can't say how much I've enjoyed the dance."

"What do you want to be called, now?"

"Baby, when you say Hank, it practically makes me melt. You could ask for anything, and I'd get it for you. But first, you need to eat before you make yourself sick or get a headache. Come on," he coaxed, walking toward me, "we'll just tell the people at the table you wanted a quickie."

"You wouldn't," I hissed, staring at him in shock.

"Nah, I prefer not to lie." He folded us back to the dining hall.

Everything all right? Lissa sent.

Just a little shocked, that's all. Smoky breath, here, forgot to tell me he's also Li'Neruh Rath, I returned.

Lissa snickered. Well, she needed a laugh.

Ashe bent time to get us back half an hour after we left. Lissa wanted to keep me with her for a while longer, but I hugged her and said I'd come back when I could. I had no idea when that might be.

Ashe also had it set up that one Larentii would accompany all investigative teams looking for rogue-engineered gates. I hoped the enemy didn't get any more creative than they already had—we couldn't risk any other lives like that.

"Sweetheart, are you all right?" Bill asked the moment we got back. He'd settled in Hank's room with Trajan, Charles and Jayson.

"Just a big snafu," I muttered. "Somebody died, and that wasn't a good thing."

"Can we go to bed now?" Bill asked hopefully.

"You want company?" I asked. I was exhausted, since we'd left in the middle of the night, but Bill looked as if he needed comfort.

"Yeah."

"All right," I nodded. "You'll know where I am," I waved a hand at the others and followed Bill through the connecting door into his suite.

~

"Sweetheart, wake up. I have to make some calls," Bill kissed me before my eyes unglued themselves.

"No," I moaned, holding onto him. His arms were wrapped around me and my head was on his shoulder when I finally blinked my eyes open. "I wanna stay in bed with you," I added.

"That's the nicest thing I've ever heard this early in the morning." Bill gently lifted a tendril of hair off my face and smiled.

"Do I look like a mess?" I asked.

"You look amazing."

"It's a good thing I love you so much," I said, pulling away. "You make me believe you when you say those things."

"Believe me. Always," he leaned in for a quick peck. "I can't tell the President that I'm late for a conference call because I couldn't stop kissing you." Bill grinned and slid off the other side of the bed. "You can go back to sleep if you want."

"I'm up," I heaved myself into a sitting position. "I just need coffee to continue that status. Would you like some while you're talking to the Prez?"

"I'd love some." Bill was snatching clothes off the inevitably useless love seat stuck in his suite.

"I'll be back." Rising, I clothed myself with power and misted to the coffee shop downstairs. Thirty seconds later, I was back with coffee for both of us. Yes, some time bending was involved, but nothing outrageous. I kissed Bill, placed the cup in his hand and opened the door to walk into Hank's connecting suite.

"Bill Jennings has disappeared completely in my visions. I can't locate him," Wildrif whined to Calhoun. "I used to get glimpses of him, but that is no longer true."

"He has become a secondary target, although this is puzzling," Calhoun admitted. "My associates have laid traps, and we saw results recently. We may focus our attentions there, and on promoting worship of the true god instead."

"I counsel against naming the new churches that," Wildrif sniffed.

"After what happened in Dallas? We are not stupid," Calhoun snapped. "We are more subtle than that, but the doors to those churches will open soon, and ours will effectively control and instruct the congregations. They are still seething over the bombings, so we will hand them those we have no use for, and tell the worshippers that they are responsible for the bombings. I await the carnage eagerly."

"Are you sure this is wise—withholding information?" Saxom asked his twin. Moxas, the Khos'Mirai, offered his brother a beaming smile.

"Chaos, brother. Isn't that what we want?"

"But it could result in our deaths," Saxom hissed.

"Have faith. I know the quarter-blood slave to Calhoun is having trouble seeing the opposition. We can claim similar troubles. They cannot fault us, when they know these difficulties are happening with others."

"Their fault, as I see it, is that they cannot see their foes either," Saxom nodded. "Brother, you have the true vision."

"We'll keep that to ourselves," Moxas grinned.

～

Breanne's Journal

I didn't realize it was Sunday morning until Hank hauled me to breakfast after a lengthy, shared shower. We found Charles already there, reading the Sunday comics. He'd gone through the rest of the newspaper already.

"Good morning," Charles closed the paper and offered me a smile.

"Hey," I leaned in and kissed his cheek. "What's for breakfast?"

"I was waiting for someone to join me," he said. "I'll order with you."

We did. A waitress walked to our table and took our orders, after pouring coffee for Hank and me. "See this?" Charles tapped a section of the newspaper he'd left on top of the others. I saw it was the religion section of the local newspaper.

"Attendance at the nation's churches still up," I read, scanning the headline.

"Yeah," Charles nodded. "They're still up in arms about those church bombings. There are interviews with several militant pastors in the article, and they are encouraging their congregations to carry weapons to services."

"Those guns won't do a thing against vampires, lion snake shifters and chimeras," Hank muttered.

"Not to mention the more powerful," I agreed.

～

"Well done, Acrimus," the General purred. "He was a target, and you managed to kill him with barely half a thought."

"It was a pleasure, General," Acrimus bowed with false modesty. "I have no idea who Ildevar Wyyld might name as his replacement, but I imagine that there will be a period of adjustment. Meanwhile, they have learned to respect our traps."

"A confused and frightened population is easy to control," the General agreed. "How is your newest minion doing?'

"Moxas suggested making the traps expandable. He also says that the Larentii and the Elemaiya would be the only ones who might detect their properties, outside the godlings or the Three. The Larentii will not consent to interfere, and the Elemaiya are now mortal and powerless. He says this is his revenge against the bitch who removed their power."

"I feel it is a great flaw in your kind that the Larentii are not traceable," the General grumbled.

"They were created when my kind was created," Acrimus grimaced. "They were created benign. Curious and powerful, but noninterfering. It was a calculated toss of the dice when I sent the Sirenali after them," he added.

"The Sirenali were created with a particular talent, although their creator considered it a flaw after the fact, that they could detect all worlds. They cannot detect the Larentii themselves, but their world was not properly guarded at the time. That has since changed and it is now closed to all, with few exceptions. It's too bad the Larentii were given permission in the beginning to protect themselves and their mates. That's how the Sirenali fell."

"*The Law* holds us back, but that will change once we destroy the Three."

"The Three made *the Law*—saying the Larentii are inviolate and to kill one will bring the wrath of the One," Acrimus shuddered. "The One has vowed to leave everything else to the Three, thinking they might be strong enough to withstand us."

"The Larentii will stand aside and observe while everything else falls," the General smiled. "They will live and the One will watch while we rule everything."

～

Le-Ath Veronis—present

Lissa's Journal

"We don't have a body to bury," I shook my head at Rigo. "Just as we didn't for Gavril."

"Tiessa, that was a necessity for your child," Rigo offered softly. "We must never allow the enemy to know that they have scored two hits against us, instead of one."

"If we live over this, we'll have a memorial for both," I sighed as Rigo pulled me against him. "Norian wasn't the best mate, but he was still a mate, when all's said and done."

"I know. The rest of us feel the same—he was one of us, although not the most popular."

"Rigo, he was the least popular, admit it," I sighed, pulling away. "The last time I saw Gavril alive, we argued. I may have done the same with Norian."

"Lissa, let that go. Don't you think they know that those are just foolish words and mean nothing? Stop wounding yourself with that. It no longer matters to them. It shouldn't matter to you, either. Focus on your love for both. That is what they have—what they take with them."

"I think I want to talk to Tybus," I said, hugging myself.

"Why?"

"To see what's left of my son."

"Are you sure that is wise? Tybus has his own worries and an Alliance to run."

"I know. I still want to see him."

"Then I will call your Falchani to transport you."

～

Campiaa—present

Tybus' Journal

I knew what she wanted when I received mindspeech from her. She didn't say it, but she had suffered another loss—a second, heavy blow. It grieved me that this was so. A part of me, too, recognized the daughter/mother that Gavril and I shared. The two were so much alike.

Drake and Drew, Lissa's Falchani mates, accompanied her inside my study shortly after I assured her that I had time to see her. So many things required my attention, but they could wait. This visit was far more important.

"Lissa, how are you?" I rose and held out my hands. She surprised me by walking around my desk and pressing herself against me. Wrapping my arms about her as tightly as I dared, I smoothed her hair.

"This will pass," I crooned. "I promise this will pass. Tybus is here. Gavril is here as well. You must trust that I am both. We care for you. You have no idea how strongly."

The first sob rocked her body. I held on tighter and murmured nonsense in the ancient language of the vampires.

∾

Earth—past

Breanne's Journal

"What is your schedule for today?" Gavin asked when Bill took a seat at the breakfast table. I got the idea that Gavin had been doing something similar to Bill and talking with Wlodek while Wlodek and he were both awake. He'd arrived five minutes before Bill.

Opal and the others had joined us while we ate—Charles had wisely asked for a table large enough to accommodate a crowd. Ashe and Kay sat across from me, and Kay seemed happy to eat beside him and talk occasionally to me, Hank and Charles.

"We have more information, but I'm worried it'll be similar to the useless intelligence we received on the sites in Arkansas and Colorado," Bill said. "Bree, this is yours." He handed an envelope down the table to me.

Those are your new credit cards—with your alias on them, Bill informed me in mindspeech. *Your accounts have all been moved*, he added. *To the outside world, it still looks as if Breanne Hayworth's accounts are frozen, except those attached to your charity. Terry is still working with those.* I watched him smile as he relayed the last bit of information.

Bill, you're a genius, I sent back. Bill's cell buzzed the moment we stopped mindspeaking. He stared at the screen for a moment before rising from the table and walking rapidly away.

"Jennings, here," he answered tersely. I knew it wasn't good news the moment he said those words.

～

Bill, Opal, Hank, Jayson, Charles, Gavin and I waded through the carnage. I felt ill, but forced my breakfast to stay where it was. Our goal was the captive who'd caused this.

Funeral attendees had been gunned down outside a chapel in Monroe, Louisiana. Few survived, and most of those were wounded.

"We have one who managed not to kill himself after emptying his gun," Bill growled as we walked inside the chapel. "The others saved their last bullets for themselves so they wouldn't get caught or questioned."

I took one look at the young man local police had captured and knew—he was obsessed. He sat on a chair before the altar—where a soldier's coffin had been only an hour earlier.

"He's from that church—you know the one that pickets funerals, hospitals and stuff," I sighed, dropping onto a nearby pew. "Instead of protesting and waving signs from the designated three hundred feet away, the attackers left the signs at home, carried concealed weapons beneath baggy clothing and opened fire as mourners were leaving the church." I saw that much, although I couldn't get to the reason for all of it—why they'd chosen this route—or been obsessed to choose this route.

"It's time to visit that church," Bill muttered. "Although this is being broadcast from one end of the country to the other by now. They may have started running like rats already."

"You fool!" Calhoun shouted at V'ili. "You know how the weak-minded react to an obsession! They'll do anything to please you, and as picketing this event was in their plans before you placed the obsession to kill, they modified their intentions in an effort to make you happy."

"You instructed me to lay the obsessions," V'ili hissed. Janine, terrified, huddled at V'ili's feet. Anger, fueled by power, vibrated from Calhoun and washed over her. If her mind remained her own, she'd have run away. Instead, she cowered at her master's feet, unable to move away from him.

"Be ready to relocate in two minutes, or I will leave you behind," Calhoun snarled and folded space to get away from V'ili.

"""

The church in question was located in Kansas, but not many there were willing to acknowledge its existence. The building was small, too, and it amazed me that so much hate could be generated inside such a tiny space.

"There is," Kalenegar began when the structure exploded in front of us. If Ashe hadn't shielded us, we'd have been obliterated with the building and the massive dungeon built beneath it.

"""

Half the neighborhood had been destroyed with the church and what lay beneath it. Ambulances and emergency teams were everywhere, crawling through the massive crater left behind after the dungeon collapsed. The immense dungeon had been hollowed out beneath streets, houses and other structures, most of which were now small bits covered in dirt and debris.

"There are none left alive in the crater," Kalenegar observed with the Larentii version of a sigh.

"I'll order rescue workers back and ask them to concentrate on those still left above ground," Bill nodded before walking toward the local police captain to share information. Gavin went with him, in case compulsion was required.

Ashe had taken Kay away from the scene, once he made sure the rest of us were all right. I was shaky as hell, but I didn't want to leave in case Bill needed me for anything. Surprisingly, Kalenegar was the one to wrap his arms around me. I looked up at his face—it was grim, and I'd never seen that expression from a Larentii before. Larentii seemed to take most things in stride, probably because they'd seen just about everything before and it no longer shocked them.

"Lara'Kayan, you are shaking," Kal turned his face toward mine. "There is nothing to fear—my shields were up, just as the Mighty Hand's were. I know you grieve for lives lost, but I feel they would have been lost anyway—this was a quicker death than the one planned by those behind this disaster."

"Yeah. I was thinking the same thing." If this dungeon held the same things the one in Dallas had, nobody is safe. They'd die—some of them happily—because a Sirenali had commanded it. Kalenegar had known there was an underground cavern and he'd been attempting to warn us when the explosion occurred.

"If there's nobody down there alive, we can wait until we get better equipment," the police captain said as he walked up with Bill. Gavin was right behind them, so I knew without reading the poor man that compulsion played a part in his cooperation. He wanted someone in that hole to be alive. Sadly, that wasn't the case.

"There's no need to risk your officers and emergency workers," Bill shook his head. "That ground is too unstable to send them in."

"You will not find whole bodies," Kal said from his position above my head. He still held me, my back to his front.

"Not good," the captain brushed back extremely thin hair, his eyes worried and sad.

Journalists and news vans were beginning to show up, too, and the captain's officers had another job to do—holding back the curious and the media. This was the local media—national news would take a bit longer, but they would all come. Likely, reporters were already flipping back and forth from the carnage in Louisiana to the cavernous, smoking pit here.

Connections between events in Louisiana and Kansas were being made, too, without any assistance from authorities. This time, the speculation was accurate. *Kal, do you think this is going on elsewhere?* I sent.

It is likely, my heart.

~

The confirmed death toll in both states currently stood at three hundred seventeen, with more coming. Heavy equipment had been moved to the Kansas site and authorities were sifting through the rubble for what remained of bodies. Teeth, bits of bone, a few pieces of jewelry—that's what they were finding. It could take a while to identify all of it. There was no sign that any of our enemy had perished in the blast, however. No surprise there.

"Was this small church behind the bombings in all fifty states?" One station—the least reliable one, was taking their speculation to a different level.

"Turn that shit off," Bill commanded when we trooped into the meeting room at the Kansas FBI office. An assistant rushed to obey, snatching the remote off the conference table and snapping off the television hanging in a corner of the room.

"We're not looking for visible construction," Bill announced, sitting heavily on a chair at the head of the table. "They're building dungeons."

"I don't think this explosion was planned," Hank began.

"I agree," Ashe said. He and Kay walked in—Hank had probably called Ashe when we left the bombing site. "I think the church members who went to Louisiana took things too literally and too far, and since one of theirs lived over it, the destruction of the source was necessary."

"Where is that one, now?" Gavin asked.

"In a secluded prison cell, but they can't get anything out of him. Breanne supplied the only information we got."

"We have one survivor, and who knows how many dead at the bottom of that pit," Opal shook her head. "These people are nothing more than murderous psychopaths."

"Psychogods," I muttered, "with dangerous minions."

"You will not recall that statement," Ashe laid compulsion on the assistant and two other FBI employees in the room. "Breanne," he admonished, "what the hell are you doing?"

"Speaking the truth," I dropped my head into my arms at the table.

"Did I hear the word *gods*?" Jayson said. I raised my head to find him blinking at me.

"Yes," Hank nodded, drawing Jayson's attention to him. "Do you think this is a one-sided fight, mortal?"

"Did you call me a mortal, bro?"

"Yes. High Demons are immortal, but that is irrelevant. You have gods among you here, at this table. Do not believe that all of them have turned against you. Many fight for you now."

"I guess that's good news," Opal breathed. "Are we outing gods at the table?"

"Not as yet. That time will come," Hank blew a curl of smoke. "Have patience. All will be revealed in time."

"Which way is this fight gonna go?" Jayson asked.

"Jayson, stop asking questions that have no answers," Hank muttered.

For just a moment, he'd been Li'Neruh Rath. In a blink, he was Hank again. I moaned and dropped my head into my arms a second time.

"We're scoping out the churches, religions and fringe groups that are a little on the extreme side," Bill said after we'd settled down and were served tea and coffee by the assistants.

"It may not do a lot of good to send locals out, since we may be dealing with Sirenali," I offered. I was tired, had been exposed to too much death during the course of the day and it was now early evening. "I suggest not sending anybody after dark, since their vampire allies will lay compulsion and send investigators on their way.

"You said before that there were four Sirenali left—that the one Hank killed in San Francisco had four buddies?" Jayson pointed out.

"Yeah."

"Doesn't it make sense, then, that there are—or were—a total of four targeted churches or facilities?"

"Sounds logical," Bill agreed.

"Even if there are more, it would make sense that those four are the most dangerous," Gavin suggested.

"True—good point," Bill said.

"I hypothesize that many of the extreme cases, as you put it, are here in this country," Kal said. "Although others might be found in additional parts of this world."

"I think we should talk to those ministers who did interviews for that article—the one in the Sunday paper," I offered. "I'll check them for obsession, too—when I'm not so tired."

"That's good," Charles agreed. "Their names and locations are listed in that article."

"I'll call Dan Kelsey. Find a place to eat. I'm starved," Bill ordered and pulled out his cell as he walked away.

Le-Ath Veronis—present

"Cass," Trajan walked alongside Casimir, "how about coming back to SouthStar for a little while? Bill and I are working on something, and we have a houseguest who needs to be entertained."

"I would be happy to do so," Casimir agreed. "At times, constant darkness becomes irritating."

"I knew you'd see it my way," Trajan grinned.

Earth—past

Breanne's Journal

"Here's the list—and the order to visit them," Bill passed a sheet of paper down the table. We'd settled on an Italian restaurant for dinner, so we could all get something we wanted. It was a family style restaurant, so Trajan ordered a plate of spaghetti meant to serve four, plus a steak. He ate all of it, with a salad and garlic bread.

Kay watched, wide-eyed, as he devoured a large piece of coconut cake for dessert.

"Sweetheart, he's a werewolf," Ashe hugged her close. Charles snickered.

"Kooper, I'm handing the reins to you and Lendill," Ildevar sighed. "You'll both share Director's duties."

"I prefer it this way—the Alliance is a big place," Lendill agreed. "My father said you might choose this path. Kooper is a trusted associate."

"I know you grieve for Norian," Ildevar told Lendill. "Do not allow your grief to dictate foolish actions. The enemy is a terrible one."

"I keep hearing that from my father," Lendill nodded. "Koop, what are your thoughts?"

"I'd like to talk with Breanne about this," Kooper sighed.

"Do you think we might convince her to visit?" Ildevar suddenly looked hopeful.

"I don't know. We can try. I'll put a message out."

Earth—past

Breanne's Journal

"Kooper wants to talk to you." That message was relayed by Kalenegar, who'd received mindspeech from Graegar, through Connegar, from Lissa, who'd been contacted by Kooper.

"Where is he?" I asked. Hank didn't like that I was prepared to go talk to Kooper, since we'd had a long, exhausting day already.

"With Ildevar Wyyld," Kal replied. "I will accompany you, as will Hank, if I read his smoke patterns correctly."

"Fine. Let's make this a short trip." I was ready to drop and Hank knew that. Kal likely did, too.

Hank let Kal bend time and fold space and we were ushered into Ildevar's presence, where Kooper and Lendill Schaff waited for us.

"Bree," Kooper stepped forward quickly and leaned in for a kiss.

"Kooper, what do you need?" I asked.

"Advice," he sighed.

"I'm not sure my advice is any better than someone else's right now," I said.

"Do you think we ought to keep looking for these gates?" Kooper asked. "The truth, Bree. Please."

"Yeah, but I think your agents should listen to their Larentii and Elemaiya helpers," I pointed out. I'd dropped my shields to read Lendill Schaff, and knew he and Kooper were now in charge of the ASD. Ildevar had chosen wisely, to make the transition of power as smooth as possible.

"I have a suggestion, too, if you need another reliable agent," I added.

"Who?"

"Bill Jennings—the one currently at SouthStar."

"Extremely competent," Hank agreed. "A wise choice, and one who'd need no training. He is familiar with the Elemaiya working with you, and they'd be comfortable together."

"I agree," Kooper nodded. "Can you get him here so I can put him to work?"

"We'll have to get Ashe," I said.

"I will go." Kal disappeared.

Kal was back in a few seconds, with Ashe and Bill from SouthStar. Bill was certainly excited, and had a comp-vid full of information to offer Kooper.

"What's this?" Kooper took the comp-vid Bill handed over.

"A listing of all new religions in both Alliances, with information and research on all of them. The ones most likely to be associated with the Sirenali or the ones that may have had undue influence from outside sources have been flagged for investigation. They have been cross-referenced, too, with unexplained disappearances near their facilities, and those are the ones I feel we should target first."

"Are you kidding?" Lendill walked to Kooper's side and stared at the information on the comp-vid.

"Ashe, Trajan and I discussed this days ago, and Trajan and I have been working on it ever since," Bill shrugged modestly.

"This is so much better than what we have," Lendill breathed while sorting through information on Kooper's comp-vid. "Can I pass this to my team and let them make a map for our investigations?"

"Kooper, why don't you introduce me to all your people involved with this—just in case," I suggested. He'd know what I meant—I wanted to make sure none of them had been obsessed.

"I can do that, but we'll have to get to headquarters on Le-Ath Veronis."

"I wish to come with you," Ildevar Wyyld spoke for the first time.

"Of course, Deonus," Kooper nodded respectfully.

That's how we ended up at ASD Headquarters, and I ended up walking through the entire place, checking for obsessed employees. We found three, but they were low-level employees and hadn't managed to get any important information.

"We'll sequester them on Wyyld," Ildevar said. "I don't want to kill them unless it becomes necessary."

I lowered my shields to read Ildevar. I couldn't. Read him, that is.

That made me sigh. I'd have to ask Lissa about him, because I felt there was something I needed to know.

"Breanne," Ildevar approached me and lifted my hand to his lips. I thought he might kiss it. He held my wrist against his cheek instead, and closed his eyes as if he found the touch of my skin blissful to him.

Yes, I definitely needed to talk to Lissa.

CHAPTER 13

*E*arth—past
     Breanne's Journal

"Breanne, Ildevar Wyyld is an ancient Ra'Ak," Hank informed me as he lifted my top over my head. I'd begun undressing myself the moment we made it back to our shared bedroom, but Hank stepped in and took the matter out of my hands.

"He doesn't kiss," Hank added, "because it is dangerous for any Ra'Ak to kiss a humanoid. Their appetite might get the better of their senses if they did. Ildevar will never harm someone he cares for. I believe he cares for you."

"Hank, I'm too tired to even think about that right now," I pouted.

"Ashe has shields around the hotel, and Bill says we can sleep until nine. We have interviews to do after that," Hank informed me.

"Okay." My eyes were closed and I was practically asleep on my feet as Hank pulled my jeans down.

"Step out, baby." Hank's breath was warm against my ear.

"Okay."

"I like it when you do what I ask," he leaned in to kiss my neck.

"Can I go to bed now?" I whined.

"Yeah. I'm gonna hold you tonight, and you'll sleep."

"I'm ready," I mumbled. I don't remember anything past that.

"These are our interviews today," Bill handed a list of names down the table. "I want to be there for all of them, and I want Breanne with me. I may need a little compulsion laid afterward so they won't think it strange that I was in so many parts of the country in such a short amount of time."

We had an interview in South Carolina, one in Mississippi, another in Texas, then two in California and the last one of the day in Ohio.

"They know we're coming?" Charles studied the paper when it came to him.

"Yeah. Dan Kelsey set it up for us."

"Could be dangerous," Charles observed, handing the paper to Gavin.

"I know that," Bill said. "How else can we get this done?"

"Good question," Charles replied.

"What are we going to do if Sirenali are there?" Opal asked.

"I'll entertain suggestions for that now," Bill replied.

Wyyld—present

"Chazi come with you," Chazi nodded at Bill. "Protect."

"I'll take all the help I can get," Bill agreed.

"I will also come with you," Reemagar offered.

"Don't forget—I have mindspeech," Kooper nodded to Bill. "Notify me if you find anything."

"One of us will contact you," Reemagar said.

"Do you have your weapons? Are they charged and ready?" Kooper checked his sidearm as he asked the question.

"Ready," Bill said.

"Lendill has already taken his teams out," Kooper said. "Jerigar, are you ready to transport me? Reemagar can take Bill and Chazi."

"Ready," Jerigar said.

"Perzi, Bekzi—ready?" Kooper grinned at the two reptanoids staying with him.

"We ready," both grinned back at Kooper. Jerigar and Reemagar folded passengers to their targets.

~

Bill studied his surroundings carefully. They'd landed in a park-like setting on Kleeg. The wide, grassy area was surrounded by trees and flowerbeds, while birds sang or called in the trees. A fountain stood in the middle, with sheets of water cascading down the sides of piled, natural stones. A huge temple lay in the background, and it, like its surroundings, seemed perfectly benign.

"What made you choose this?" Reemagar asked. "This is a well-established temple for the god of air and light."

"I know. But Trajan and I noticed some changes in their purchases lately," Bill said. "You see there's no activity outside the temple, too? Usually this is prayer time for the priests and acolytes, and they'd all be outside chanting prayers in the sun."

"What they buy?" Chazi asked.

"Weapons," Bill replied grimly. "That, combined with a few unexplained disappearances in the area certainly drew my interest."

"A recent excavation has been made beneath the temple," Reemagar said.

"All the more reason to get inside," Bill drew his weapon. "I wish Breanne was here—she could mist us inside."

"I will call Lissa," Reemagar said.

~

Le-Ath Veronis—present

Lissa's Journal

Reemagar sent mindspeech as I was going over reports in my study. He sounded worried, and that wasn't like my Larentii mate. I folded space to Kleeg quickly.

"Bill?" I was surprised to find him, Chazi and Reemagar about a quarter mile from a temple dedicated to the god of light and air. We stood in a grassy park; not surprising as it was the usual setting for this type of temple.

"Lissa, good to see you," Bill nodded to me. "There's something going on inside that temple, and we need to find out what it is."

I already knew Reemagar found it troublesome—I'd read that in his mindspeech. He wouldn't come out and express those worries to Bill, but I knew.

"Need mist," Chazi said.

"I can do that," I said, studying the temple. Made of pure white marble, it gleamed in the early morning light on Kleeg. Devotees of the god of light and air liked tall, wide domes and spires. This temple was covered in domes and spires.

"Watch out for rogue-engineered gates, too," Bill cautioned.

"This is turning into a mess, and we haven't even gone inside," I pointed out.

"Then let's take care of that now," Bill muttered. "Everybody ready?"

~

Earth—past

Breanne's Journal

The minister in South Carolina wasn't obsessed, had no dungeon beneath his church and ruined any innocence he might have in my mind when he said that all other religions would "burn in hell."

He also seemed to think that he had God on speed-dial. In his less than normal mind, maybe they had breakfast together on Saturday mornings, too.

Poor Bill had to listen to an almost-sermon after asking whether the minister had been approached by anyone recently who might want to use his church building. After ten minutes, Gavin took over, laid compulsion and we were on our way to Mississippi.

~

Kleeg—present

Lissa's Journal

Weapons, many of them not legal in either Alliance, filled two rooms inside the temple. In the rectory, tables were shoved aside so some could practice firing those weapons. Weapons masters had been brought in and they were busy training the temple residents to kill living targets.

What we found in the oval sanctuary was more frightening than that. Genley Reith had taken over the temple. If I hadn't seen his image before and known that he was Sirenali, I would have imagined him a normal member of the population.

Genley stood at the edge of a huge, indoor pool that was nearly finished, watching while former priests and acolytes applied a coat of pale-blue paint to the structure before filling it with water. His new army was as busy as an anthill, making sure their new master would have a comfortable saltwater pool in which to swim.

I knew Genley was using a Sirenali's talent for disguise to hide his true nature, but the thing that worried me most was that all the people inside the temple were likely obsessed. Those dedicated to the god of light and air would never be tempted to purchase or use weapons otherwise.

I'll have to set you down somewhere, so I can attempt to get him to remove his obsessions, I sent to my passengers.

Set me down in those rafters over the sanctuary, Bill said. *I can cover you from there.*

I will keep Chazi and myself shielded on the floor, in case our help is needed, Reemagar said.

Good enough, I agreed. *Bill, don't hesitate to shoot if things don't go well.*

I won't, don't worry about that, Bill replied.

I misted Bill onto a broad beam in the rafters over the pool, where he'd have a clean shot at Genley if things didn't go as planned on the ground. I dropped Reemagar and Chazi onto the narrow space between the pool's edge and a wall, where someone was least likely to walk into Reemagar's shield.

Remaining mist for a few seconds, I pondered what needed to be done. If Genley didn't respond to threats, then he and everyone else in the temple would have to be killed. I hated doing that. The residents weren't acting on their own accord, but who knew the extent of what they'd been instructed to do? Those instructions would outlive Genley if he failed to remove them.

"Hello, Genley," I purred as I appeared before him and held the tip of a deadly claw beneath his chin.

~

Earth—past

Breanne's Journal

The minister in Mississippi bore an obsession. I felt itchy about the whole thing, so I'd asked Bill to let me go inside the church as mist before he walked in for the meeting. He and Hank insisted on riding in my mist with me. We hovered before the minister, who had gray hair, cloudy green eyes and a permanent frown.

He's obsessed, I sent to my passengers. They could see for themselves the piles of explosives in the minister's study.

He's waiting for us to get here, so he can kill us the minute we walk in. Bill's mindspeech was a low growl.

Let's check the basement, but if my hunch is correct, the rats have already deserted this ship, I returned.

Check the basement by all means, but I believe we should destroy the explosives and take the minister in, Hank suggested.

Bree? Bill sent. I destroyed the explosives by turning them into harmless sparks while the minister leapt from his chair in terror. His shriek was cut off as he was swallowed inside my mist.

The basement, enlarged and modified to hold a dungeon, had been vacated and all equipment removed. Charles was right—letting them know we were coming was a mistake. Chances were, too, that Bill was still on their list of targets. Who knew what—or who—might be waiting for him at the other facilities?

We'd seen enough, and as there were no others inside the church, I misted toward the parking lot outside. I warned Opal, Jayson and Trajan that I was dropping a prisoner and dumped a frightened and obsessed minister at their feet. How thankful was I that I'd supplied everybody with Ranos technology? Very thankful, when two Blackhawk helicopters flew over our heads and opened fire.

Kleeg—present

Lissa's Journal

I should have known better. I should have. Isn't that how hindsight always works—you figure you should have known what might happen before the fact? Genley had been instructed on what to do, should he find himself in this situation. He changed to his natural form and fought me, knowing he'd either die or hurt me in some way. Both those things happened.

Bill couldn't get a clear shot at Genley Reith as he and Lissa fought, the Sirenali's dark scales gleaming dully in the light filtering through high windows as he struck at Lissa with sharp claws. Lissa's movements were swifter than the eye could follow, and Genley's body was covered in superficial cuts. Bill knew Lissa wanted the obsessions removed and that's why the Sirenali still lived.

Temple residents were moving in on the fight, their weapons drawn and pointing toward the combatants. Bill jerked as a weapon discharged. Blood sprayed from Lissa's left arm. Bill fired at the one who'd wounded her, killing him quickly. Chazi's lion snake, escaping Reemagar's shield, began whipping through the humanoids surrounding the fight and biting any who carried weapons. They began dropping quickly.

"Hello," hands jerked Bill's pistol away. Bill turned to find someone grasping the adjoining rafter with sharp, dark claws. Before he could stop himself, he was mesmerized by the eyes of a second Sirenali. "You'll do everything I tell you to do from now on," the female Sirenali purred. Bill didn't want to, but found himself nodding anyway.

～

Lissa's Journal

If Reemagar hadn't noticed, who knows what might have happened? He also released the particles of the female Sirenali, but it was already too late—she'd managed to obsess Bill. That's when I went into hyperdrive, killed Genley with barely a thought and turned nearly two hundred humanoids to sparks. I stood next to Genley's pool afterward, panting and holding my bleeding left arm. Chazi came back to himself and stood naked nearby, watching as Bill was transported from the rafters by Reemagar.

Who knew what he'd been instructed to do? If Breanne couldn't see it, the rest of us couldn't, either.

～

Earth—past

Breanne's Journal

Ashe and I were inside the FBI offices, discussing the remaining churches on Bill's list and working out which of us would mist through them and whom we'd carry with us when Graegar and Barrigar appeared inside the room with us.

Bill, Opal and Jayson had escorted the minister to a holding cell— he'd have to be held until we could determine whether his condition was permanent. If we couldn't find the Sirenali or the Sirenali died, we couldn't let the man live.

He'd been instructed to kill Bill and anyone with him; he'd shouted

205

that often enough after Hank and Jayson shot down the helicopters from the church parking lot. Kal had shielded us from their bullets, and they'd flown low enough that Ranos pistols destroyed them easily. Graegar's appearance worried me greatly, however.

"Dearest," Graegar began, "we have terrible news."

~

Le-Ath Veronis—present

Lissa's Journal

Connegar and Reemagar held a shield around Bill, who sat quietly inside my study. Reemagar sent a message to Graegar through channels, and he'd been informed of Bill's obsession. Graegar sent a reply, saying he was going to Breanne.

I waited for her to arrive. This might upset her greatly or destroy her—she loved Bill. Drake, Drew and Gavin walked in to wait with me. It wasn't long before Graegar, Barrigar, Breanne, Hank, Ashe and Ashe's mate, Kay, appeared.

Bill's obsession wasn't difficult to determine once Breanne arrived —he went from docile to terrifying in a blink, and if my Larentii hadn't kept him behind strong shields, he'd have attacked my sister.

She'd come as herself, dropping her disguise, but I felt it didn't matter—Bill knew who she was in either guise.

"Bill," Ashe pulled Breanne behind him—Bree looked ready to cry.

"Ashe?" Bill turned to the Mighty Hand. The obsession centered on Breanne; that much was obvious. Hank pulled Breanne away and settled her on a chair in a corner of my study.

"Bill, tell me what happened. As much as you remember." Ashe motioned for Bill to sit. Bill sat and stared at the Mighty Hand.

"That woman jerked my gun away. She couldn't fire it—Ranos pistol tuned to my DNA," Bill said. "She said something to me, but I can't—I can't say what it was." Bill offered Ashe a puzzled frown.

"Bill, we may have to sequester you for a while," Ashe sighed and shook his head. "I'm sorry."

~

Breanne's Journal

Was I upset? Upset couldn't begin to describe how I felt. That word was too tiny and insignificant. Bill wanted to kill me, and the Sirenali responsible for this travesty was dead. All sorts of things went through my mind, but primarily I wanted to *Change What Was*, bring that bitch back to life, force her to remove the obsession and then kill her slowly.

"Breanne," Hank breathed a warning against my ear. He knew—perhaps from my rapid breathing and the trembling of my body, exactly what I was considering. It was either that or scream my grief for all to hear. Bill, in this time frame, was dead to me. With the obsession he carried, he wanted to kill me. He'd keep trying, too, if I didn't *Change What Was*.

"Ashe?" Kay's voice was timid.

"What is it, sweetheart?" Ashe asked, turning to her and holding out his hand. Shyly, she went to him and he pulled her close.

"I can see Bill's lines," Kay said.

"What?" Ashe asked, puzzled. I struggled out of Hank's grip and stared at Kay. Hank, following my lead, stared too.

"I saw them before, too," Kay went on. I held my breath.

"I know what's different now," Kay said. "I can try to change it, if you want."

"Oh. My. God. Please try, Kay. Please," I begged.

"Breanne, come here," Ashe beckoned me toward him. "I'll shield you so Bill won't see."

"What do you want me to do?" I asked.

"Connect with Kay. See through her eyes. I'll do the same—I don't want Kay placed in danger."

"Yeah." I knew he didn't want Kay placed in danger. I didn't matter so much, but I didn't want Kay harmed, either.

Ashe surprised me by putting his free arm about me when I went to him. I did as instructed and connected with Kay so I could see through her eyes. With the talent I had, I could see Bill's aura lines just as easily as Kay could, and knew without having to ask which ones were different. If Kay could do this for Bill, then she could do it for others who didn't deserve to die. I wanted to whimper with fear—and hope. Ashe's arm tightened about me.

Don't be afraid, love, his voice filtered into my mind. I felt that message was meant for Kay, and I'd heard it since I was connected to her.

I think Ashe and I both held our breath as Kay reached out with her talent and turned graying lines back to their natural colors. I was afraid to hope as Bill's lines glowed with soft, healthy color instead of the drabness they'd held after the obsession was laid.

It gave insight, too, into what the Sirenali were capable of doing and how their obsessions were accomplished. Kay's talent was almost a mirror image of theirs, and I wondered at the complexity of it.

"There, all done," Kay sighed and sagged against Ashe. What she'd done had worn her out.

"Where am I?" Bill stood and looked around him, as if he'd wakened from a deep sleep.

I'd always been able to read Bill, and I was grateful for that fact now. He was back to himself, but what I saw in him was more than disturbing. I saw the Sirenali through his eyes, and she'd pulled the knowledge that I was alive straight from his mind. She'd likely passed that knowledge up the chain of command immediately, so the enemy knew everything.

Then, not only had she instructed Bill to kill me when he saw me again, but to send mindspeech that he'd accomplished that deed to her —and to others. They knew now that he could mindspeak, and were also aware of his other talents. That was terrifying.

Ashe, they know—the enemy, I said. *When she placed the obsession, she pulled all of it from Bill's mind. They know I'm still alive and what I look like, through him.*

Ashe cursed himself softly. *I didn't think my compulsion was necessary not to reveal your identity*, Ashe returned. *This is a horrible turn of events. I don't want Bill to feel worse than he already does*, he added.

Me either, I agreed.

"The Sirenali can read talents in those who don't hold a lot of power." I said aloud and shivered in Hank's arms. The Larentii had removed their shields since Bill was back to himself, and he'd given us information we never thought to get from any victim of obsession. Once Kay worked her magic, he could remember and talk coherently about the experience.

"I felt dirty," Bill, unaware of my silent conversation with Ashe, shook his head in disgust. "Bree, I'm really sorry. There's no way I'd ever do anything like that when I'm normal," he added.

"Don't worry about it—I know what happened," I said. My heart was still beating faster than it should, and I felt more than grateful that Kay had pulled him away from an obsession that could have destroyed both of us, although sensitive information had fallen into enemy hands.

"Will you come to me, sweetheart?" Bill asked.

"Yeah." Hank let me go and I walked to Bill. He pulled me onto the chair with him.

"Baby you're shaking. You're not afraid of me now, are you?"

"No. I was so scared I wouldn't get you back." I struggled not to cry. Bill didn't need to read everybody after touching my tears. Graegar said only those I couldn't read would be unaffected.

"What if," Hank began, "we pretended that Bill accomplished his task?" I jerked around and stared at him. "The Sirenali obviously still think you're alive, and that information is now everywhere, unless I miss my guess."

Ashe and I should have included Hank in our mental conversation —that was apparent—but he had the beginnings of a good idea.

"You're saying that Bill ought to send mindspeech, to draw them out?" Lissa broke in.

"Yes, but we have to plan this carefully. We can't rush this or they'll suspect, don't you think?"

"Yes. There's no valid reason that he should see her for a few days, at least. They'll believe the obsession is still active, I think, since the one who placed it is dead and can't tell them otherwise." Kalenegar appeared inside Lissa's study, his well-muscled arms crossed tightly over his chest. I guessed that Graegar and Barrigar had included him in the conversation through a mindlink, and he'd chosen to show up so he could talk with us.

"Meanwhile, one hundred seventy-nine obsessed people died in the temple on Kleeg," Lissa moaned and dropped her face in her hands. She'd attempted to convince Genley Reith to remove his obsessions, but it was likely that he could only remove about half of them. The others were probably placed by Bill's Sirenali attacker.

"I think we should all ponder this and meet here again in two weeks to make suggestions," Ashe said. "If we work this out carefully, there's no reason we can't lay a trap for anybody who shows up to check on Bill's handiwork."

"I don't want Breanne placed in danger," Hank blew a cloud of smoke. "So plan carefully if you intend to include her."

The idea that I might be included in the plans frightened me, and that shouldn't be. My beating and subsequent death at the hands of the General had taken a greater toll than I wanted to admit. If he showed up a second time, I could be too terrified to do anything about it.

Baby, I'll do everything I can to protect you, Hank sent. *I can tell you're worried. We still have to go back and help Bill in the past. Hold your chin up, Avilepha. We have much to do.*

I gave a slight nod in reply—I felt ill and didn't want Hank to sense that in my mindspeech. Ashe had both arms wrapped around Kay, I noticed, and I knew she was tired and shaky after healing Bill's tainted aura lines.

"Ashe, why don't you take Kay to Southstar?" I said, my voice wobbling only a little. "She's tired and hungry."

"I think I will," Ashe said. "We'll catch up with you and Hank later." Ashe folded Kay away from Lissa's study.

"Now," I said, shivering against Hank, "Kay just became one of the most valuable people in either Alliance. The Sirenali think their obsessions are infallible. Kay proved that wrong earlier. What can we do to protect that knowledge from the enemy?"

CHAPTER 14

Earth—past
Breanne's Journal

Ashe explained that his compulsion overrode anything anybody else might do, and even a Sirenali couldn't get to information if Ashe commanded that it not be shared or released with anyone. Once he'd arrived on Earth again with Kay, he set about placing cautionary compulsion on everyone before telling them what Kay could do.

At least Kay would be protected in the future, if anyone who knew of her talents encountered a Sirenali.

It was decided, too, to leave the two obsessed people we had in custody as they were, so as not to tire Kay. After all, if we found someone more important who'd been obsessed, her energy would be better spent there.

Kalenegar then explained what had happened in the future—up to a point. He didn't tell Bill that he'd been the one obsessed. He merely said that Kay had managed to heal the one obsessed and left it at that.

I, on the other hand, still felt shaky and had no way to combat that feeling. In my experience, it was a runaway horse that you had to ride until it ran its course. Meanwhile, the terror of the ride could threaten to overwhelm at times.

"How many more churches?" I asked.

"Three, sweetheart," Bill said.

"I'll take two, if you'll stay with Kay," Ashe told Kalenegar.

"I will," he agreed.

"That leaves the one in Ohio for you, baby," Hank said. "Bill, Opal and Jayson can come with us."

Charles, Gavin and Trajan went with Ashe to the two churches in California, but I was worried. So far, only the church in Mississippi had held a Sirenali at one point, and that meant there was likely three more at churches somewhere. I didn't think those three were the ones we traveled to now; the odds were against it. It didn't keep me from thinking that one or more of them could be booby-trapped, just as the one in Mississippi had been.

"I suppose they're more difficult to kill than I originally thought," the General grumbled.

"I think you did kill her. I don't know what wizardry they employed to bring her back. At least the one our Sirenali read believes it to be her."

"If it is a doppelgänger to make us believe we didn't kill her, then I will reward the one who brings me confirmation of this. How is the obsessed one doing?"

"The Sirenali who placed the obsession was killed, but that only means the obsession cannot be removed. He was instructed to notify us should his target be eliminated. Then we may determine whether it is an impostor."

"Very good," The General nodded. "I greatly anticipate this news."

Breanne's Journal

The church was in a suburb on the outskirts of Akron; a tidy, white frame church nestled in a neighborhood. That sent warning signals through me immediately the moment I set my passengers down outside the building. *Bill*, I sent, *I don't feel good about this one.*

Bree, are you being overly cautious? Hank asked. He and Bill were both staring at me while Jayson and Opal cautiously drew their Ranos pistols.

Honey, I don't know, I returned. *I just feel shaky right now*. I started to say something else when prescience kicked in. When the entire community of Delvano, Ohio exploded in a huge fireball, I already had my passengers hundreds of miles away.

"I think they didn't want us to take any more of their slaves as prisoners. Something set off their alarms the moment we landed outside that church," Hank paced and blew smoke. We were in Bill's D.C. office—that's where I'd taken them when I'd fled the Akron area. Bill sat behind his desk, Jayson and Opal stood near the door as self-appointed guards, and I sat in one of Bill's guest chairs.

"What set them off? Sight? Sound?" Opal asked.

"Could be anything," Hank shrugged. "Bree, what kind of shield did you have up?"

"Just one to keep bullets or something like that from passing through." My shakiness hadn't subsided—in fact, it was getting worse. I knew I was close to a panic attack; too many things had happened and it frightened me that Bill had been a target twice. It terrified me that the enemy knew I was still alive as well, and that they were aware of my disguise.

"Hey," Jayson knelt in front of me and took my hands in his. "What's wrong with my girl?"

"She's had a long, bad day," Hank rumbled, kneeling beside Jayson. "Baby, do you need to lie down? Something more than that, maybe?"

"Bree?" Bill rose from his seat and walked around his desk quickly.

"Baby, tell me what you need," Hank pleaded.

I blinked at Hank, struggling to keep his handsome face in focus. "What happened?" A new voice joined the others. Kevis had arrived.

≈

Hank's Journal

Nearly four thousand people died in Ohio. That, coupled with Bill's obsession in the future, the knowledge that the enemy knew she was alive and the destruction of the church in Mississippi on the same day triggered Breanne's PTSD. I was forced to call Graegar, who transported Kevis to us.

"I worry continuously about this," Graegar shook his head at me as we watched Breanne sleep. If she'd been awake, she might have been frightened by the number of people inside her room. Kalenegar glowered in a corner while the rest of us—Graegar, Barrigar, Jayson, Trajan, Charles, Bill and I, either sat or stood and watched Breanne after Kevis placed a healing sleep.

"We're placing temporary patches on a leaking boat and hoping they hold until we don't need it anymore," Kevis grumbled. That's when I knew he loved her, too. Graegar offered a sly smile as that realization hit me.

"Kay's asleep. How's Bree?" Ashe folded in beside me and asked the question we all wanted to ask.

"We're hoping she's better when she wakes," Barrigar spoke for the first time. Graegar's Protector had sat in silence, watching Breanne carefully. I knew Trevor, Kooper and the reptanoids would be worried, too, if they knew about this. The last person I might have suspected showed up as I was considering all this—Ildevar Wyyld.

"I have my sources," Ildevar sighed as he stared at Breanne.

I didn't miss the gesture when he nodded slightly at Kalenegar, however. Somehow, those two knew one another.

"How long will she sleep?" Trajan asked.

"Four more hours, then I'll get her up and see if she wants to eat. We'll assess the damage then," Kevis replied.

"Damage?" Trajan sounded lost.

"Just a figure of speech," Kevis soothed, patting the werewolf on the shoulder. I could tell Kevis was worried, though.

"Look, why don't we get dinner and leave the Larentii here with Breanne?" Charles suggested.

"That sounds good," Kevis steered Trajan away from the bed. The suggestion was sound—Kevis was considering what the rest of us needed while Breanne was down, and talking about it over dinner was a wise idea.

~

Breanne's Journal

Disorientation clouded my vision when I woke and for a moment, I had no idea where or when I was. "Lara'Kayan, you are safe with us," Kalenegar soothed. A large hand covered my heart, convincing it to slow its pace to a more natural rhythm. I found myself surrounded by Larentii; Barrigar, Graegar, Kalenegar, Renegar, Garegar and Pheligar stood around the bed, all of them studying me with interest.

"Hey," I held out my hand and grasped Pheligar's hand in mine. Actually, I was only able to hold a couple of fingers, but he smiled at me anyway.

"Much better," another Larentii, one I didn't recognize, walked into view.

"Breanne, this is Lenigar," Graegar introduced the newcomer. "He and Renegar are our finest healers."

"Really?" I stared at Renegar, who was Pheligar's son and Graegar's father. He was also Garegar's grandfather, so I had four generations of Larentii at my bedside. I kept my shield up and didn't read Lenigar—I figured it was only polite to ask before reading most Larentii.

"Yes." Lenigar smiled at me, too. "We have done what Kevis said and placed a patch on a leaking boat," his smile widened.

"Okay, what does that mean?" I asked.

"It means that some of your memories have been muted," Renegar replied. "Until a time comes when you might deal with them a little better. Muting certain memories places time and distance between you and them, so they cannot do too much harm."

At first I didn't believe him, but when I dredged up the memory of

Bill's obsession (it took some work to do it) it seemed as if it had taken place long in the past and no longer frightened me so much.

"This requires several Larentii working together to accomplish," Lenigar said. "And at least two of them must be well-versed in healing humanoids." His last statement was accompanied by a smile.

"Thank you," I nodded to him.

"You are welcome," he replied.

~

Kleeg—present

Lissa's Journal

"So many things happened, I didn't think about the gate," I said. Reemagar and I had returned to Kleeg to search the rest of the temple. Chazi remained on Le-Ath Veronis with Bill, who was working out the next world to visit.

"We did not have time to search properly," Reemagar agreed.

He and I walked through the sanctuary and past the large, unfinished pool. He'd watched while I separated the particles of all those at the temple, then healed my arm afterward. The marble floor was nearly spotless beneath our feet, except the area where Genley and I had fought. There, dried blood spattered the floor—his and mine.

"Where do you think they'd put a gate?" I looked up at Reemagar.

"Somewhere so their slaves wouldn't accidentally wander into it," Reemagar said.

"True," I agreed. "That means it's probably near the statue of the god."

To those who worshipped the god of light and air, the statue, once placed and consecrated, couldn't be touched by anyone except the High Priest. All others had to stand back a respectful twelve feet or so. That meant there was likely twenty-four feet of dangerous space surrounding the sculpture.

We walked through widely spaced columns and into the chapel of the god, where the statue was positioned at the center. Reemagar and

I both recognized the gate—it vibrated with a dark malevolence, waiting for the unsuspecting to come closer and be swallowed up by it.

"Those who disappeared didn't wander into this one," Reemagar observed. "I believe they were pushed into its waiting vortex."

"I agree. Everybody knows not to get too close to the god's likeness." I shook my head as I stared at the gate. "What should we do, now?"

"I have an idea," Reemagar said and held out his right hand. Light formed around it as he gathered power.

"Lissa, that's incredible," Bill breathed as he studied the images I showed him on comp-vid. Nobody would be able to pass through the thick mass of sharp, steel needles that formed a dome over the god's statue at the temple on Kleeg. Reemagar had placed it far enough back that the gate couldn't pull anyone into the barrier, and the sight of it would put anyone off—its long, sharp spikes were lethal.

"We should place these over every gate we find," Bill breathed.

"I think so, too," I agreed. "Reemagar placed one around the gate that killed Norian as well, once we were finished on Kleeg. Reemagar set alarms on them—every Larentii will know if the barriers are destroyed or fall to any kind of power."

"Handy," Bill sounded impressed.

"Definitely," I agreed. "We just need to get with Kooper, Lendill and Jett, to let them know we have a temporary fix. If the team has a Larentii, the barrier will go up immediately around any gates they locate. If they don't have a Larentii, all the team has to do is send a message and they'll get a Larentii quick."

"The Larentii don't see this as interference?" Bill seemed puzzled.

"It's really not," I grinned. "They have no problem providing transportation—or in forming anything they might consider art."

"So a needle thicket shaped as a dome is art?" Bill chuckled.

"I think it's damn fine artistry," I said.

~

Earth—past

Hank's Journal

"It's not so much the amount of power as the level of skill involved," Kevis explained. Ildevar listened raptly as Kevis told all of us that Graegar had sent mindspeech—their attempt to mute some of Breanne's memories had been successful.

Their worry was that as Breanne was the Mighty Heart, it might prove impossible. The task had been difficult but not impossible, but then the Larentii were occasionally modest about their accomplishments.

"Are the memories gone?" Opal asked. She worried about Breanne's mental health, but didn't want her mind tampered with in any way.

"Not gone," Kevis shook his head. "They're still there; just a little harder to call up and not nearly as harmful. The Larentii don't do this often, as you might imagine. Breanne is their Vhanaraszh, so of course they'll make the attempt for her."

"I'm glad it worked—that scared the hell out of me," Jayson said. "When she gets like that, I'm terrified we won't get her back."

"I have bad news," Bill broke in.

"What's that?" I went on alert immediately.

"Vernon Clark's best buddy troublemaker has started up the website again."

"It makes sense, now that they know she's still alive," I pointed out.

"I was hoping he'd be hiding in a cave so deep he'd never see the light of day again after Vernon was killed," Bill tossed his cellphone onto the long table where we'd had dinner at the hotel restaurant. He'd asked for—and received—their banquet table in a private room so we could talk freely. I'd placed a shield around it, too, just in case. It always paid to be cautious.

"So Marc Cummings is letting loose with the conspiracy crap again?" Opal asked.

"Yeah. That message was from Dan Kelsey," Bill nodded toward his phone. "The website is claiming again that the whole Breanne Hayworth book is a lie, that Ross Gideon vomited that mess for Rome Enterprises and they're offering a reward to anybody who can bring down the woman posing as Breanne Hayworth, or to kill Ross Gideon or your father, Jayson." Bill's gaze turned to Jayson, who stared back in alarm.

"How much?" Jayson's question was forced. Bill's announcement had stunned him—no matter how much he disagreed with his old man, a part of Jayson loved his father.

"A million for each. You know that'll lure in the professionals and the crazies."

"If they're blatantly offering that for the obvious targets, how much do you suppose they might be offering for you, Director Jennings? It's apparent that they want you as well, after two attempts at two different churches." Bill's head jerked in Charles's direction, but the observation was an accurate one.

"I've got people doing research," Bill sighed. "It seems to be a private vendetta against me, because none of our sources know anything."

"Wlodek says that there are rumors circulating that Gavin was killed in San Francisco," Charles continued. "We've chosen not to refute them."

"That's good—we don't need more targets among us," Bill said.

I knew, whether anyone else at the table did or not, that Opal had been a target as well—that she'd actually died in Austin and Breanne had revealed herself to the enemy by *Changing What Was* and restoring Opal's life. I'd learned that when I'd connected to Breanne with our first kiss. I never intended to divulge that—Breanne didn't want Opal to know, and I felt that was reason enough.

"This means," Bill's voice interrupted my thoughts, "that we can't officially schedule anything else until this is over. They'll be waiting for us if we do."

"Young man," Ildevar spoke for the first time, "if you wish to keep your father and his associate safe, I can take them to Wyyld when I leave. They will be under the protection of my palace guards while there."

His offer was made to Jayson, who wasn't sure who—or what—Ildevar actually was. A wise concern, actually, but Ildevar would never offer protection lightly.

"Hank?" Jayson turned to me.

"Jayson, this is Deonus Wyyld, Founder of the Reth Alliance and Master of the Grand Alliance Council," I said. "They'll be as safe at his palace as they can be anywhere."

"I don't give a damn about Ross, but Dad does," Jayson muttered. "Yeah—if you don't mind," he nodded to Ildevar. "They won't like it," he added.

"I have had unwilling," Ildevar hesitated for a moment, "guests—in the past," he smiled slyly. "My guards know how to keep them comfortable in their confinement."

"I'll help you pick them up," I offered.

"I'll accept that," Ildevar replied.

Breanne's Journal

All heads turned as I was ushered into the private banquet room inside the hotel restaurant. Kalenegar had shortened and disguised himself again and held a protective hand at my back as we walked through the door. The other Larentii had left, but not before Graegar and Barrigar gave me warm kisses.

The good news was that I was only feeling slightly shaky, and most of that stemmed from finding a crowd waiting for me and that I hadn't eaten anything for too long. Two chairs were left between Hank and Kevis, so Kal and I took those.

"Baby, how do you feel?" Hank's mouth gently brushed my temple.

"A lot better," I said, lifting the menu lying in front of me.

"Here, drink this first," Kevis passed a bottle of strawberry protein drink to me. Kal opened it with power, Hank stuck a straw in the bottle and I drank nearly half of it before stopping for a breath.

"What happened with Ashe and those other two churches?" I asked.

"Same thing that happened in Ohio," Bill said. "We just didn't want to tell you before."

"Fuck." I rubbed my forehead; Hank rubbed my back.

"Ashe is fine—he had major shields in place so nobody was hurt," Trajan said. "At least nobody with him," Trajan amended.

"Baby, don't ask right now, okay?" Hank tilted my chin in his direction and I stared into dark eyes. "You've had enough for today."

I couldn't argue with that so I went back to my protein drink while I studied the menu.

James Rome Sr. followed Quin, his bodyguard, into the parking garage beneath the Rome Enterprises building in Los Angeles. He'd been made aware of the threats against his life. It wasn't the first time he'd been threatened.

His car and driver waited in a private bay to take him home. The chief of security had hired extra guards for the building, too.

"Mr. Rome," Alan, his driver for more than ten years, nodded as he slid out of the driver's seat to open the back door. Alan nodded to Quin as James Sr. moved to slide onto the back seat. Without hesitation, both pulled weapons from pockets and opened fire.

Ross Gideon was bored, but there wasn't any way to escape his comfortable prison. Guarded night and day by FBI agents, he couldn't go to the bathroom without someone taking notes. Television programs were monitored and he wasn't allowed a phone, a computer or anything else that might be used for communication. Except paper —Ross had paper. He hadn't written anything on paper in a decade. He was writing on paper, now.

"Gideon." Ross' least favorite agent stalked into the room and addressed him gruffly.

"What is it, Weathers?" Without looking up, Ross kept writing, his ballpoint pen moving steadily across the notebook page.

"This," Sherman Weathers replied, firing a single shot and hitting Ross Gideon in the head, killing him instantly.

~

Hank's Journal

Breanne knew before anyone else, and she was standing and shrieking as Ross Gideon and Jayson's father died simultaneously.

~

Kevis had his hands full with Jayson's meltdown after he learned of his father's death. Trajan, Kalenegar and Ildevar were taking Breanne in hand so Bill and I took Opal, Gavin and Charles with us. Breanne had seen who'd committed the murders in that strange prescience she often displayed, so we were going hunting.

~

"They'll come hunting," Moxas assured Calhoun. "I suggest you have your Sirenali ready and waiting when they find those they instructed to kill your targets."

"This is easier than I thought," Calhoun gloated.

"I warn you, I only see that some will come hunting these obsessed murderers of yours. Like your quarter-blood seer, these things are often unclear to me."

"Then I'll place a vampire, a chimera and a lion snake shifter with each set of Sirenali, to ensure we take them down."

"If that is your wish," Moxas shrugged. "As I said, I cannot see nor predict who might come."

~

Breanne's Journal

Ildevar's gentleness was difficult to reconcile with the fact that he was Ra'Ak. Granted he was an ancient Ra'Ak, turned long before their descent into evil, but it was still somewhat perplexing to associate a giant, flesh-eating serpent with the man who held me so carefully against him, you'd think I was made of fragile glass.

"How are you feeling now?" Ildevar's blue eyes twinkled at me. He had thick, blond hair, a dimple that he didn't show often and was quite handsome, in build and features.

"Better," I said.

"Good. Very good. Lay your head here," he pulled my face against the hollow of his shoulder, where it was comfortable. "Now, I will tell you of how I and twenty others broke away from my race and formed the Reth Alliance."

~

"She's asleep. That story will bore even the most avid listener," Ildevar said softly as he closed Breanne's door behind him. "How is the young man doing after the loss of his father?"

"Kevis says he and Kalenegar placed a healing sleep," Trajan sighed. "A few months ago, I might have said all this was impossible. I may never say those words again."

"I believe I said something similar perhaps a hundred thousand years ago," Ildevar smiled.

~

Hank's Journal

Sherman Weathers was holed up in the suite where Ross Gideon had been held. In addition to killing Ross, Sherman had shot two other agents. Without an obsession, he'd never have done any of those things.

"Hold on," I placed a hand on Bill's shoulder—he gripped his Ranos pistol tightly and prepared to kick down the suite's outside door.

"What is it?" Bill's eyes held concern as he turned to me.

"It's not just Sherman in there," I warned. I didn't add that this information had been passed mentally to me seconds earlier.

There's a chimera, a lion snake shifter and two Sirenali waiting inside, I sent. *Weathers is dead already.*

What's the plan? Bill returned.

How about you skip us inside and we open fire? Opal joined our conversation.

Chimera, I reminded her. *They can blast fire with a dying breath. Don't need to burn the building down if we can help it.*

How about I freeze everybody inside and you can do whatever the hell you want with them afterward? Someone new joined our party. Yes, he'd likely been called to come to our aid, and freezing a moment in time was one of the talents inherited from his Elemaiyan ancestors. That talent had been enhanced, once he'd become Saa Thalarr. Griffin, also known as Brenten Arden, appeared beside us.

The Sirenali die first, I said. *Then the others. We can't question any of them; it's too dangerous.*

I'll mist inside and place the freeze, Griffin said. *Then you kill.*

Agreed, Bill checked the charge on his pistol.

Yeah, Opal added. I turned my gaze toward Gavin and Charles—both nodded.

Griffin became mist and pulled us inside it before traveling through walls to find those waiting for us in the suite.

CHAPTER 15

Earth—past
Hank's Journal

Charles and Gavin decapitated the Sirenali in a fraction of a second, leaving the lion snake shifter and the chimera to the rest of us. Opal shot the lion snake immediately while my smaller Thifilathi gripped the chimera's throat and crushed it, preventing it from blowing fire. I tossed its body away the moment I realized it was dead. The enemy should have left Sherman Weathers alive; we would have happily killed him as well.

"Dan Kelsey's on the way," Bill said after ending the call on his cellphone.

"I'll check him for obsession," I growled. I hadn't turned back—I realized it when I spoke. My voice is always lower, the growls easier to form when I'm Thifilathi.

"No, keep that," Opal held out a hand. "If somebody shows up who's obsessed, then we need to scare the hell out of 'em," she smiled.

Dan Kelsey and two agents arrived twenty minutes later. He wasn't obsessed, but both his agents were. Dan swore when Gavin and Charles disarmed both after their first shots went wild—vampires were so much faster than any human might ever be. Hands grasping weapons had been knocked aside before pistols were snatched away and two agents were held—one-handed—by two vampires with red eyes and fangs showing.

"Obsessed," Bill explained quietly. FBI Director Dan Kelsey stared at two agents whose faces were tinged with blue as their feet hung inches off the floor.

"Fuck me," Dan muttered. "Anybody got cuffs?" Three sets were handed over immediately.

"I want in on this one," Dan Kelsey checked the gun in his shoulder holster before slipping into his suit coat. We'd dropped off the two agents at a local holding facility and placed them under heavy guard before going back to the hotel, briefing Dan and considering our next target. Griffin actually offered good advice as we discussed our plan of attack.

Ildevar joined us—Breanne was asleep and he was as deadly as any Ra'Ak ever was. He, like many others of his race, wasn't susceptible to any kind of compulsion or obsession. Older Ra'Ak, like older vampires, built up an immunity over time and Ildevar was very, very old.

"I've asked my people to hold off on announcing James Rome's death," Dan Kelsey said. "To keep the murderers from running away so fast. Maybe that'll help when we go after that bunch."

"It's likely they'll bring in additional firepower after they learn their Sirenali died here," Griffin pointed out.

"What do you suggest, then?" Bill asked.

"Bending time and taking these before the others. They won't suspect. It's an old Saa Thalarr trick."

"You're willing to do this?" my voice betrayed my surprise.

"I was instructed to do as much as possible," Griffin replied coldly. "It was also pointed out to me that my daughter saved my worthless hide, and I owe her. I do owe her," his shoulders slumped. "I have no legitimate power to properly repay that debt."

"I think acting like a parent would go a hell of a long way," Bill growled.

"As my past indicates, I have extremely poor skills at parenting."

"Then it's time you learned," I snapped. "In the meantime, get us to the Rome house in Los Angeles, at the proper time."

∽

SouthStar—present

"Casimir? I've never met anyone with that name," Kathleen almost giggled as Casimir took her hand and kissed it.

"That has been my name for centuries uncounted," Casimir smiled. "How do you like SouthStar?"

"It's lovely. Adele, Sharon and Lavonna helped me unpack, and they told me all about the gishi fruit and the groves. Cori and Dori brought my breakfast this morning, and then invited me for a tour. Did you know that there's a unicorn and a white wolf who live here? They're shapeshifters. I've always loved unicorns, but I never thought they were real."

"My lady, there are many wondrous things at SouthStar," Casimir said. "Come. Have tea with me and we will discuss some of them."

∽

Earth—past

Hank's Journal

"I thought you might need help," Kalenegar said stiffly as he appeared with Trajan.

"I didn't mean to upset you," I held up a hand. "I was just surprised, that's all." I'd asked him why he'd come the moment he'd appeared with the werewolf.

"I understand that—up to a point."

"Then we welcome the assistance," I said. "Is Ashe with Kay and Breanne?"

"Yes. He has moved both of them into his suite of rooms and is guarding them while they sleep. He brought his vampire father, plus Amos Thompson, Bear Wright and Salidar DeLuca to help."

I couldn't help smiling when he mentioned Amos Thompson and Bear Wright—the white buffalo and grizzly bear shapeshifters. Who wouldn't be surprised by those two guards? I hoped Breanne got the opportunity to see both.

"Ready?" Griffin asked.

"Ready," I nodded to him. He transported us to Los Angeles, four hours earlier.

~

"I don't like those people," Quin offered a beer to Alan. They'd helped themselves to what was inside the refrigerator after tying up James Rome's housekeeper and locking her in the laundry room.

"The job's done, why do they want to come back?" Alan asked. "The money's already in my new account; they don't have access," he added. "So it's not for the obvious reason."

"My ride to Mexico will be here in an hour, so I hope this little visit doesn't interfere with that," Quin sucked on the bottle of beer.

"Yeah—I was offered a place with somebody in Juarez," Alan agreed. "I'll check that out."

"Too bad Rome's dead, we could rub it in his face," Quin laughed.

Alan jumped when the one who'd commanded him to kill James Rome Sr. appeared beside him, accompanied by several others.

He screamed when the room was suddenly filled with many others, and the giant serpent who gulped down his new master made Alan fall to the floor in petrified horror.

~

Hank's Journal

Ra'Ak are terrifying when they're angry. Ildevar was angry. It's too bad a Sirenali has no recourse against a Ra'Ak's teeth or appetite. Gavin removed the head of the second Sirenali before he could place an obsession. Like before, I grabbed the chimera and squeezed the life from it, but the lion snake shifter turned humanoid and dropped to his knees, begging for his life.

"No." I tossed the chimera aside and held out my hand to keep Opal from shooting him. "This is Norian Keef's brother, and he was involved in Norian's death. This justice belongs to Queen Lissa."

Since Yaredolak didn't understand English, I spoke to him in Alliance common, telling him he would face justice on Le-Ath Veronis for his part in Norian Keef's death.

"If Lissa does not kill you herself, I will," Ildevar hissed at Yaredolak after coming back to himself.

"Bro, want to clean out the bodies or leave 'em here?" Trajan asked. He and Charles had dispatched the obsessed humans who'd murdered Jayson's father.

"Leave the humans; I'll tell the department they're here for pick up," Dan Kelsey grimaced. One body was headless, the other savaged. "I'll let my people know they ah, resisted."

"Where would you like the others delivered?" Kal asked. "And someone should release the housekeeper who is locked in the closet."

"Take the shifters to the lab in D.C. if possible," Bill said. "Dan, why don't you tell your locals to free the woman after we're gone?"

"Good enough," Dan jerked his cellphone from a pocket to make the call.

"Inform your people the bodies are coming," Kal replied and swept out a hand, causing the chimera and Sirenali bodies to disappear.

"Who wishes to help me deliver this one to Lissa?" Ildevar frowned at Reedy.

"I will come," Kal offered.

Ashe's Journal

"I had to place a healing sleep," Kevis sighed. "He just kept rambling about how he and his father never really got along."

Sali stood near the door of the adjoining hotel room, where Kevis had taken Jayson Rome. Sali had both Falchani blades strapped to his back as he stood guard; Caylon Black had instructed him the art of the blade more than fifty years earlier, after Trajan and Trace taught him everything they could about hand-to-hand combat. Sali was lethal, and not just as a werewolf.

Sali had likely heard all of Kevis' conversation with Jayson, just as I had. At least Kay and Breanne had slept through it—I had an extra shield around them so their sleep wouldn't be disturbed.

"I heard from Hank—he says they got the others, and managed to take a prisoner—Norian Keef's brother."

"Seriously?" Kevis asked. "Another lion snake shifter?"

"Looks like he was involved somehow in Norian's death. They're taking him to Lissa for judgment," I said.

"Good place for him," Kevis agreed. "Norian wasn't popular by any stretch, but to have his own brother involved in the murder? That's bullshit."

"Kevis, I'm not sure I've ever heard you say bullshit," I grinned at him.

"Dad always says to save those words for when they'll have the most profound effect," Kevis grinned back.

~

Le-Ath Veronis—present

Lissa's Journal

"Well, Reedy, I always knew you'd end up causing more trouble," I said.

Ildevar and Kalenegar dumped a quaking Yaredolak before me seconds earlier, and Kalenegar held a shield around the troublesome lion snake shapeshifter so he couldn't get away.

"I just never suspected you'd help somebody kill your own brother," I went on. "You sold him out twice, you filth. You didn't care if he died either time. I'll let Ildevar and the Vampire Council decide your fate this time."

I was glad Reedy didn't offer excuses. He didn't look me in the eye, either, keeping his head down and staring at his bare feet. Perhaps the obsession a Sirenali had laid prevented it. It no longer mattered; he was a dead shifter, I knew that much. Ildevar would make sure of that.

"I will place a shield around his cage in your dungeon," Kalenegar offered. "He will not escape by turning and slithering past the bars."

"Thank you," I nodded at Kal. "Saves me the trouble of doing it myself."

Your sister is fine—she is resting and guarded by the Mighty Hand, Ildevar sent mindspeech after Kalenegar folded us to the dungeon and tossed Reedy into a cell with power. He then placed the appropriate shield; it wouldn't keep me or my guards out—it merely held Reedy in. The Larentii were quite talented in the use of their power.

Is there a problem with Bree? I asked Ildevar. *Did something happen?*

Too many responsibilities weigh upon her and she is not strong at the moment, Ildevar replied. *The Larentii helped a great deal, however.*

Tell them to let me know if there is anything I can do, I said. *This is my only living sibling. The other two are dead.*

I know this, and it matters to me a great deal, as your sister holds my heart. I never thought a M'Fiyah would come to me, and to have it be her, his sending held a great deal of reverence. *It also gives me hope in a very dark time,* he added.

Let's hope we have enough strength to withstand the dark time, I replied.

"It is most fortunate we brought a replacement for my brother," V'ili stroked Janine's head in seeming affection.

"Most fortunate that Moxas advised us to do so," Acrimus agreed. "I am greatly incensed that our slaves have been killed and your cousins murdered by the filth who oppose us."

"We will bring others of my kind, and together we will devise a way to destroy our enemy," V'ili hissed. "Slave, bring towels. I wish to swim and think. Let none disturb me in my pool." V'ili stalked away, leaving Janine behind to do his bidding.

"Moxas, how might I reward you for your foresight?" Calhoun asked. "We lost some, that is true, but we always allow for such losses. It makes our revenge sweeter in the long term."

"We have comfortable quarters and the best of food," Moxas swept out an arm to include his twin and their surroundings. "However, we feel somewhat lonely. Saxom would very much like his love delivered to him."

"I wasn't aware you had a companion," Calhoun turned to Saxom.

"A love for the ages," Saxom nodded.

"Who might that be? I will bring her to you."

"Her name is Kiarra," Saxom smiled malevolently. "She belongs to the race known as Saa Thalarr."

Earth—past

Breanne's Journal

I remember waking once before to find Charles kneeling at my bedside, his face propped on his hands while he watched me sleep. He was doing it again, only he grinned when I opened my eyes this time and said, "It's about time, sleepyhead."

"Are all hyperactive vampires this insufferable?" I asked. Yes, my grumpy side is always in control when I wake. It's the law of inevitability, sort of like death and taxes.

"I'm insufferable?" He pointed to his chest in mock disbelief.

"No, honey, I'm just teasing," I pulled myself into a sitting position and raked tangled hair away from my face.

"I like it when you call me honey." Charles rose and settled on the side of my bed so he could put an arm around me.

"Yeah." I leaned my head on his shoulder with a contented sigh. "Where's everybody else?"

"Having breakfast. I offered to get you up," he kissed my forehead. "But I wanted to watch you sleep for a few minutes first."

"Sounds like a chore," I muttered.

"No—none of that. It makes me happy. Fills my heart with good feelings," Charles murmured before kissing me again.

"Can the good feelings extend to the bathroom, so I can clean up and brush my teeth?"

"Haven't you discovered you can do that with power yet? The Saa Thalarr do it all the time."

"Really? What do you know about that?" I asked. Yes, he'd know that in the future, but this Charles? That puzzled me.

"I'll have you know that Adam Chessman, our former Chief Enforcer, is Saa Thalarr. Wlodek knows it. Merrill knows it and my sire Flavio knows it. I'm naturally curious. Haven't you figured that out, yet?"

"So you admit you're nosy," I pointed out.

"With an enormous amount of pride," he chuckled. "Now get with it, clean up with power and let's get to breakfast before they eat everything."

"If Trajan orders, that's a real possibility," I said. Charles laughed.

"We killed four Sirenali, but I'm still concerned that they might bring in more," Hank said during breakfast. I sat across the table from him, squeezed between Charles and Jayson. Jayson looked like anyone might after losing a parent, so I'd sent him *Love* the moment I took my seat at the table.

He'd perked up a little afterward, so I resolved to send him more *Love* later. Kevis was seated on Jayson's other side, so I figured somebody had deliberately placed him between the two who might do him the most good.

"They may have already done that," Kal said. "If the Khos'Mirai is operating true to form, he may have advised such."

"That's not good," I said. I knew from reading Lissa how dangerous Saxom's twin could be. "Who knows how many Sirenali he might tell them to bring? How much danger do you think we're in because the Khos'Mirai is interfering?"

"I think it's one of his clones, but the results will be the same." Hank blew an aggravated stream of smoke. "There is no way to tell how many Sirenali were rescued from their destruction in the past by our enemy. With the Khos'Mirai directing the movement of Sirenali, that will be a convenient way for the enemy to trap the unsuspecting and pull them into their forces. If all are eventually obsessed, what might we do to intervene?"

I stared at Hank in alarm. Somehow, I wasn't sure he wanted that information revealed—at least in the way it was. "I understood that the Khos'Mirai's agenda was to cause destruction—for everybody, and not just for the opposition," I said. "That his heritage makes him desire chaos. To think he might be on your side is to court disaster."

"What heritage are you talking about?" Bill leaned in so he could see me from farther down the table.

"He's half Bright Elemaiya and half Dark Elemaiya—just like his twin, Saxom. I worry that since Saxom appears to be back in business, that his obsession with Kiarra may manifest again." I shook my head— how easy would it be to blame Griffin for that? He'd chosen Saxom as a healer long ago. For a time, Saxom had performed his duties and hid his true nature. His obsession with Kiarra finally caused him to reveal himself, and he'd died for it.

Except he was back again, and likely ready to create havoc again. This time, however, he had powerful, rogue gods at his back. I shivered, just thinking about it. Well, there wasn't anything else I could do except send mindspeech to my sister.

Lissa? I'd had to gauge the time difference, but it wasn't difficult.

Bree? Where are you?

Same place, I sent. *I just wanted to warn you—with Saxom likely back in the saddle, I worry that he'll ask for help to get to Kiarra. Has she been warned? Are they taking precautions?*

Adam and Merrill are keeping her at NorthStar as much as possible, because Ashe has it shielded, in addition to SouthStar and EastStar, Lissa replied. *I'll let her know you're concerned, too, in case she feels like escaping for a while.*

Yeah, I said. *We don't need anybody else captured or killed.*

I hear that, Lissa agreed. *I'll tell Merrill, Adam and Pheligar, too.*

Thanks, I said and ended the conversation.

NorthStar—present

Adam's Journal

"Sweetheart, it's not just this timeline—what if they come after you back then? It's only us in that timeline where Breanne is, now—you, me and Justin in Fresno. How can we protect you better?"

Kiarra frowned at me. That meant she was irritated and studying the problem at the same time.

"I see you have discovered the difficulty in all this," Pheligar appeared beside us. Kiarra and I stood on the deck outside her suite in the early morning light. A thin fog lay over the gishi trees below us as we considered the problem.

"You and I were doing a difficult dance back then," Kiarra pointed a finger at Pheligar. "You muted the M'Fiyah between us, remember?"

"I recall it perfectly," Pheligar said. "I regret the wasted time."

"I regret more than that, and one of those things I regret is Saxom. Fucking Saxom. Bastard asshat shit-sticky Saxom," Kiarra muttered. She was never one to hold back the profanity; Pheligar had gotten used to that fact long ago. I was still coming to terms with it, especially as she often invented new expressions.

"Shit-sticky?" One of my eyebrows lifted minutely.

"Don't ask," she shuddered.

"I only wanted to make sure I wasn't traveling in the wrong direction."

"Ah, fecal expressions. How little I enjoy them," Pheligar sighed.

"That doesn't solve our problem in the past," Merrill walked onto the deck where Kiarra, Pheligar and I were having our conversation.

Pheligar had likely included him in the discussion wherever he was, and he'd chosen to join us now.

"It does not solve the problem," Pheligar agreed. It's surprising how he can express irritation without actually traveling the entire distance to that emotion.

"We can't pull ourselves out of there—can we?" I asked. "Wouldn't that change too much?"

"It could," Pheligar said. "It is better not to disrupt that time, as any changes could result in catastrophe later. Only the Three might involve themselves and still make things turn out as they should."

"What about placing guards? Ashe and Breanne appear to have their hands full, and we still don't know about Wisdom. He or she could be doing important work elsewhere," Merrill said.

"I can ask for Larentii guards," Pheligar said. "They can be discreet and disguise themselves as humans. Traveling in time will not be an issue for them. Shall I ask Ferrigar?"

"That's the best solution I know," I agreed. "Saxom and any Sirenali pets he has can't get past a Larentii—with power or obsession. If a rogue god shows up, the Larentii can send a message to Ashe or Breanne."

"I will visit Ferrigar now." Pheligar disappeared.

"This is crazy," Kiarra shook her head.

"That much is certain." I pulled her into my arms.

Earth—past

Breanne's Journal

He needs you. Hank's words were a plea for me to take Jayson back to the room Hank and I shared, only this time, we'd be alone. Hank wouldn't be there, to make me feel safe with Jayson. The thought of being alone with him and his desires frightened me.

Baby, don't be scared. Don't you think he knows not to hurt you? He needs sex, not play time, Hank attempted to reassure me.

"Come on," Jayson grabbed my hand and hauled me toward the

elevator. It was obvious he and Hank had already had a conversation, and I'd been excluded until now. We rode up the elevator in silence, but Jayson hadn't let go of my hand. I knew I was shaking. He didn't comment. Maybe that's how he did things—how did I know? I still couldn't read him, and I'd never read Belinda—I was too afraid.

"Take off your clothes," Jayson demanded the moment he shut the hotel room door behind him.

"Jayson," I broke away from him and held up a hand.

"Breanne. My love. My heart. My unexpected. Please take off your clothes. I need your warm body beneath mine. Now."

I blinked at Jayson. He'd never called me anything like that. I stared at him. "And just for right now," he added, "I'd like to be me when we fuck."

I breathed a sigh as I removed his disguise—he now looked like the Jayson Rome I'd met on a cool night in San Rafael. He turned to study himself in the mirror outside the small closet. He was taller. Blond. Handsome, with brown eyes. "Yeah. This is the face I want you to see when I make you come. Take off your clothes, Bree. I want to touch every part of you before we fuck."

"Bree, it's lunchtime." Jayson brushed hair back from my face. I'd fallen asleep half-sprawled across his body, the fingers of my right hand curved around his neck.

I wasn't coherent when I mumbled a reply, I know that much.

"Here, now, what's this?" Jayson's fingers lazily stroked my face. Yes, I'd bitten him the first time we had sex—he wanted it really bad. For those people who are just dying (pun intended) to be vampire, let me tell you, the taste of blood in your mouth is no good thing to wake up to.

Need to brush my teeth, I sent. I didn't want to open my mouth, that's for sure.

"Then get to it," he patted my behind before sliding off the bed and dragging me with him.

~

Bill had used the hours Jayson and I spent in bed to catch up on phone calls and track down more leads for obsessed humans. Four Sirenali had been killed, but their obsessions would outlive them. Janine was still out there unless I missed my guess, and who knew what she might end up doing?

The search for rogue-engineered gates continued on other worlds, and I had no idea how those investigations were progressing.

"At least the disappearances seem to have stopped, but we now have a shortage of plumbers, masons and such in the country's midsection," Bill grimaced. "I figure most of the missing may be at the bottom of that pit in Kansas."

"That dungeon took up a lot of space beneath the community. All of it imploded, taking the homes and businesses topside with it," Dan Kelsey said. He was still with us, although Griffin, Kal and Ildevar were gone. I'd missed seeing Griffin, and I couldn't really say how I felt about that. Yes, I was grateful for any help, but it made me feel more than uncomfortable. As for Kal and Ildevar, Hank said they'd left to run an errand and just hadn't come back yet.

"What about unusual activity—or increased crimes—murders and such?" Jayson asked. I'd given him more *Love* while he'd worked off some of his grief in bed with me, and he was ready to take anybody down who might have had something to do with his father's death.

Yes, Hank had already explained about the bodyguard, the driver and the Sirenali, but Jayson knew, just as the rest of us did, that this was a small portion of a larger plot. I was still a target, too, and I needed a new disguise to fool those hunting me.

Ashe and Kay walked in to join us for lunch—we were waiting for them before deciding where to go. I was tired of the limited vegetarian choices offered by the hotel restaurant, and the protein drinks were getting old, too.

"Let's go to NorthStar," Ashe sighed. "I got an invitation."

"But what about," I began. I didn't want Trajan or Bill placed in danger, because they were close by.

"Bree, we're with them. They'll be protected," Ashe said without mentioning names.

"Yeah," I hunched my shoulders. Ashe had been in the Mighty business for around four hundred years. I was still getting used to it. He'd recognized his power at age sixteen. I hadn't realized what I was until I was nearly sixty. Even then, somebody had to tell me. Just as Graegar said, it was a given I wasn't the Mighty Mind.

Bree, Ashe sent, *your circumstances interfered. Stop worrying about that, okay?*

How did you know what I was thinking?

Sweetheart, I love how your thoughts are on display at times.

Oh, sure, I returned. *Make fun of me, why don't you?*

Hey, if you two will stop mind texting, we can go eat, Salidar DeLuca informed both of us.

Sal, are you hungry? Ashe teased.

Dude, you ought to know the answer to that already, Sali declared. *I can hear Trajan's stomach growling from across the room.*

You know this isn't the same Trajan? I asked.

Just like I know it's not the same Bill. So do Mr. Thompson, Bear Wright and Mr. Evans. We've been briefed, Sali replied dryly.

So you wore underwear today. Big deal, I teased back. I wasn't prepared for Salidar DeLuca to start laughing.

"He loves underwear jokes," Ashe muttered.

"A werewolf ninja who laughs at juvenile humor?" I shook my head at Ashe.

"We all have our weaknesses," Ashe replied. "That part of him just never grew up."

"I like it," I said.

"Awesome," Sali walked over and draped an arm over my shoulder. "Let's blow this joint. I'm starved."

"A Ra'Ak has never stood upon the Larentii homeworld." Ferrigar,

Head of the Larentii Council nodded to Ildevar Wyyld. "I am pleased to welcome you as the first."

"You called me, Father?" Kalenegar said. Ferrigar had greeted Ildevar first before turning to his only remaining child.

"Yes. Pheligar informed me that security is required to protect Kiarra in the past. I have offered the services of four Larentii for that task. We will blend in with the humanoid population of Earth's past and place shields should they become necessary. We will be prepared to send information to the Mighty should Kiarra be attacked. She is a member of the Larentii Council, after all, and is deserving of our protection."

"You say we, father, as if you include yourself in that number," Kalenegar observed.

"That is because I do include myself in that number. I have chosen three others, and together we will provide hidden security in the past. The Khos'Mirai cannot see us, and neither can rogue gods. It is the way we were made."

"Father, are you sure this is wise?" Kalenegar had his differences with Ferrigar, but he couldn't hold back the concern he felt for his parent.

"It will be easy, and I have not left the Larentii homeworld for any length of time in millennia. I grow somewhat bored, child. I hope you understand that."

"I do." Kalenegar nodded.

"I must say, you are not as cold toward me as you usually are," Ferrigar said.

"Father, I recently observed one whose last words with his father were unkind. He grieves for the loss of his parent, now."

"Understood. I will be leaving before the sun sets at my home," Ferrigar said. "The Wise Ones will be in charge in my absence."

"Good choice," Kal said. "They will inform you, should your assistance be required."

"Of course," Ferrigar replied.

∼

NorthStar—present

Breanne's Journal

I'd been to NorthStar before; the last time for the biggest barbecue ever. This time, only Grace, Devin, Kevis, Karzac, Graeger and Barrigar were there, in addition to Kiarra, Adam, Merrill, Franklin and Shane.

"You're kidding," Jayson swore as he stared at the miles of gishi trees below the enormous house.

"SouthStar is bigger," I sighed.

"Four times this size," Kevis agreed, handing a drink to Jayson. "SouthStar covers a third of the Southern Continent on Avendor."

"I can't see the end of the trees," Jayson said.

"They're lost in the mists," Ashe said, clapping a hand on Kevis' shoulder. "Can I talk to you for a few minutes?" he asked.

"Sure." Kevis walked away with Ashe. Hank took his place. He already had a drink—an old fashioned. No surprise.

"How did you get addicted to those things?" I asked.

"When I fought in World War II, somebody introduced me to it," Hank said, chewing on red drink straws. "I like it. It takes a lot of alcohol to even give me a slight buzz."

"You fought in the second World War?" Jayson stared at Hank.

"And in the Korean War, Vietnam, Desert Storm, Afghanistan—had an assignment and things to learn. Drank old fashioneds the whole time. Come on, let's sit on one of those porch swings and enjoy the day. Someone will bring food out as soon as it's ready."

Others joined us as if called. Kevis and his parents, Grace and Karzac. Devin. Graeger. Barrigar. Trajan and the others from Earth. Dan Kelsey, who'd been included, was seeing things he never imagined he might see, including Larentii in their natural form.

Sali removed his sheaths and blades to sit on the deck nearby. Werewolves tend to be graceful when they move, but Sali's movements were works of art. I knew it was the blade master's training, but it still fascinated me.

Kiarra, Merrill and Adam joined us and small talk occurred all around me. I was happy just to listen while we waited for the meal to be served.

~

Ashe's Journal

"She'll let me hug and kiss her, but when I get a little past those things, she freezes up," I huffed.

"I believe Bree will tell you what I'm about to tell you—that Kay was virgin when she died, and that's who you're dealing with. Kalia is asleep, and even if she were awake, she'd be more nervous than Kay." Kevis shook his head and emptied the glass of bourbon he carried. I'd folded us to SouthStar for our talk—I didn't want to take the chance that Kay might come looking for me. Dad and Mr. Thompson were keeping an eye on her while I was gone.

"I've never been to bed with a virgin," I said. "Now what?"

"Talk to Hank. I believe he has made an extensive study of sex," Kevis ducked his head to hide the grin.

"Of course he has," I tossed out a hand in helpless surrender. "Do I really need to consult the dark side?"

"Breanne will go to Hank before she'll go to anyone else—have you noticed? If he crooks a finger, she's there."

"There is that," I nodded. "Don't you have any idea what he might suggest?"

"None."

"Fine. There's something else, too."

"What's that?"

"We're sort of in the same boat, you and I," I began.

"What do you mean?" Kevis had no idea.

"Kay keeps asking me to let Bree live with us. She wants her close. Even suggested that we bring Breanne into the room with us a couple of times."

"And you don't want Breanne?"

"No, that's not it. I do. I just had no idea what was in front of me when I hurt her. Now, every time she comes close, she's

243

uncomfortable. Both times she's bitten me, it was the best sex I ever had and my clothes were still on."

"Yeah. I heard that from Jayson, too. Several times." Kevis was grumpy about that fact.

"Kevis, don't wait. Don't be an idiot like I was. Tell her. Tell her she makes you harder than a titanium rocket."

"I didn't say that," Kevis said.

"It's true, though, isn't it? I think Sali has the hots for her, too, and I have no idea what she'll think about that. Although she did say she liked his preference for juvenile humor."

"How does Trajan feel about that?"

"He doesn't know, yet, but he and Sali get along pretty good. The big question comes back to Breanne."

"And Kay. Talk to Hank—I'm serious. See if he has any ideas."

"Let's talk to him together, then," I said.

"Feeling uncomfortable?" Kevis probed. He was his father's son, all right, as well as being the best psychiatrist in either Alliance.

"You know it," I said. "Come on, I'll send mindspeech to Hank."

CHAPTER 16

NorthStar—present
Hank's Journal

"I never expected to be asked for advice on sex by one of the Mighty," I said. I covered the smile in my voice—Ashe wouldn't take it well. At least I doubted that he would.

"You seem to know a lot," Kevis picked up the conversation. I'd found myself cornered by both of them shortly after we'd eaten.

"I do."

"Then what's your suggestion—for Kay? To make her comfortable with this?"

"Let her make the moves," I said.

"That sounds great, except I don't think she'll ever do that," Ashe said.

"How comfortable are you being naked?" I asked.

"Comfortable enough. I'm a shapeshifter," Ashe shrugged.

"Good. Show her the bumblebee bat. Tell her all about it. Tell her about shapeshifters being comfortable in their natural state. Sit beside her naked, or get in the pool with her naked. Don't be bothered if you have an erection the size of a baseball bat. Trust me, it makes them curious."

"Are you kidding me?"

"Look, what will it hurt? If she says she's uncomfortable, then cover up. It's a simple fix. Talk about sex if she asks. Tell her it feels good. Hell, maybe she'll ask Breanne or somebody else about it."

"I want to talk to Breanne, anyway. I think Kay is uncomfortable about her scars. Bree can fix that."

"Then do that first. She won't get naked with you if she's ashamed or embarrassed about her body."

"Yeah. Good point."

~

Breanne's Journal

"Bree, we need to talk to you," Hank said. He, Kevis and Ashe stood beside my chair as I was about to doze off in the afternoon sun at NorthStar.

"Huh?" I jerked awake.

"Baby, we didn't mean to scare you," Hank said, putting a hand on my shoulder. "We need a favor. A big favor."

"What's that?" I rubbed my eyes—the brightness of the light was a little painful at first.

"Can you take care of Kay's scars?" Hank asked. "I think they're preventing her from having sex."

"Oh, yeah. I wanted to do that anyway," I leaned forward in my chair, preparing to rise.

"You, ah, have to go by yourself, and uh, make it seem like your idea," Ashe said.

"Seriously? I thought she was asking," I said. "Never mind," I said after getting a good look at Ashe and Hank's faces. "I'll see what I can do." I stalked away from all three of them. I knew where Kay was—sitting on the flagstones and soaking her feet in the swimming pool.

~

"Bree!" Kay was definitely glad to see me as I sat beside her and folded my jeans up to put my feet in the water.

"Hey." I put an arm around her. "How are you? Seems like we hardly see each other."

"I'm good. Probably better than I've ever been," she said, pulling a leg up so her toes would stick out of the water. Even her toes were perfect.

"Great. I have a question for you," I said.

"What's that?" Bright-blue eyes studied me carefully, wondering what I might ask.

"I know you have those scars, and I know you don't like them," I said. "I can get rid of them, if you want."

"Really?" Kay stared at me, now.

"Yeah. That way, you could wear a bikini if you want. You'd look amazing in a bikini. A blue one—to match your eyes."

"Yeah," she breathed. "Will it hurt?"

"Nope. All I have to do is *Change What Was* just a little, and presto, you'll be perfect."

"Can we do it here, or should we go somewhere else?" she asked.

"We can do it here, but I shine pretty bright when I do this, so maybe you ought to close your eyes."

"Oh, yeah." Her eyes closed immediately. I gathered power and light shone around me.

Hank's Journal

"I think Breanne could ask for anything, and Kay would do her best to get it," Ashe breathed as we watched from a distance. Ashe had to shield us; Breanne's light is blindingly bright.

"Breanne never asks for anything," I muttered. She didn't and hadn't.

"What are we discussing?" Opal approached us. "What's Bree doing now? I need sunglasses around her."

"She's fixing Kay's scars," Kevis said.

"Oh. Kay has scars?"

"Let's talk," Kevis took Opal's elbow and led her away.

Ashe and I watched as Bree's light faded. Then, to our surprise, Kay lifted her top to examine her stomach. She squealed with delight and hugged Breanne. "There it is. It's done," I said.

Breanne's Journal

Kay was so excited, she squealed and hugged me. If we'd been standing, she might have danced, too.

"Bree," her eyes became huge, "tell me what it's like."

"What?"

"Sex. Tell me."

"You don't want to tap into Kalia's," I began. "Wait. Never mind. That's not sex."

"Yeah," her joy dimmed for just a moment. "Please?"

"Look, as long as you're with somebody who cares about you, and who you care about, it doesn't matter," I said. "It's nice if you can have a climax right away," I added, "but that doesn't always happen."

"But the way Hank looks at you," she said shyly.

"Huh?" I blinked at her in surprise.

"Well, when you're not watching, he sometimes looks as if he'd like to grab you up and haul you away. You know. Like that."

"Uh, okay. That sounds like how Ashe looks at you, sometimes."

"Really?" She was definitely interested now.

"Oh, yeah."

"Wow. Uh, what should I do about that?"

"Well, you can invite him to go swimming. Or get in the hot tub. Have you kissed him—you kissing him, and not the other way around?"

"He's so tall," she sighed.

"Yeah. He's that, all right."

"I know he wants to go farther, but until now, I didn't want him to see the scars and well, I just feel nervous. I'm afraid I'll do something wrong and he won't like it."

"Trust me, you won't do anything wrong," I said. "He knows what to do—let him guide you. I had no idea what to do when Hank and I had sex the first time. I told him that's how it was, and he wasn't shy about explaining everything as we went along. He made sure I enjoyed it as much as he did."

"You think Ashe will do that?"

"I don't know. Everybody's different, and nothing seems to embarrass Hank."

Hank's Journal

I wasn't aware of Ashe's hypersensitive hearing until he eavesdropped on Kay's conversation with Breanne. He linked me in on the conversation, too. I didn't care that Breanne explained things— I came out of it in a very positive light. I found myself smiling, in fact.

"Breanne's doing all the work," Ashe breathed beside me. "Kay wants me. Is that amazing or what?"

"Breanne has done more for you than you can possibly imagine," I reminded him before walking away.

Ashe's Journal

"I want to go back," Sali informed me. "When you do. I can help."

"Are you sure?"

"I want to."

"It could be dangerous, Sal."

"I know. I'm willing to take the risk."

"You know," I motioned for him to sit with me in the arboretum at NorthStar, "we still ought to take the car out for a spin—on a real highway."

"I know." Sali sat across from me, his dark eyes searching my face.

"A lot of things came between us back then. It was stupid. I was stupid. I can't say I'm not still stupid, because I manage to make mistakes. I just try to think them through before I choose stupidity."

"Is that Falchani wisdom?" I grinned at Sali.

"I paraphrased," he grinned back. "Three syllables." He laughed, then. That was an old joke between us.

"Did Caylon really enter your name on the rolls as a Falchani warrior?" I asked.

"Yeah. If you fight in a war and come out a hero, that option is made available. I hear it was offered to Queen Lissa, too. She refused."

"Are you the only werewolf on their list?"

"I think so." Sali was back to grinning. "If I wanted, I could get a full set of tattoos. I'm entitled. Obviously, I'm listed as a member of the Wolf Clan."

"I can't imagine you'd belong to the flamingoes," I said.

"I don't think there is a flamingo clan," Sali chuckled.

"Probably a good thing. I don't think pink bird tattoos will instill fear in anybody."

"Chewie was a shapeshifter," Sali said. We both burst into laughter.

Breanne's Journal

"Baby?" Hank's arms slipped around me as I stood on the highest balcony of the NorthStar mansion.

"Hi." I turned in his embrace and put my arms around his neck. He leaned in to kiss me. How happy was I he'd finally decided to do that? Hank's kisses are mesmerizing. Maybe he knows that. I didn't care. All I cared about was his mouth on mine, his tongue exploring, his teeth nipping my lower lip gently before pulling away. Somewhere along the way, Henry Hank Bell had learned how to kiss—in addition to learning how to fuck.

"So, where did the Henry come from?" I asked. That was the name on his driver's license, after all—he just went by Hank.

"Reverse nickname," he grinned before rubbing my nose with his. "I wanted to use Hank, but that's a nickname for Henry."

"Really."

"Yeah." He bent his head and nipped my neck before placing a kiss there. A hand slipped down and unbuttoned my jeans. Fingers made their way inside. I gasped when they made contact with a sensitive area.

"I'm gonna fuck you against that wall back there," Hank backed me up. "I don't care who sees or hears it."

At that moment, I didn't care, either. Some people might call it passion. Some might call it the heat of the moment—or an inflamed desire. It was a dance as old as time itself, and might take something stronger than both of us to stop. That's when Kalenegar arrived with Graegar and Barrigar. Hank and I were about to be included in energy sex—while having actual sex. I had no idea how that might turn out. I didn't care, either.

～

Ashe's Journal

All he'd said was *bring Kay*. That's it. I realized soon enough as we landed on the high balcony at NorthStar. The Larentii were joining in and I stared—Hank already had Breanne against the wall and she was holding onto him with all her strength, her legs wrapped around his hips.

"Are they?" Kay began before gripping my hand.

"Yeah. Sweetheart, the Larentii are about to join in, and that's the best and most intense sex you can ever have. Say you'll do this with me."

"I," she hesitated. "Yes. Let's do this. I will." Kay seemed determined, suddenly.

"I won't hurt you. I won't ever do that," I promised, lifting her top over her head. "You are the most beautiful thing I've ever seen," I leaned in to kiss her. Her hands gripped my face as she deepened the kiss. To hell with clothing. I made it disappear with power.

~

Adam's Journal

Pheligar stalked into the room and lifted Kiarra into his arms. That's when I felt it—the building of power toward a climax that might touch anyone at NorthStar. Ashe had us shielded, and I imagined that shield would protect the rest of Avendor from energy sex.

Too bad—they'd definitely enjoy it. Pheligar added his power to the rest, and it was customary to provide power in return. Kiarra and I did so.

~

Hank's Journal

In later years, it was known as *the earthquake that rocked the Southern Continent.* Nothing was destroyed, but it was described as a great jolt followed by a quick series of intense aftershocks. If Ashe hadn't already had shields in place, it likely would have destroyed the planet in a climax felt by other worlds light-years away.

~

Kay's Journal

I won't ever forget my first time. It wasn't Kalia's first time, but it may have been the first time her body felt pleasure. Ashe's eyes opened shortly after mine did, and he smiled. Our bodies were still connected, although spent.

"That was amazing," I whispered. His smile widened.

"That was more than amazing," he replied. "I'm not sure there are words to describe it properly."

He was right—there were no words. Anything that might be written or said would fall far short of the reality. Only the lingering sensation and the memory of it remained.

"Ready?" Ashe asked.

I didn't want his body to leave mine, but eventually it had to happen. "We'll do this again?" I asked.

"You and me for sure—whenever you want. We have to invite the Larentii, or they'll have to volunteer," he added while his body disconnected from mine. "I know a place," he said, and before I could blink, he'd transported me elsewhere.

"Where," I turned to look. We were immersed in water beside a waterfall. Yes, it was a fantasy. A dream most anyone might have. Ashe made it happen for us.

"SouthStar—on the southern edge of it, before the jungles begin," he breathed against my mouth. That let me know he wasn't quite done for the day.

Breanne's Journal

"Avilepha?"

Hank's voice, but not Hank's arms. "Huh?" I said. My vocabulary never improves until I'm fully awake. Coffee generally helps.

"Wake, Lara'Kayan."

Kalenegar.

"She's coming back to us."

Barrigar.

"Did you like that?"

Graegar—with a smile in his voice and gentle fingers on my face.

"Honey," I opened my eyes and stared at the concerned faces around me, "I want to do that again. Just not right now. I don't think I'll survive that if we do it again so soon."

Kal was the one who held me, and we were in bright sunlight—the Larentii were feeding and replenishing their energy. No surprise—a lot of it had been expended in energy sex. In this case, it should probably be termed *explosive* energy sex.

"Hank?" I blinked at him—the sunlight on Avendor was blindingly bright.

"Here." He pushed a pair of dark sunglasses onto my face. "Better?" He grinned.

"Oh, yeah." I relaxed in Kal's arms. Were we naked? Yep.

"Juice?" Barrigar offered a glass with a straw. I sipped it and shuddered with pleasure—pineapple-gishi fruit juice. "You like that, don't you?" Kal said.

"It's amazing."

"I'll make sure you have it every day if you want."

"We'll save it for once a week," I reached up to pat Kal's face. He smiled and kissed me.

"It is our responsibility to make sure our mate is tended to after sex of any kind," the corners of Kal's lips curled up slightly. "Next time, I wish to be the one connected directly with you."

"Are we really talking about this?" I made a face at him.

"There is no subject that cannot be discussed," Graegar said. "Embarrassment, you will discover, has no meaning to a Larentii."

"So the rules of conversation don't apply to Larentii?" I asked, turning to Graegar.

"The rules?"

"Never discuss politics or religion," I said.

"Which aspects of each? We can argue both sides," Barrigar said. "Or make a case for a middle ground," he added.

"Forget I said anything about that," I sighed.

"We can talk anytime you wish," he said. "About anything. Send mindspeech if we are not together."

"What if you're busy?"

"I can bend time, dearest," Barrigar smiled at me.

"Bree, Bill says we need to go home," Hank interrupted.

"Honey," I grumped as his handsome face replaced Barrigar's beside me.

"I know. Someday, we won't have this mess hanging over our heads," he said.

"I need to dress," I pointed out.

"No," Kal breathed as Graegar ran a hand over my body—he was washing me with power. My clothes appeared afterward—I should have expected it. In less than half an hour, we were back on Earth in the past.

∿

Earth—past
  Fresno, California
  Humanoid construction is generally designed to keep light out, not allow it in, Ferrigar sent to Connegar as they walked through the large house together. Ferrigar formed a large skylight overhead as they wandered through the widest room in the house.
  It is fortunate that this house was empty and close by, Connegar replied, enlarging the windows in the house until they covered almost every inch of wall space. *It will make our work simpler.*
  Does Lissa know you're here? Ferrigar asked.
  She does. I informed her before I left. When will Evagar and Diagar arrive?
  Soon. Do you want the first watch?
  I have already placed my shield around the shields Kiarra and Adam have in place. I will know if she leaves by vehicle or folds space.
  The child is nearly nine years of age, as they measure time, Ferrigar sighed. *He attends a local school, and she transports him there by vehicle most mornings. We should guard him and his father as well.*
  Already in my plans, Connegar returned.

∿

Earth—past
  Breanne's Journal
  Ashe and Kay didn't come back with us. Hank grinned when I mentioned it. "Did everybody get sex?" I asked.
  "Every adult inside Ashe's shield got sex," Hank said. "Unless the Larentii put up a shield or deliberately lock you out, you'll be included. They never include anyone who's under the age of consent. Usually, energy sex covers a fifty-yard radius if no shield is in place.

With that much power involved, it would have involved the entire planet plus a few other celestial bodies."

"So Ashe and Kay got hooked up. They're probably in a tropical pool somewhere, with a waterfall and everything, having fun," I pointed out. "While we're here."

"You want a waterfall?" Hank's left eyebrow lifted.

"Honey, I want lots of things. Wanting hasn't gotten me very far in the past, so I ignore it."

"What if I want to make my baby happy?" Hank asked. "What would that take?"

"Can we discuss this another time? If we do it now, it'll just point out what I don't have."

"What's wrong?" Kevis, Charles and Salidar DeLuca walked in. Salidar—Sali—had the twin Falchani blades strapped to his back again. Dressed completely in black with only a few white highlights on his close-fitting shirt, he looked like a ninja.

"Hey," I said. "I didn't think anybody could see ninjas."

"Are you sure you're seeing me, then?" Sali grinned, likely because I spoke to him, first.

"I'm probably talking to myself, too," I nodded. "In addition to not seeing you."

"Now you're getting it," he laughed.

"Thanks for the, uh, you know. Earlier," Kevis said.

"According to the Larentii, there is nothing that cannot be discussed," I told him.

"Then thanks for the mind-blowing sex. Next time, make sure I'm not sitting close to my mom and dad, okay?"

"Oh, jeez, I'm sorry," I said.

"Breanne, do not apologize. He enjoyed it, the rascal," Hank blew a curl of smoke.

"I think we all had a jolly good time," Charles grinned. "Opal said she hadn't had sex in a while, and that made up for it."

"You know, I wasn't embarrassed at the time, but I am, now." I slapped a hand over my face and walked away.

256

~

"Bree—Breanne?" Charles had come to find me. I was doing what Lissa often did; sitting on the roof of a building. It wasn't even our hotel—it was the dome of the nation's capitol. I'd shielded myself. If I hadn't, I imagine I'd have been stormed by Secret Service and the military by now.

"How the hell did you get up here without getting shot?" I stared at him. Even a vampire couldn't fool the guards for long; eventually they'd realize he was there.

"Kal provided a shield for me. He wanted to come, as did Hank. I said they'd had enough of your time recently."

"So you haven't gotten enough face time?" I asked as he settled beside me and pulled me close.

"Not nearly enough. Never enough." He cupped my cheek and pulled my head into the hollow between his neck and shoulder. "Comfortable?" he asked.

"Yeah. You smell good," I added.

"You think I smell good? What do I smell like?"

"Cinnamon and sugar. Like the best cinnamon roll ever, with a dash of cayenne pepper to make things interesting."

"Do you remember when I said you got to decide the ending to the story?" he asked. "What would you like the ending to be?"

"That all this was over," I sighed. "That you and I and Hank and all the others I love and who love me could live in the most amazing house ever. It would have enough room for everybody—with places to be together or alone, depending on how we feel, and a kitchen where everybody could have breakfast together if we wanted, and an ocean outside with the best view ever."

"That's what you want, love?"

"Yeah. That's what I want." I sighed. It wasn't likely to happen.

"That's a tall order," Charles breathed against my temple.

"It's an impossible one," I replied. "I guess we ought to get back."

"No, let's sit here for a little while longer and dream," he whispered.

~

"Recognize this one?" Bill held up a photograph. I stared, as did Hank. Janine Webster's image was shown as she walked out of an upscale department store with shopping bags in hand.

"Where is this?" Hank demanded. We'd been called to Bill's suite for a meeting the moment Charles and I returned.

"Fresno, California," Bill said. I was standing and sending mindspeech to Lissa in half a blink.

~

"I'm surprised I didn't think of it," Calhoun gloated. "Why didn't I realize that all we had to do was relocate and send that worthless human out on an errand?"

"Don't forget that this is where my brother's love lives," Moxas sniffed. "This will bring your targets to you—never fear. Be ready for them when they arrive."

"But the dance before death is always a sweet one, is it not?" V'ili observed. "If I or one of my people cannot obsess the enemy, you will kill them." He nodded to Calhoun.

"Acrimus or I will do it," Calhoun insisted. "And we will capture the woman for your brother, Moxas, as that is your expressed desire."

"Perhaps we will share her," Moxas examined his fingernails. "If my brother permits."

"I will permit—but only with you," Saxom said.

~

Le-Ath Veronis—present

Lissa's Journal

"Some of the enemy is in Fresno in the past, where Kiarra and Adam live," I said. "I've already sent a message to Adam, but he says the Larentii are guarding the area. Breanne says that she and the others are going there, to attempt to track the enemy. Ferrigar says he and the other three Larentii are staying, in case extra shields are required."

"Do you think we ought to warn Kiarra and Adam in the past?" Gavin asked. "And I have memories now, of Bill requesting that Breanne and Hank relocate our group from Silver Spring to Fresno."

"Are they still being written as things progress?" I asked, rising from the chair behind my desk. "Your memories, I mean?"

"Yes, just as before. The memories are forming as things move along. The past is being rewritten, cara."

CHAPTER 17

Earth—past
Breanne's Journal

Fresno, even in mid-September, can be hotter than Hades. In fact, the folks who came up with the idea of Hades were probably referring to Fresno. Or Phoenix, maybe. Bill asked Hank and me to transfer our group from Silver Spring to Los Angeles—he wanted to bring in a few extras to help run down leads and to borrow a fleet of SUVs.

That fleet was presently driving through Fresno, with an outside temperature of one hundred six degrees. Even Hank didn't like the heat and he was High Demon on the outside.

"I'm surprised our tires aren't melted to the pavement," Jayson grumbled as we stopped at a traffic light on our way to a borrowed building.

Ashe, who'd finally shown up with a smiling Kay in tow, promised that he could renovate anything large enough to hold our group with the power he held. Well, I suppose I could, too. Ashe was the better architect, though, because he'd built the monstrous house at SouthStar, with very little help or input. I knew that from reading Aedan Evans—he'd been one of the few who'd provided input for the house, along with Casimir and Nathan Anderson.

"What kind of building is it?" Opal asked. She and Charles rode in the third row of seats in our van. Hank, Jayson and I took up the middle row. Bill rode up front while Trajan drove us through afternoon traffic in the California Valley.

Kalenegar had folded ahead to visit the Larentii already stationed in Fresno, while Dan Kelsey, Ashe, Kay, Sali and Gavin followed us in a second van. Kevis hadn't come to Fresno with us—he'd gone back to be with his parents at NorthStar.

Driving before and behind us were two SUVs, filled with the agents Bill and Dan requested. I'd verified that none of them were obsessed. They were armed to their hairlines and carried an extra arsenal in the backs of their vehicles. Bill made sure we all had our Ranos weapons, too—he'd learned to respect them greatly after two pistols brought down two helicopters.

Our mission was to track the enemy as discreetly as possible, but with four shiny black vehicles traveling through Fresno together, we may as well have announced ourselves with the sounding of trumpets.

"At least the AC works," Opal sighed behind me. She liked the cooler environments, just as I did. That's one of the reasons I'd chosen to settle in San Francisco a few years earlier. I had no idea when I did that things would come to this.

"I feel like we're heading to the O.K. Corral," Jayson muttered beside me.

"Tombstone," Hank muttered. "Not Fresno."

"Please tell me you didn't fight in that battle, too," Jayson grumped.

"I didn't. I'd have won it for our side," Hank teased.

"Are you suggesting you'd throw a third party into the mix?" Opal tapped Hank on the shoulder.

"Maybe."

"Stop teasing," I wrinkled my nose at him.

"Stop wrinkling your nose. You know how that makes me feel."

"Irritated?"

Horny as hell, he replied in mindspeech.

～

The building was an empty shell in Clovis, a city almost surrounded by Fresno. The large structure had once been home to a construction company, but the business had moved to a new location and the old building was now for sale. Plenty of space was available for the vehicles, as long as Ashe could make the rest of it livable for us.

He did. All of us watched in wonder as he formed interior walls and covered them with sheetrock and paint. Flooring, bathrooms and bedrooms followed. A kitchen came last, but it was almost a work of art. Kal showed up to help with that and to add air-conditioning, water heaters, linens and pipes throughout for clean water.

I felt almost worthless next to the skills required to build all that. Maybe someday, I'd try it for myself. When I was feeling stronger and more confident.

"Baby, he can't *Change What Was*, no matter how hard he tries," Hank whispered next to my ear. "Only you can do that."

"He called Lissa back from death," I said softly.

"He only pulled her mist back together before it scattered too far," Hank informed me. "We talked about that—he and I. It was her choice to return to her body, once it was reformed. He called to her spirit, it's true, but the choice was hers. He couldn't do what you do, baby, and *Change What Was* for her. That's why she was somewhat in between for many years and had to go to energy to replenish herself. Did you know that's no longer true after you *Changed What Was* and brought her back after Cheedas stabbed her?"

"How do you know that?" I stared at Hank in shock.

"I know Kifirin—perhaps better than he likes. He knows it, because he loves her. He used to catch up with her while she was energy, just so he could watch her. That no longer happens. I believe she is grateful for it, too."

"She doesn't hate him," I said, lowering my head to stare at my shoes. They were black canvas with white rubber soles and went well with the black jeans I wore. I might have to consider dressing much lighter in the Fresno heat. "She loves him. But he messed up a few times too many. She doesn't really know how to reconcile her love with his mistakes."

"He made promises he couldn't keep himself," Hank blew a thin stream of smoke. "So he placed the burden on other shoulders. That burden weighed too much and almost broke the life-giver."

"Would he have taken that burden away from her if he could?" I turned my face up to Hank's. "Or was he just taking the easy way out?"

"Avilepha, I don't have an answer for that," Hank shrugged.

"I think a lot might depend on that answer," I said. "If he could have taken the burden away and didn't, then punishment might be deserved, don't you think? If he couldn't take it away, then he should have supported her any way he could. Did he do that? It's my understanding that he made her suffering worse by alienating her mates."

"That's why I was sent to become his overseer," Hank replied. "I was approached by the Ear and instructed to take over the ruling of the Dark Realm, because Kifirin had obviously lost control of it. I must govern it until such a time as Kifirin is deemed capable of handling it again. I have already placed others there to help—as should have been done in the beginning. They cannot deny me if I outrank them, and only the Three outrank me." He smiled as he leaned in to kiss me after that statement.

"Does that mean you outrank Acrimus?"

"He and I are equal," Hank blew more smoke. I could see that irritated him greatly. "Had I been there when you found him, he and I," Hank didn't finish.

"That might have been a fight for the ages," I sighed. "I should have destroyed him. I had time. Instead, I dithered and gave the General time to show up."

"We all have hindsight, do we not?" Hank pulled me close. The new air-conditioning system hummed around us, and I found we were inside a bedroom.

"I should have jumped your bones the minute I saw you," I huffed. "Instead of buying you coffee." Hank's bellow of laughter could likely be heard throughout the building.

"So we don't know where she went after walking out of that store." Opal shook her head.

"These are the only camera images we have, and they don't extend past the parking lot in front of the business," Bill said. He and Dan Kelsey had gotten more images from other cameras in the same shopping center, as well as footage from inside the store, but all Janine purchased was a swimsuit and six large bath towels.

"That tells me we still have a Sirenali," I said.

"How?" Jayson asked.

"Sirenali are amphibious," I said. "Janine can't swim. I read her, remember? She doesn't do swimsuits generally, because it might show —well, you know." I hunched my shoulders.

"Tattoos?" Bill asked.

"Uh, no. Janine is into flogging and whipping," Hank said. "She usually has bruised flesh. Enjoys the ache of it."

I rubbed my forehead as Hank explained Janine's fetishes and habits. I knew from my reading that she didn't want her associates arrested for abuse, so she didn't dress in skimpy outfits unless she was walking into a club.

It's the differences in people, sweetheart, Ashe sent. *Don't let it upset you. What one person loves might terrify another. You know that, don't you?*

A part of me knows that. A part of me cringes and wants to curl into a ball whenever this stuff is mentioned.

I'll make sushi out of anybody who tries that shit with you, a new voice joined the conversation. It was Sali.

I can see the arguments between you and Jayson now, I sent to both of them.

Already been there, they both chorused. *Jayson was angry that we'd even suggest he wasn't trustworthy enough to be with you. He knows where to draw the line,* Ashe added.

I wasn't sure whether to be pleased or upset that they'd done this without my knowledge. After a few moments, I realized I appreciated the thought behind it. With multiple mates came a system of checks and balances. I hoped that continued to weigh in my favor.

Here's my question, I sent to both of them. *Why would you argue with Jayson on my behalf?*

Well, Sali began.

Sal has the hots for you, Ashe said. *I sort of do, too. Kay wants you as part of the family, and frankly, so do I. Hank, Jayson, Bill, Trajan, Sali and I discussed this while you were sitting on top of the capitol building.*

Seriously?

Don't be upset, Sali said. *That's not what we want. We just needed to make sure everybody was cool with us making our bid to be included in the herd.*

Were they?

If you are.

I wouldn't mind seeing where this might go, I replied.

Great. Want to go to a movie?

Yeah, but I want to share a large popcorn. I love popcorn.

I don't know whether we can afford a large popcorn, Sali teased.

"Breanne?" Bill said.

"Huh?" I was brought back from my private conversation with a bang. Going by the frown on Bill's face, I felt as if I'd been caught passing notes in class.

"We're splitting up tomorrow to scout the areas around the Griffin household. You'll be with me, Opal and Jayson. Hank will be with Gavin, Director Kelsey and Trajan. Ashe will be with Salidar, Charles and Kalenegar. Two human agents will join each of our groups, leaving two agents behind to guard our headquarters. Any questions? Dan and I will be sorting through information and possible leads tonight, and assignments will be handed out in the morning."

"Those agents aren't gonna be wearing red shirts, are they?" I turned to Sali. His eyes widened before he covered a loud snicker.

"This is better than going out." Sali dipped his hand in the popcorn bowl, pulling out a cluster of popped kernels. We watched a cable movie on a wide-screen television in our new family room. I sat on a sofa between Bill and Sali, while Trajan lounged at my feet. We'd popped so much popcorn, there were huge bowls of it scattered throughout the room.

"I love this movie," I sighed. We watched *Young Frankenstein*—it was the choice everybody settled on. Kay had never seen it, poor thing.

❧

Ashe's Journal

I had my arm around Kay, who seemed perfectly comfortable with that. *Sali,* I sent, *I think I dreamed about this when I was sixteen.*

Me, too, he said. I didn't want to point out that when we were, his parents were still alive. They'd survived another hundred years or so after he arrived on Avendor with me, but I'd informed him and Marco when they passed. We'd gone to separate funerals, three years apart. It was the way things were, more often than not.

I watched as he pulled Breanne's hand into his and kissed it. Sali was serious when he wanted or needed to be, in addition to being a deadly warrior. He fooled people often enough with his casual ways and goofy sense of humor, but he wasn't anyone to cross lightly. At least we were working to repair a friendship that had suffered through the years, and I was glad.

❧

Hank's Journal

I'm taking Bree to bed tonight, Bill informed me.

Gonna fight DeLuca for her? I teased.

I don't think she's ready for that, yet, Bill said. *I won't keep her awake all night, either.*

The Saa Thalarr set up calendars, I said. *Depending on how many mates they have, they get nights, weekends or weeks, sometimes.*

How do they decide the order?

Draw names from a hat or cut cards, I offered a mental laugh. *You cheat, you get sent to the back of the line.*

Let's worry about that when things are more stable. I watched as Bill pulled Breanne against him and leaned in for a kiss.

～

Breanne's Journal

Bill asked me to go to bed with him. I wasn't going to turn him down. He had a lot on his plate and definitely needed a distraction. Did I mind being that distraction? Hell no. Bill always treated me like the most important thing in existence when I went to bed with him, and I was completely comfortable going to sleep and waking up in his arms. We had a long day scheduled for tomorrow, and Bill's bed might be the best place for both of us.

～

"This will be quite simple. We know where she'll be and when she'll be there. All we have to do is incapacitate her and bring her to Saxom and Moxas."

"Her child's school will be the perfect place for the abduction. V'ili, have you placed your obsessions?" Calhoun turned to the Sirenali.

"I have. If things go wrong, all you have to do is transport yourself away from the vehicle and leave the human driver and passenger to answer questions and take the blame."

"The Saa Thalarr all have an abnormally strong desire to save those who are weaker. V'ili, have the vehicle's driver aim for a child. You know she'll intervene, making this ridiculously simple for us," Acrimus said. "Our power is greater. Kiarra cannot resist when we pull her in."

～

Breanne's Journal

Two of Bill's extra agents brought in breakfast for us as we gathered around a huge kitchen island to eat. "Where are we going first?" I asked Bill. He and I rubbed elbows at the island as we ate a hurried meal and drank coffee from a local restaurant.

"There's a new school being built on the east side of Fresno," Bill said. "The only people there will be construction workers, and we've seen how they've been obsessed in the past. Easy enough to do and the enemy moves right in. The school swimming pool is already built, it just needs water."

I could see that Bill and Dan Kelsey had put a lot of thought into our search. A few old motels were also on the list, because they had swimming pools. Several very large homes with pools, which were empty and listed for sale were also targeted. Others were on the list, too—anything that might be big enough to hold part of Acrimus' army.

Somehow, I guessed that the General wasn't involved in this mission—he didn't care that Saxom or his brother might get what they wanted out of this. He only cared about having everything under his control. Acrimus realized that pacifying the Khos'Mirai and his brother might result in better information in the long term, and that was a frightening prospect.

Construction workers stood aside as we walked through the school an hour later. I put it to the sniff test, too. It was free of any scent of Sirenali or Janine. I shook my head at Bill as we stared at the empty swimming pool—the school moving into the new facility had a championship swim team, so the pool was regulation length to hold swim meets.

"Nothing here," Bill sighed. "Let's go."

"Slave," V'ili snapped, "test the water for me."

Janine stepped into the water at Shaver Lake and shuddered. "Cold," she said, closing her eyes and shivering.

"Then come in with me. You can keep me warm," V'ili said.

"Can't swim," Janine's voice was flat.

"Too bad. Perhaps I'll keep you alive if you endeavor to keep me warm."

Breanne's Journal

"We're coming up empty everywhere," Bill placed his cellphone on the table and shook his head at me. He was worried, that was plain enough to see. He'd gotten off the phone with Dan Kelsey after we'd stopped for lunch at a local restaurant.

"We're basing this on what we've seen in the past," Opal offered. She sat opposite me in the booth where we'd been seated by the restaurant hostess. Jayson sat beside her while I was seated next to Bill. The two extra agents had a table near the door so they could watch who came and went and guard Bill at the same time.

"What are you saying?" Bill turned to Opal.

"That we're assuming the Sirenali wants warm, clean saltwater to flex his gills. What if they want to throw us off? There are a couple of lakes near the mountains."

"What do you know about the Sirenali? Do they require saltwater?" Bill turned to me.

"I don't know," I shook my head. "But how hard would it be for a rogue god to add salt to a body of water? Especially if they wanted to mislead us?"

Bill lifted his phone and dialed Dan Kelsey. He answered right away. "Dan," Bill said, "How difficult would it be to get area lakes tested for salinity?"

"No problem," I heard Dan's reply. "I can get someone on it right away."

"Thanks, Dan," Bill said and ended the call. "I don't like this," he raked fingers through his hair in frustration.

Hank's Journal

"He asked Dan to get his people to check the salinity of area lakes," Trajan said. We'd watched as Dan answered a call from Bill. He'd walked away from us as he talked, but that didn't prevent Trajan from hearing the conversation. A werewolf could detect cellphone conversations from yards away.

"Then they're not finding anything either, and we're widening the search," I said.

"If they're camped at a local lake, that's an even bigger problem," Trajan said. "I wish we had more wolves—we could sniff around. Maybe pick up a trail."

"Would the Grand Master consider contacting the local Packs?" I turned to Trajan.

"Yeah. Let me get Winkler on the phone. I'll see what we can do."

In less than an hour, Weldon Harper had called for volunteers from the Fresno and Sacramento Packs and werewolves living in the lake areas were already on their way. Dan Kelsey blinked at the efficiency of the Grand Master and offered his thanks as soon as Trajan gave him the information.

~

Fresno, California

Adam's Journal

I was supervising a local construction job, so I'd gone home for lunch. When Kiarra's cellphone rang, I looked up from the chicken tetrazzini she'd made to listen in. She seldom got calls and hated the phone. She only kept it because I asked.

"Hi, Martin, what's up?" she said when Martin Walters identified himself.

"Can you pick Mack up from school when you go for Justin?" Martin asked. "I have an emergency job up at Shaver Lake this afternoon."

Martin built custom cabinets for businesses and wealthy clients. He was good with his hands and his work was excellent. It didn't surprise me that someone might be calling from that area—there were plenty of nice cabins on Shaver Lake.

"Sure, Martin. Justin will love it if Mack comes home with us."

"I'll pick him up later, after this job is done," Martin said. "Thanks, Anna. I owe you."

Everybody in Fresno knew Kiarra as Anna. She'd used that name when we first met, and it was a good disguise while we lived in Fresno. I'd changed my last name to match that of my alter ego—Griffin. It was one of the disadvantages of being Saa Thalarr—you had to hide behind a mask most of the time.

"I'll pick up fried chicken for dinner—Mack loves fried chicken," Kiarra sighed as she placed the cell back in her purse.

"Have I told you lately how much I appreciate the fact that you'll cook or serve meat for the rest of us, when you don't eat it?" I asked.

"Adam, it's a choice. I'm not gonna lose it if you, Justin and Mack have fried chicken for dinner."

"What if other vegetarians picket our house?" I grinned at her.

"Don't even start," she held up a hand.

"Come here, sweetheart." I reached for her.

"After you finish your lunch," she said.

Breanne's Journal

The Grand Master was sending werewolves to the area lakes to sniff around and report anything unusual back to him. Dan had experts on the way to test the water for salt. We had an old motel to visit in the Fresno heat.

"That looks unsanitary," Jayson muttered as we walked up to the abandoned motel. It looked as if it had melted and rusted shortly after it was built in the 1960s. The sign bore an arrow beneath the word "Motel," which pointed toward the building. All the bulbs were broken or missing in the arrow's lights, and parts of it had rusted away.

The office was tiny; the glass walls making up a corner of it were so scratched and filthy you could barely see through them. The inside was impossibly worse. I couldn't imagine anyone hiding inside—except perhaps rodents, cockroaches and crickets.

Nevertheless, we went through each of the sixteen rooms attached, plus the pool area. "They can't possibly hope to renovate this; their only hope is to bulldoze it," Opal grumbled as we stared at the bottom of the pool, where weeds struggled to survive between narrow cracks and only a hint of peeling blue paint remained.

"It's been on the market for four years," Bill said, consulting the notes on his cellphone. "No offers."

"I can see why," Jayson said. He wore expensive sunglasses to protect his eyes, but the shake of his head reflected my feelings about this one—it was an eyesore and needed to be destroyed immediately.

"Do you think it'll petrify if they leave it?" Bill joked.

"It's there already," Opal said.

"I will go to the school and wait in disguise," Ferrigar informed Connegar. "If you will monitor the microscopic cameras in the vehicle from here, I will protect the child while you watch Kiarra."

"Of course," Connegar inclined his head. The other two Larentii had left to feed so they could take the evening shift. So far, the work had been uneventful. Ferrigar folded away.

Ashe's Journal

Up to now, we'd found nothing. There was no word from the werewolves searching the area lakes and Dan Kelsey's people were on their way to test for water salinity. Everything was taking time, and I felt in my heart that time had somehow slipped away from us. A heavy weight settled on my mind and I couldn't shake the feeling that something could go horribly wrong at any moment.

"I'm getting a bad feeling all of a sudden," Sali walked up beside me and spoke softly.

"Me, too, Sal," I nodded. "I just don't know what it might mean. Too much is shielded or hidden by that weird talent the Sirenali have, and that worries me. It tells me they're here, and I'm afraid our time may be running out to find them."

"Have we heard anything from the Larentii? They're still guarding Kiarra, aren't they?"

"Yeah. No word yet, so I'll assume that means nothing is happening on that front. Who knows what may happen? It could all be a trap, and we just haven't realized it, yet."

~

Hank's Journal

Something sounded an internal alarm in my mind, and I couldn't determine what it might be. I sent mindspeech to Ashe, who replied immediately.

Something's wrong, he agreed. *I just can't get to the root of it.*

Sirenali and rogue gods, I returned. My mental voice sounded as angry as I felt. The feeling became stronger that we were all in danger and I didn't like it. I had the urge to find Breanne and carry her away to the farthest habitable reaches of the universes.

We can't back down, now, Ashe cautioned. Somehow, he'd known how I might react to extreme danger—especially if Breanne were involved. I never wanted to feel her broken, unresponsive body beneath my hand again.

I won't back down, I said. Smoke curled away from my nostrils at the sending. *I only worry for Breanne.*

I worry for her, too—and all the others. What can we do? We can't run every time things get dangerous.

Breanne didn't run last time. You know how that ended.

I know. We weren't with her—remember that.

I remember that all too well, I snarled mentally while more smoke floated away.

~

Father, where are you? Kalenegar sent mindspeech to Ferrigar.

I am at the child's school in disguise, waiting for Kiarra to arrive, Ferrigar replied.

How are you disguised, father?

As a child. It seems appropriate, as this is a school for young humans. Why do you ask?

The Mighty Hand grows agitated. That cannot be a good sign, Kalenegar replied.

Can you determine a reason? All seems calm here at the moment.

Father, we cannot read the Mighty. Unless I ask, there is no way to determine a cause.

Then keep watching for further signs and keep me informed, unless you wish to ask questions.

Father, I care for you. You make that extremely difficult at times.

No more than you have made it for me in the past, Ferrigar replied. *Perhaps we should discuss this at a later time. Connegar informs me that Kiarra's vehicle approaches.*

As you wish it, Father.

~

Wisdom's Journal

Without his knowledge, I was connected to Ferrigar and saw what he did. Kiarra's vehicle pulled into the long, U-shaped driveway leading up to the school. Nothing seemed amiss, although my senses screamed otherwise. Breanne had better prescience, but we all had it in some measure. Mine had increased since I'd bitten her, but hers was still sharper.

Kiarra's vehicle parked halfway down the U, as she waited for Justin and the werewolf child, Martin Walters Jr., to walk out of the school. It was nearly three o'clock in the afternoon and the school bell would ring in seconds.

Ferrigar stood at the top of the U, disguised as a child waiting for someone to pick him up. He and I both noticed the car driving the wrong way up the U and picking up speed.

Calhoun didn't like that they'd allowed Janine to drive instead of one of the five other humans V'ili brought with him. A second human sheep—a middle-aged male, sat in the passenger seat while Calhoun and Acrimus were seated in the back. Acrimus, at the last moment, had decided to accompany Calhoun and the humans, just as a precaution. Neither had dealt with the Saa Thalarr before, and Kiarra was designated as First among them.

V'ili's argument—that a female and a male could better represent a child's parents when driving toward the school made sense—after a bit of consideration. Neither Calhoun nor Acrimus had ever dealt with or given thought to human education before.

"Saa Thalarr reflexes are just as quick as a vampire's. Drive faster," Acrimus snapped at Janine. Janine complied by pushing the accelerator to the floor.

Breanne's Journal

I wanted to scream as prescience kicked in, but my mouth could only gape at the horror that enveloped me. Everything fractured around me and I saw stars falling. I wasn't even aware when I was pulled to the scene, and had no idea whether it happened in and of itself or whether I was transported by another.

Hank's Journal

We were pulled as if by a very strong magnet. There wasn't anything we could do to prevent it or escape. Inevitability had come and there was no denying it this time.

We arrived just in time to see that the other two teams had been tossed toward the scene as well, dumping us on the grassy yard surrounding a grade school in Fresno. The speeding car—the pale-haired woman running—the tremendous push by a Larentii in disguise; all of it seemingly happened at once.

The car crumpled as if it had hit a rock wall before it reached the disguised Larentii, and both humans inside died quickly. Had any of us counted on the fury—or the willfulness—of an angry, rogue god?

Acrimus and an underling appeared outside the vehicle, unharmed, while the humans inside it bled and died.

Without thinking or investigating, Acrimus raised a hand and leveled a blast at the disguised Larentii. That's when space and time fractured—and hope died.

CHAPTER 18

reanne's Journal
All of us watched, helpless to prevent it. I saw Ashe across the U-shaped street—he stood between Sali and Charles. My body was gripped, as if in a tight fist, and drawn forward. Ashe was pulled toward me, just as I was pulled toward him. I blinked when I saw Charles; his face changed, followed by his body. He became taller. Darker-haired. Gray-eyed. If I could have gasped, I would have.

Wisdom was drawn toward me—and toward Ashe. Somewhere, deep inside me, I knew it was because a Larentii died. That Acrimus, evil fool that he was, had done this with the power he possessed.

The Larentii are my children, filtered into my mind. *It is forbidden to kill them. It will bring the wrath of the One.*

Our bodies were no longer our own as light and stars fell about us, and we rushed toward one another with no power to stop the momentum.

~

Report for the Archives

Submitted by Kalenegar of the Larentii, now duly elected Head of the Larentii Council and Vhirilaszh of the People.

Prophecies are strange and malleable entities, and often grow or twist out of shape in their telling and retelling. The Prophecy concerning the Three in the Larentii Archives all say the One created the Three. It never said anywhere that the One created the Three by splitting itself.

I can only report on what I witnessed that day, and give an accounting from my perspective. I saw the Three; Wisdom revealed himself at last as Charles of the vampires, as they were pulled together and fused into something so bright none could look upon it.

Acrimus, come, a voice boomed in a language none had heard before. I watched as the rogue god Acrimus dropped before the newly reformed One. Ferrigar, Head of the Larentii Council, as well as my father, had died at Acrimus' hand.

It is only known to the Larentii—and the gods—that it is forbidden for any god to take a Larentii life. The One had created the race, through the Three. Many cares were placed in Larentii hands, and only the One and the Larentii know these things.

I watched my father die on a hot day in the city of Fresno, California, on old Earth as many refer to it now. I watched the One reborn, who took my heart—and my love—with it. Acrimus was destroyed by a flick of the One's mind. The other rogue god escaped— he had not participated in my father's death.

This was not how it should have ended. There are still rogue gods creating havoc under the General's command, and we no longer have Strength, Wisdom or Love to combat them.

The Larentii race will survive. I feel none will tempt fate a second time by killing another of my race. I fear all others will die, however, and there is little any of us might do to prevent it. The God Wars have been waged—and lost.

~

Le-Ath Veronis—present

Lissa's Journal

"There are still rogue gods, and we might be able to capture and contain them, but the General remains and he may protect them," Belen sighed as he sat in one of my guest chairs.

"That doesn't include the Sirenali and anyone they might obsess," I pointed out as I watched Belen carefully. I'd never seen his radiance so subdued or his manner so defeated. Inside, I wept. Yes, my sister might still live, but never again as my sister. She was the Heart of the One, now, and I could do nothing about it.

"Will we watch everything die?" I brushed a tear away.

"I fear that may be," Belen shook his head. "The shield still stands around the gishi groves on Avendor and we are welcome there—I received mindspeech from Trajan, telling me to consider it a haven if it is needed. It will only sustain and protect a few, however."

"Yeah. Belen, I'm going hunting," I stood and pulled in a deep breath. "I may not be able to destroy rogue gods, but I can destroy Sirenali and their minions. They have no hold on me."

"Then perhaps all of us still adhering to the Light should do the same. Call if you need assistance. I need time and space to think." Belen disappeared.

~

Avendor—present

Hank's Journal

Of the two highest-ranking Koh'Ahmari, I am the one remaining. When I was handed the assignment—and the rule of the Dark Realm from the Ear—I was given permission to do what was necessary to bring it in line. I was about to test that permission to the limit.

King Jayd was about to receive a visit from the new Lord of the Dark Realm and his servant, Kifirin. No High Demon would refuse the service I would now demand of him or her. I had rogues to hunt—Sirenali, vampires, shapeshifters and gods alike. The General, however, had never been made by the One, the Three or any god. He remained a problem.

"I will hunt him anyway, avilepha," I promised. Breanne wouldn't return to me, but I held her memory in my heart so it would never fade.

The End